The Lost Ticket

Titles by Freya Sampson

THE LAST CHANCE LIBRARY

THE LOST TICKET

THE
Lost Ticket

FREYA SAMPSON

BERKLEY
NEW YORK

BERKLEY
An imprint of Penguin Random House LLC
penguinrandomhouse.com

Originally published as *The Girl on the 88 Bus* in the United Kingdom by Zaffre,
an imprint of Bonnier Books UK, in 2022.

Library of Congress Cataloging-in-Publication Data

Names: Sampson, Freya, author.
Title: The lost ticket / Freya Sampson.
Description: New York : Berkley, [2022]
Identifiers: LCCN 2022006174 (print) | LCCN 2022006175 (ebook) |
ISBN 9780593201404 (hardcover) | ISBN 9780593201411 (trade paperback) |
ISBN 9780593201428 (ebook)
Classification: LCC PR6119.A475 L67 2022 (print) |
LCC PR6119.A475 (ebook) | DDC 823/.92--dc23
LC record available at https://lccn.loc.gov/2022006174
LC ebook record available at https://lccn.loc.gov/2022006175

Printed in the United States of America
1st Printing

Interior art: London street and bus © Franzi / Shutterstock.com
Book design by Kristin del Rosario

For my parents,
Alison & Roy

The Lost Ticket

April 1962

Frank spotted her out of the front window as the bus pulled up at Clapham Common Station.

She was standing at the bus stop, wearing a pair of wide-legged trousers, what looked like a man's tweed jacket, and a black beret, set on a sideways angle to reveal a shock of red hair underneath. The whole ensemble was unlike anything he'd ever seen a girl wear before, both boyish and feminine at the same time. From his seat at the front of the top deck, Frank saw a flash of green eyes under the beret and felt his heart quicken.

The 88 stopped and the girl boarded, disappearing from view. Frank could hear the conductor downstairs greeting passengers as they paid their fares, and he imagined the girl taking a ticket and finding a seat on the lower deck. Should he move downstairs? He paused, struck with indecision. And then he felt a movement behind him and caught a glimpse of tweed to his right. Frank kept very still, his head facing the front window, but out of the corner of his eye, he saw the girl

sit in the vacant seat across the aisle from him. She put her bag
down by her feet, closed her eyes, and let out an audible sigh.

The bus pulled away from the stop and set off up Clapham
High Street. The girl didn't move from her position or open her
eyes, so Frank was able to steal glances at her. He guessed that
she was slightly younger than him, maybe eighteen or nineteen,
although she held herself with the confidence of someone twice
her age. She was surprisingly tall, with a long, slender neck and
a sharp, pointed chin. Her skin was so pale it looked like por-
celain, and up close he could see that her hair was the color of
the orange marmalade his parents sold in their shop. As the bus
approached Stockwell, she still hadn't moved and Frank was
beginning to wonder if she'd fallen asleep, when all of a sudden
she opened her eyes and turned her head toward him.

"Do you make a habit of staring at girls on the bus?"

Frank was so taken aback that he felt himself blush.

"Oh, I'm . . . eh . . ." he stumbled, sounding like the schoolboy he suddenly felt like. "I'm sorry."

She looked at him with her olive green eyes, and Frank saw
a flicker of amusement dance across her face. Oh god, she was
laughing at him. "It's rude, you know. Didn't your mother
teach you any manners?"

"I'm sorry," Frank said again. His pulse was racing, and he
reached into his pocket and pulled out his book, desperate to
end this excruciating moment. He could feel her watching
him, so he hurriedly turned to a random page and pretended
to read.

"What's the book, then?" she asked.

"Eh . . . it's *On the Road*. By Jack . . ." He hesitated, unsure
how to pronounce the surname. "Ker-ooh-ick."

"Any good?"

At once, Frank had an urgent sense that how he answered this question was vital; that he had one chance to make up for the terrible first impression he'd made. But the problem was, he really didn't like the book. He'd been lent it by a friend who loved all things American and had ordered it all the way from New York. His friend had raved about the book's modern style and said something about Beat poets, but Frank had been struggling with its chaotic and strange narrative and had barely got past the first ten pages.

"Yes, it's great. It's from America. The author is part of the Beat generation."

Frank hoped that sentence made him sound grown-up and sophisticated, but he saw she still had that same faintly amused expression on her face.

"What happens in it?"

"Oh. Well, he goes on a journey. On the road."

"Yes, I'd got that much from the title. Then what?"

"He meets some people and goes to parties and . . . eh . . ."

Frank tried to remember what else he'd been told about the book, but this girl was making his brain turn to jelly. She was watching him silently, with no intention of putting him out of his misery.

"To be honest, I've not got very far with it yet," he said, and heard a sigh of defeat in his own voice.

The girl didn't say anything, just reached into her bag, pulled out a large notebook and pencil, and began to scribble something down. Frank waited for her to speak again but realized with a sinking sensation that she'd got bored of him and their conversation was over.

The bus trundled on, up South Lambeth Road toward Vauxhall Junction. Frank desperately wanted to observe her some more, but whenever he glanced over, she seemed to sense it and looked back at him, so he resigned himself to staring out the front window instead. He was painfully aware that she might get off at any moment, and as they approached each bus stop, he held his breath in case this was the one. But she didn't leave, and the only sound was the scratch of her pencil on the paper.

Finally, when he could bear it no longer, Frank turned back to her.

"What are you writing?"

"What's that?" she said, not looking up from the page.

"I said, what are you writing?"

"I'm not."

"But you're—"

"Here." With a flourish she ripped the page out of her notebook and thrust it toward him. Frank took the piece of paper and turned it over cautiously, unsure what he was about to see.

It was a sketch of a young man, and with a jolt like an electric shock, Frank realized it was him. She'd caught his hair perfectly, the way he styled the front with wax so it stood up high, and there were his too-big ears and the crooked nose he'd inherited from his mother. Yet somehow she'd taken all his odd features and still made him look, well, handsome.

"This is . . ." His voice came out in a boyish squeak, and Frank winced.

"It's very rough," she said, pulling a pack of cigarettes from her bag and extracting one.

"I can't believe you did it so quickly."

"I like to sketch on the bus." She struck a match and lit the cigarette, inhaling deeply. "There's always an interesting selection of life models, with the added frisson that you never know when they'll suddenly bugger off."

"It's wonderful."

"It's not one of my best," she said, dismissing the compliment with a wave of her cigarette. "Do you like art?"

Again, this answer felt important, and Frank opened his mouth to bluff, then stopped himself. "I don't really know much about it, I'm afraid. My family have never had much interest in art."

He waited for her to mock him, and was surprised to see her smile, warmly this time. "My old man's the same. His idea of art is the cartoons in the *Daily Mirror*. He tried to stop me going to art school."

"It's not that I'm not interested. I just don't know where to start. It's all a bit . . . intimidating."

"I know it can seem like that, but it's not really. Anyone can enjoy art. That's why it's so exciting."

Frank wasn't sure he agreed. His parents' attitude to art was the same as their attitude to the pictures or the theater: that it was something frivolous that only those with too much time or money could enjoy. "So, how did you learn to draw if you don't go to art school?"

"Oh, I do go."

"But I thought you said your father stopped you?"

"He tried, but I left home and went anyway," the girl said. "I moved in with a friend in Clapham, and I have a part-time job in a clothes shop so I can pay the rent—that's where I'm headed now. My family have pretty much disowned me."

She dropped her cigarette on the floor and ground it out with her shoe. Frank watched her in awe. Even though he was twenty-two, he could never imagine disobeying his parents like that. His father would kill him.

"You're much braver than me," he said, but she shrugged.

"It's not really bravery. I didn't have a choice. Painting is all I've ever wanted to do."

"And what will you do when you finish your course?"

"I'll be an artist." The way she said the word sent a thrill down Frank's spine. He'd never met an artist before, and it only made her seem more exotic and wonderful.

The bus passed through Parliament Square, and Frank stared out the window at Westminster Abbey. His parents had brought him here when he was thirteen to join the cheering crowds at the Queen's coronation. It was one of the few times Frank could remember them ever closing the shop. He imagined turning round to his parents now and telling them that he didn't want to work there anymore, that he had bigger dreams than standing behind a counter for the rest of his life. He glanced across at the girl, who was lighting another cigarette. What must it be like to be her, to have such a strong sense of purpose that you'd risk your whole family for it? He wanted to reach out and touch her arm, to soak up some of that unbridled confidence.

"What about you?" she said as the bus turned onto Whitehall.

"Oh, I just work in my parents' shop."

"Do you enjoy it?"

"No, I hate it. But they expect me to take over the business."

"And what do you want to do?"

"Promise you won't laugh?"

"Cross my heart and hope to die," she said, her face so solemn he smiled.

"I want to be an actor." As he said the words, Frank realized this was the first time he'd ever spoken them out loud.

"I'm sure you'd make a fine actor," the girl said. Frank looked across to see if she was teasing him, but her face was still serious. "You even look a bit like Rock Hudson in *Pillow Talk*."

"Oh, I loved that one. I saw it twice."

The first time, he'd taken Rosamund Green, and the second time, he'd gone on his own, sneaking in so no one saw him going to a romance flick without a girl.

"I go to the pictures as much as I can," he said. "I've seen almost everything they've shown at the Electric Palace."

"Well, then, you've begun your acting education already," she said. "Now you just need to tell your parents."

"I wish it were that simple."

"It won't be, but I swear you won't regret it. You only get one life, after all."

The bus had reached the top of Whitehall, and Trafalgar Square came into view in front of them.

"You know, if you're serious about wanting to learn about art, this is a good place to start," the girl said as the bus turned left in front of Nelson's Column.

"Trafalgar Square?"

"No, the National Gallery." She pointed at a large, domed building at the far side of the square. Frank had seen it dozens of times before, but never paid it any attention. "It's got over two thousand paintings inside, from all round the world."

"Two thousand? How are you meant to see all of them in one visit?"

"You're not," she said. "It's free, so you can go as often as you like. I could spend hours there staring at just one painting."

Frank looked at the girl in disbelief. "Hours looking at one painting? Don't you get bored?"

"God no. There's a painting called *Bacchus and Ariadne*, by an artist called Titian, that I must have spent days looking at. Every time, I see something new."

"Goodness," Frank said.

"Sometimes I wonder why I'm bothering with art school. Spending time in that gallery is like being taught by the greatest art masters in the world."

"I suppose I should go and take a look, then." Frank couldn't believe he'd lived in this city all his life and never even known the gallery existed. How small his world suddenly felt.

They were passing through Piccadilly Circus now, under the huge neon signs advertising Coca-Cola and Cinzano. The girl began to gather up her belongings and, with a start, Frank realized that she must be about to get off the bus. He felt such a rush of emotion that for a moment he couldn't speak. He'd asked girls out before, and some of them had even said yes, so why did he feel so nervous now?

"Look, this might be presumptuous, but . . ." He faltered as she turned to look at him with those bewitching eyes. "I was wondering if perhaps you'd like to go to the National Gallery next Sunday? With me, I mean. You could show me that Bacchus and Adrian painting you like so much."

She squinted at him, and Frank braced himself for rejection.

"Why not?" she said, and in that instant he thought his heart might explode.

"Wonderful! That's . . . Thank you!"

"You can call me if you like," she said. "There's a phone in my building and you can always leave a message with one of the girls."

"I will do." He reached into his pocket, then realized he didn't have a pen or anything to write on.

"Here." She produced her pencil and bus ticket, scribbling her number at the bottom of the small rectangular card. She held it out to him and then stopped, pulling the ticket back. "You're not one of those boys who like to collect girls' numbers, then never call, are you?"

"Of course not!" Frank said. "I swear, I will call you tonight, and every day if you like."

"Just the once is fine," she said, but she smiled as she handed over the ticket. Frank's thumb brushed against hers as he took it, and he felt like he'd been burned.

He put the ticket into his jacket pocket and then went to hand her back the drawing. "Thank you for showing me this. It's wonderful."

"You can keep it if you like."

"Really, are you sure?"

"'Course. It's just a scribble."

"Well, then, I should give you something in return." He felt in his pockets but all he had was his friend's copy of *On the Road*. "You can have this, if you like? I'm not sure it's for me."

"Thanks. I'm intrigued to see what this Mr. Kerouac is like."

The way she said his name was completely different to how Frank had pronounced it, and he felt himself blush again.

"I'll give it back when we meet," she said, taking the book off him.

The bus was approaching Oxford Circus, and the girl stood up to disembark. Frank watched her, savoring every last detail to remember until he saw her again. He wanted to say something profound or funny, something that would make her smile when she remembered him later. Something they could talk about in years to come.

"It was lovely meeting you," he said, feeling once again like a hopeless schoolboy.

"You too, Rock Hudson. See you soon."

She turned and walked down the aisle toward the stairs, not looking back.

1

April 2022

This is the 88 to Parliament Hill Fields."

The electronic announcement rang round the bus as Libby heaved her two rucksacks on board. There was a queue of passengers behind her, and she heard an impatient tut as she rummaged in her handbag to find her wallet. Finally she located it and tapped her card to pay, but not before she heard someone mutter, "Bloody tourist." Libby hurriedly scooped up her bags and began to maneuver toward the one free seat on the lower deck, but she'd gone only a few paces when a teenage boy pushed past, almost knocking her into the lap of an elderly woman, and threw himself into the vacant seat.

Libby gave the boy her best death stare, then turned and climbed the narrow stairs toward the front of the upper deck, clinging to the handrail so she didn't fall as the bus swerved out of Vauxhall Station. When she reached the top, she was relieved to see that the nearest seats in the first row were available, and she dumped her bags on the floor and sat down.

The bus edged its way through the London traffic, and Libby looked out of the front window. Everyone seemed in such a hurry: crowds of pedestrians streaming along the pavement, car horns honking like angry geese, a cyclist gesturing and swearing at a taxi driver. As the bus drove onto Vauxhall Bridge, Libby turned right to get a view along the River Thames. She recognized the Tate Britain art gallery, and behind it the London Eye, its glass pods glistening in the late April sunshine. Simon had taken Libby on it once as a birthday treat, three or four years ago. They'd drunk prosecco as the wheel had rotated them high above the city, and afterward they'd bought hot dogs and walked along the South Bank, hand in hand. It had been one of their rare day trips to London, and Libby remembered feeling so lucky to be there with Simon. And yet—

"Oh my goodness, it's you!"

A voice to Libby's left made her jump, and she swung around to see an elderly man sitting across the aisle, wearing a burgundy velvet jacket that had seen better days. His face broke into a grin when he saw her.

"It really is you, isn't it?"

Oh god. She'd been in London only ten minutes and already she'd picked up a weirdo.

"I'm sorry. I think you've mistaken me for someone else," Libby said, and she turned away from him.

"Oh . . . oh, I am sorry."

Libby pulled her phone out of her handbag. Usually, if a stranger tried to make unwanted conversation, she'd ring someone for a chat instead. But who on earth could she call now? Certainly not her parents, and all her friends these days were Simon's friends too, the wives and girlfriends of his mates and the last people she wanted to speak to. Libby slid her phone back into her bag.

"I'm sorry I disturbed you," the man continued, his voice shaky. "I get a little confused sometimes."

There was something in his tone that made Libby turn back around. He was staring at his lap, looking so utterly dejected that she had a sudden urge to make him feel better.

"Don't worry. Strangers are always mistaking me for someone else. It's my face, I think. I look very average."

"Average?" His head snapped up. "You don't look average. With that marvelous red hair, you look like Botticelli's Venus."

Libby ran a hand though her long, thick curls. Her hair had been called many things over the years—ginger nut, Weasley, carrot top—but never compared to a Renaissance painting, and she couldn't help but smile.

"Sorry. You must think I'm very strange," the man said. "I don't usually accost young women on the bus and tell them I like their hair, I promise."

"It's fine. I needed a compliment today, so thank you."

"Bad day?"

"You could say that."

"I'm happy to listen if that would help?" He ran a hand over his own hair, which was bright white and stuck out at all sorts of unruly angles from his head. "People often tell me their problems, especially on the night bus. Once they've had a few drinks, complete strangers confess all sorts. You wouldn't believe the things I've heard on here."

For a brief second, Libby considered pouring her miserable story out to this stranger, but where to even begin? "That's a kind offer but I'm okay, thanks."

The man nodded and turned to look out of his window, and Libby returned to hers. The bus wound its way behind Tate Britain and along toward Parliament Square. It was busy this morning, crowds of tourists queueing to get into Westminster Abbey, a small huddle of protesters with placards outside the Houses of Parliament being monitored by some bored-looking police officers. Libby checked her phone; it was two fifteen, and according to Google Maps she should be at her sister's house around three.

The thought made Libby shudder. When she'd turned up at her parents' house late last night, still numb with shock, she had assumed they'd let her stay with them for a few days while she worked out what to do. But this morning, over a strained breakfast at which her father could barely look at her, Libby's mum had announced that she'd called Rebecca, who had offered Libby her spare bedroom. This had struck Libby as odd, given the two of them weren't exactly close, but when she'd tried to argue, her mum had brushed her protests aside. And so here she was a few hours later, on an unfamiliar bus in an unfamiliar city, with her life packed into two ancient bags.

"Excuse me." The old man from across the aisle was looking at her again.

"Yes?"

"I'm sorry to be nosy, but I couldn't help noticing that. Are you an artist?"

Libby looked to where he was pointing and saw an old, battered sketch pad stuffed in a side pocket of her backpack. She hadn't even realized it was there; that showed how long it was since she'd used this bag.

"I'm afraid not. That's from years ago when I was at school."

"Did you draw back then?"

"I did, but I haven't done anything artistic in a long time."

"And why is that?"

Libby opened her mouth to answer and then stopped. Why

was she about to tell her life story to a complete stranger? The old man was right; there was clearly something about him that made people spill their secrets.

"I haven't had time" was all she said.

"Nonsense, there's always time to draw. You could sketch me now if you like?"

"Thanks, but I think my drawing days are long gone."

The bus pulled up outside Downing Street and more passengers boarded, their voices a jumble of languages under Libby's feet.

"It's never too late to start drawing again, you know," the man said. "Did you study art at school?"

"Yes, and I wanted to go to art college but . . ." There she went again, about to spill out her guts to him. "I did medicine at university instead."

"Medicine? Lordy, you don't strike me as the doctoring sort. No, I wouldn't trust you with my dickey hips for one minute."

Libby looked up in surprise, but the man winked at her.

"I'm only joking. I'm sure you're a wonderful doctor."

"Actually, you're right. I'm not the doctoring sort. I hated medical school and left before I could do damage to anyone's dickey hips."

The man chuckled and Libby smiled despite herself.

"So, what do you do now, then, if not medicine or drawing?"

She didn't reply, unsure what to say. Up until twenty-four hours ago Libby had worked for Simon, doing the accounts and admin for his gardening firm. But now who the hell knew?

The bus was approaching Trafalgar Square and Libby saw the four majestic lions sitting as defiant sentries, accompanied by a flock of fat pigeons. In the middle, Nelson's Column rose tall above the crowds of tourists and buskers, the admiral on top watching over London like a disapproving parent. Behind him stood the grand pillars and domed roof of the National Gallery. At the sight of it, Libby felt a memory stir. She'd been to the gallery once, on a school trip. Most of her classmates had got bored quickly and complained they wanted to go to Madame Tussauds instead, but Libby had been in awe of the huge building with its ornate ceilings and room after room of extraordinary paintings. But that had been back when she still held out hope of going to art school, before her parents put their foot down about her doing a "proper" degree so she could get a "real" job.

Libby looked at the old man and saw he was lost in thought too, his eyes misty as he stared out the window. He must have sensed her looking at him as he shook his head, as if waking himself from a dream.

"You know, someone once told me you didn't need to go to art school to learn how to draw. She said all you needed was to spend time here, at the National Gallery, and it was like studying under the greatest artists in the world."

"Really?"

"She used to practice sketching on the bus too. She said it was the perfect place to learn life drawing because there's always a choice of interesting models."

"I think I'd find it impossible—far too bumpy."

The man turned to look at Libby. "Have you ever been to the National Gallery?"

"Once, when I was a teenager. I've always meant to go back."

"Well, in that case, why don't we go now? We can start your art education right away!" He reached to the pole behind his seat and hit the stop button with force.

"I'm sorry. I can't," Libby said, and she saw his shoulders sag.

"Of course, silly me."

"I have somewhere I need to be. Plus, I've got these beasts." She indicated her two bags.

"I'm sorry. I don't know what's got into me. I'm behaving very strangely today."

"Not at all. And I will go another time, I promise."

But the man had stopped listening to her, staring back toward the gallery. The bus pulled up at a stop, letting out a low moan as its doors opened. He was still looking out the window.

"You know, I think I'll get off here," he said, pulling himself up into a standing position. "There's a painting I'd like to go and see."

Libby watched as he shuffled out from his seat, clinging to the pole for support. He looked as though he might topple over at any moment.

"Do you need a hand on the stairs?"

"No, thank you. I'll be fine." The man looked down at her. "My name is Frank, by the way."

"It was nice to meet you, Frank. I'm Libby."

"Libby." He smiled as he repeated her name. "Why don't you give drawing on the bus a go? I have a feeling it might suit you." And with that he turned and made his way slowly down the stairs.

2

Libby stood outside her sister's house, looking up at the tall, imposing Georgian building, then took a deep breath and climbed the steep steps. A moment after she rang the bell, the front door swung open and there was her older sister, dressed in yoga leggings and an expensive-looking gym top, eyeing Libby up and down.

"Wow, you look knackered." Rebecca leaned forward and gave her a bony hug.

"Yeah, it's all a bit of a shock." Libby tried to hand one of her bags to Rebecca, but she'd already turned and swept back into the house.

"Take your shoes off, will you?" she called as Libby struggled in.

Libby dumped her bags on the floor and kicked off her shoes, then headed down the hallway into the large open-plan kitchen, which occupied the back of the house. Everything in here was bright white, down to the identical china mugs hanging in a row on hooks and the crisp white tea towels folded over the oven handle. Libby was amazed Rebecca allowed bananas to sit in the fruit bowl, given they didn't match the color scheme.

Libby perched on a narrow stool at the central island, awaiting the inevitable.

"So, tell me everything," Rebecca said. "Mum gave me a brief outline but I want to hear it all from you."

"Okay." Libby swallowed. "So, Simon had suggested we go out for dinner last night to this new Italian place. I thought it was a bit strange, because we usually have takeaway on a Friday, and we haven't been out for a meal for ages. But he'd booked the table, so I got dressed up and out we went."

"And?"

"We had a nice meal, but I could tell Simon was distracted—he kept checking his phone and he went to the toilet three times. I thought . . ." She trailed off, embarrassed to say it out loud.

"What?"

Libby closed her eyes and she was back there, watching Simon across the candlelit table, the way he was chewing his thumbnail as he did when he was nervous. The bubble of excitement that had risen in her throat as it occurred to her what this meant.

"Lib?"

"I thought he was about to propose," she said in a quiet voice.

"Oh my god!"

"I know." Libby felt the emotion coming up again, and she took a breath to push it back down. "But it turns out he wasn't working out how to propose to me. He was working out how to break up with me."

"The total bastard," Rebecca said, with a little too much relish. "What did he say?"

"He said that he still loved me but he's been unhappy for a

while. That things have got stale and he's been questioning whether he wants to be in a relationship anymore. He said he thought it was best to be honest and tell me how he felt, rather than—what did he say?—'suffer in silence any longer.'"

"And why did he take you to a romantic restaurant to tell you all of this?"

"He said he thought it was easier. That at home I'd have got upset, but he knew I'd never make a scene in front of other diners."

"I have to give it to him—that's some Machiavelli-level planning," Rebecca said, shaking her head in admiration. "And you really thought he was going to propose?"

"We'd always said we'd get engaged when we turned thirty, and my birthday's soon, so . . ."

"You know what this is, don't you?" Rebecca said. "This is a classic midlife crisis."

"At thirty?"

"Men do all sorts of weird things around big birthdays. Tom wanted to get a motorbike when he turned forty; I didn't let him, of course, but this is exactly the same. They freak out about getting older and less virile, and feel they need to do something radical."

"He seemed pretty serious about it," Libby said.

I'm so sorry, Simon had mumbled, not meeting her eye across the tiramisu. *I can't help feeling there should be more to a relationship than this . . . Our life has become so organized and predictable . . . I miss spontaneity.*

"So, what are you going to do now?" Rebecca stood up and walked across to the kettle.

"Simon said he needs some time to figure out what he wants . . . a break, he said. And I was so thrown by it all that

I agreed to move out for a bit, to give him space. But I'm think-ing maybe that was a bad idea."

"No, I think that's a good plan. Give Simon one week of living on his own and he'll see what a mistake he's making."

"But what if he doesn't? What if—"

Libby was interrupted by a loud roaring sound as Rebecca turned on the coffee grinder. There was no such thing as in-stant coffee in this house; every cup was hand brewed—a pro-cess that took ages. Simon used to find it hilarious, watching the palaver Rebecca and Tom went through to make a simple hot drink, and would always try to catch Libby's eye to make her laugh too. At the memory, Libby felt a stab in her chest. They were a team, she and Simon, always there for each other, especially around their crazy families. How could he want out?

"What were you saying?" Rebecca said, when the grinding had finished.

"I said, what if he really is serious? What if it's not some midlife crisis and he actually wants to end it?"

"Come on, you two have been together for eight years. He's not going to throw it all away just like that. He'll see sense."

"And if he does, do you think I should go back to him? I mean, what if he does this again in another few years' time— how can I ever trust him again?"

"Of course you can trust him. This is Simon—the man is hardly Casanova. I swear, this is just some silly little blip, and in a few weeks' time, you'll be back in your little home, watch-ing TV together like the pair of boring old farts you are."

Before Libby could say anything, there was the sound of thundering footsteps down the hall.

"Auntie Lib!" Rebecca's son, Hector, came charging into the kitchen, his arms spread wide as he threw himself at Libby.

She scooped her nephew up into a hug, burying her face in his hair and inhaling his comforting scent of apple shampoo and rice cakes.

"I can't believe how big you've got," she said, releasing him. "What are you now, eighteen?"

"You know I'm only four," he said, frowning at her. "Mummy says you're going to look after me for the rest of the Easter holidays."

"I am?" Libby looked at Rebecca, who was busying herself dripping hot water over the coffee.

"Can we go to the Natural History Museum? I want to see the dinosaurs."

"Hector, why don't you go and finish that drawing for Granny? And then you can show it to me and Auntie Libby," Rebecca said.

The boy ran out of the room. There was a long silence as Rebecca focused intently on the coffee.

"So that's why you offered for me to stay here," Libby said eventually. "You need me to look after Hector for you."

"No! I offered for you to stay here because I'm a kind sister who wanted to help you out." Rebecca's voice was full of indignation, although her ears had gone slightly pink.

"So you don't need me to look after Hector, then?"

"Not if you don't want to. But I thought you might enjoy hanging out with your nephew—you hardly ever see him, after all."

"I thought you had a live-in nanny?"

"We do, but she's had to go back home—family emergency, most inconvenient. That's why we have a free room for you to stay in."

So, there it was. Libby had known that there had to be an

ulterior motive for her sister's invitation; Rebecca never did anything unless there was some benefit for her.

"How long do you need help for?"

"Only a week or two, until Rosalita's back. And it's perfect timing, really, as by that point you and Simon will have got over all this nonsense and you'll be home again." Rebecca handed Libby a cup of strong-smelling coffee.

"I don't know, Bex. Obviously I'd love to hang out with Hector, but I'm not sure my head's in the right place. I mean, look at me. I'm a mess."

Her sister let out a long sigh. "How many times have I asked for your help since Hector was born?"

"Well, never, but—"

"And do you or do you not have free time at the moment, given I assume you won't be working for Simon while you're on this break?"

"I do, but—"

"Well, there you go, then. Besides, it'll do you good. Hector will be a distraction from wallowing over Simon."

Rebecca had always been able to overrule Libby like this, ever since they were kids; no wonder she was so successful in her job as a corporate lawyer. Libby took a resigned sip of her coffee. "Mmm, this is delicious."

"It's Kopi Luwak, from Indonesia. The beans get eaten by civets, who then defecate them out, and they get fermented in the process. It costs a fortune because we only buy beans from totally free-living civets."

Libby grimaced and put her mug down.

"So, will you look after Hector, then?" Rebecca said.

Libby paused before she answered. Maybe it wasn't such a

bad idea? It would be good to keep busy; besides, she loved Hector, who was the only member of her family who didn't treat her like a complete moron. "Okay, sure."

"Excellent." Rebecca picked up a piece of paper that had been resting on the counter and handed it to Libby. "I've printed out his schedule for you. Every morning he's got football club, and then there are various activities in the afternoon. His tutor comes on Tuesday. He has piano on Wednesday and you've got tickets for an exhibition at the Science Museum on Friday."

"Wow."

"What?"

"Well, you know I'm all for a schedule, but this sounds exhausting."

"It's not exhausting. It's enriching," Rebecca said. "And he needs to get ahead if he wants to get into the right pre-prep school."

"Okay. Well, I'll do my best with it all."

"Tom and I don't get home until six, so you'll need to cook meals for Hector too. I order everything on Ocado, so all you'll need to do is follow the meal plan. And remember, he doesn't have red meat or dairy, and we try to only give him refined sugar at the weekends."

"Righty-ho." Libby was feeling sorrier for Hector by the second.

"I know what you're thinking, Libby, and no sneaking him off to McDonald's for chicken nuggets and milkshakes. You may not care about your body, but in this household, we treat ours with respect."

"No Big Macs, I promise."

Rebecca's phone buzzed and she picked it up. "Oh, and no

screen time either," she said as she read the message. "I saw a report recently about the damage it can do to developing brains."

Libby couldn't help but roll her eyes at this, and at that exact moment Rebecca glanced up from her phone, catching Libby midroll.

"Is there a problem?"

"No."

"Because that eye roll suggested you don't agree with me."

"It's not that. But we watched loads of TV as kids, and I'm not sure it did our brains any damage."

Rebecca was staring at Libby with a look she remembered from her childhood, a withering mixture of boredom and contempt. "Remind me, Libs—how many kids do you have?"

Oh, here we go.

"Exactly," Rebecca snapped. "If and when you do have children, you're welcome to let them spend all day staring at screens and eating crap. But while you're looking after *my* son, I ask that you please respect my parenting rules. Okay?"

Libby started to reply, but Rebecca had already swept out of the kitchen, leaving her staring openmouthed at the civet-poo coffee.

3

The following week was one of the most exhausting of Libby's life. Hector woke her at quarter to seven each weekday morning by bursting into her bedroom and jumping on the bed, and from then until the moment he fell asleep, twelve hours later, he kept up an almost constant barrage of questions: *What's the capital of Mongolia? Why do girls have boobies but boys don't? What's the opposite of "hamster"?* By the time Rebecca and Tom got home from work each evening, Hector was still bouncing off the walls, but Libby was ready to collapse.

The one upside was that Libby's days were so full, she had no time to think about Simon. It was only when she went to bed, drained and desperate for sleep, that the reality of her situation came crashing back. Two days . . . Three days . . . Four days and still no word. Their conversation on Friday night played over and over in Libby's brain like a bad pop song on loop. *I still love you but I feel like we've grown apart . . . We're more like housemates than lovers . . . You used to be such fun, but things have grown stale.* And every time, Libby felt the same sucker punch of surprise crushing the air out of her lungs. How had she not seen this coming? All this time she'd been so content in their life together, their Friday night takeaway and

Sunday morning sex, dreaming of the future they'd carefully planned for themselves, completely oblivious to the fact that the man she loved was deeply unhappy.

On Saturday morning, Hector woke his parents up instead of Libby and she slept in past nine. When she sat up, her whole body ached and she had a tight knot in her chest. She reached for her phone and flicked to Instagram. Libby had avoided it for the past week, not wanting to torture herself by looking at Simon's feed. Now she clicked on his name, holding her breath for what she'd find. Thankfully, Simon had posted only one photo since she'd last checked, a shot on one of his runs. Libby studied the new image carefully. His skin was flushed and his hair disheveled, and he was squinting into the sun as he grinned at the camera. He looked so rugged and handsome it made Libby feel sick. Surely Simon should have been missing her by now, but he looked so alive and carefree in this photo. What if he'd already realized he was happier without her in his life?

Libby jumped out of bed, showered, and dressed, then snuck out of the house before her sister could give her any commands. She had no idea where she was going, only that she couldn't spend the day moping in bed, staring at Simon's Instagram and panicking. When she reached the main road, she went into a café and bought herself a cappuccino and a chocolate croissant. As she stepped back outside, she saw a bus pull up at the stop in front of the café and its door swing open. Libby watched for a moment as passengers disgorged onto the pavement. She had no idea what number bus this was or where it was going, and she didn't have a coat or umbrella with her in case it rained. If she got on this bus, then she could end up anywhere, in one of the many dangerous areas of the city her sister was always telling her about. She was about to turn and walk past when she remembered Simon's words. *Our life has become so organized and predictable.* Libby took a deep breath and jumped on board.

She found an empty seat in the back section of the lower deck and sat down. How's *that* for spontaneous? she thought as she took a satisfied bite of her croissant. Although as she did, she glanced toward the electronic noticeboard to see where the bus was headed. 88 TO CLAPHAM COMMON, it read. Fine, Clapham Common it was, then.

As the bus set off, Libby looked around her at the other passengers. In the row in front were two teenage boys, their heads bent together as they shared a pair of earphones, the tinny beat of their music leaking out. Across the aisle from the teenagers was an older lady with silver hair under one of those clear plastic rain hoods; she was gripping the handle of a wheeled shopper. Sitting behind the pensioner, directly across from Libby, was a young woman with her hair pulled up in a bun, her lips moving as her eyes scanned across the page of a battered copy of *Pride and Prejudice.* She was completely lost in the story, absentmindedly playing with a button on her cardigan as she read. As Libby watched her, she suddenly remembered Frank, the old man she'd met on the bus last Saturday. What had he said? *A bus is the perfect place to practice life drawing because there's always a choice of interesting models.*

"Camden Town Station / Camden Street," the automated voice announced. The reading woman stood up, not taking her eyes off the page, and made her way toward the exit. Libby watched her step off the bus, impressed to see she didn't even look up from the book as she started to walk off down the pavement. More passengers were boarding at the front, and Libby glanced toward them and almost did a double take.

A tall, skinny man with a row of spiked black hair down the center of his head had boarded the bus and was making his way along the aisle in long strides. He must have been in his mid-thirties and was dressed in a black leather jacket, tight jeans, and Doc Martens boots, with a chain attached to his belt that jangled as he walked. Was this an actual punk? Libby hadn't realized that was even a thing anymore. The two teenagers in the row in front were nudging each other and staring at the man, but he seemed oblivious to the stir he was causing. He slumped down in the seat that the bookish woman had vacated, his long legs jutting out into the aisle.

Frank's words ran through Libby's mind again. Here was someone who was definitely interesting enough to draw, but could she do it? She'd not drawn anything for years, and besides, she didn't have a sketchbook with her and . . .

Spontaneous.

Libby opened her bag and rummaged through the contents. She usually kept it tidy, but after a week with Hector, it now contained several toy cars, a half-eaten box of raisins, a small notepad, and a pack of coloring pencils. Libby pulled out the notepad and a black pencil, then looked over at the man.

Because he was sitting directly across the aisle from her, Libby could see only the left-hand profile of his face. He had a strong, angular jaw and dark eyes, and his ear was lined with small silver hoops. A tattoo was creeping up his neck from under the collar of his jacket, although Libby couldn't make out what it was. Aside from his Mohawk, his head was closely shaved, and it looked like it would be almost soft to touch.

Unlike Libby, who tended to slouch, this man was sitting tall in his seat, with the confidence of someone who didn't care what anyone else thought of them. He really was extraordinary-looking. Libby glanced down at the blank white paper on her lap, then took a deep breath and pressed her pencil onto the page.

When she next checked out of the window, Libby was surprised to see they were driving down a busy shopping street, and an underground station sign told her they were at Oxford Circus. She stared down at the sketch and inwardly groaned. She'd made the man's body a weird shape and his hair looked like it had been stuck on with glue, and there was a big line across his chin where the bus had hit a pothole and her pencil had skidded across the paper. It was the kind of thing Hector would draw, and he was only four. Libby ripped out the page and was about to screw it up when she noticed the profile of his face. It was far from perfect, but she'd managed to capture the shape of his skull, the sharp jawline and brooding eye. It was very rough, but with more time maybe she could make the sketch better? Libby glanced back up at the man. He'd barely moved all journey, staring forward as if in a trance. But he could get off at any minute, and then her chance to finish the sketch would be over. If only there was a way she could get a photo of him so she could carry on working on it at home.

Libby looked around her. All the other passengers were in their own worlds, staring out the windows or at their phone screens. She reached into her bag, pulled out her phone, and as discreetly as possible, lifted it up and took a shot.

"What the fuck are you doing?"

At the sound of the camera click, the man she'd drawn had

swung round in his seat and was staring at her. Libby stuffed her phone back in her bag.

"Were you taking photos of me?" His black eyes were fixed on her, and Libby could feel other passengers turning to look.

"No . . . I mean, yes, but sorry."

The man scowled. "You think I'm some kind of tourist attraction, here for your entertainment?"

"No, I was . . ." Libby felt the color drain from her face. "I'm sorry. I'll delete it."

"Imagine if it was the other way round, and some random guy took a photo of you on the bus. How would you like that?"

The old woman sitting in front of the punk was looking at Libby and shaking her head. Libby felt a burn of shame, and she snatched up her bag and stood up to leave. As she did, the piece of paper slipped off her lap and, as if in slow motion, floated toward the floor in the middle of the aisle.

Shit! Libby watched as the punk leaned down and picked up the page as it landed by his feet. She closed her eyes, preparing to hear his roar of rage. But there was only the muffled sound of music from the two teens in front, and when Libby opened her eyes again, he was staring at the drawing with a look of disgust on his face.

"I'm so sorry," Libby said, and she heard a tremor in her voice.

He didn't say anything and carried on studying the piece of paper. She could sense the passengers around them were holding their breath, waiting to see what he would do.

"It's a really bad drawing," Libby said in a half whisper.

The man glanced up then and caught Libby's eye. For a moment she stared back at him, unsure what to do. Then she ran toward the open door, humiliation coursing through her body.

4

PEGGY

There's nothing I love more than a bit of drama on the bus.

Did I ever tell you about that time, back in the sixties, when I saw a full-blown fight on the top deck of the 74? There were a couple of mod lads on the bus and then these rockers got on at Earls Court. It started as a few swear words chucked here and there, but before I knew it, they were facing each other off in the aisle, tossing empty beer cans like missiles over the seats. Most of the other passengers scarpered at the first sign of trouble, but you know me. I stayed up there, enjoying the free show until the police turned up and escorted them off.

And do you remember when we were on the 205 and we saw that skinny lad in a cheap suit get down on one knee and propose to his girlfriend? I remember how all the passengers held their breath while we waited for her to answer, and then she said no, and it was so awkward, the poor bugger had to get off the bus.

Well, let me tell you about yesterday's drama. It started with great promise. I looked up as soon as I heard a raised voice, and I knew straightaway it was the young man sitting in

the row behind me. I'd clocked him as soon as he got on the
bus, of course; you used to see a lot of punk rockers in London
back in the day, but I've not come across one in years, apart
from that nice man who works at Oxford Circus Station and
once helped me when my shopper got caught in the ticket bar-
rier. This lad on the bus was far too young to be an original
punk, but he looked the part with his spiky hair, dark clothes,
and angry face. He was glaring at a girl sitting across the aisle
from him, who was clutching a piece of paper in her hands,
quaking like a leaf.

Well, at first, I thought the punk was being inappropriate,
and I was about to give him an earful when he started speaking, at which point I stood down. Turns out, I'd got it the
wrong way round and the girl had taken *his* picture on her
mobile phone. Well, that's all very well, but if you're stupid
enough to get caught, then you've got to be prepared to take
the consequences. The girl looked like she was about to burst
into tears, and I'm sorry, but I couldn't help shaking my head.
Honestly, young people are so soft these days it's no wonder
the world's going to hell in a handbasket.

Anyway, the girl stood up to get off the bus, and as she did,
the piece of paper fell off her lap onto the floor. I leaned down
to get it, but before I could, the lad reached over and snatched
it up. But I got a quick look at it, and you'll never guess what
it was. It was a pencil sketch the girl had done of him, right
there on the bus.

Can you believe it, of all the things?

And then the strangest thing happened. At the sight of this
drawing—which wasn't half bad, by the way—I had this sudden flashback. It was almost as if I could feel a pencil in my
hand, the sensation of it passing over rough sketching paper,

the jolts and bumps as the bus rumbled along. And it was like I was back there, all those years ago, and I just sat there, letting the memories wash over me. Then, all of a sudden, they burst like a bubble, and I was an old woman again, back on the 88, heading down toward Piccadilly Circus.

The girl had got off the bus by then, and I turned back to look at the man. He was still staring at this sketch, and I waited for him to screw it up and chuck it away. But instead, he folded it in half, ever so carefully, like he didn't want to damage it, and slipped it into his jacket pocket. And then he looked up and I had to turn back round so he didn't think I was being nosy.

So it wasn't quite up there with the fight or the marriage proposal, but still, I knew it was a story you'd enjoy. So little of excitement happens these days, and I hate to admit it, but sometimes I struggle for things to tell you. It's why I'm grateful for my bus journeys. On the 88 there's always the chance for a bit of drama or a brief chat with a stranger, a nugget of something new. And then, with a little bit of creativity and elaboration on my part, I can turn it into a story to share. But if nothing happens on the bus, if no one wants to talk to me and everyone's staring at their phones, well, that's when I struggle.

Remember the other week, when I was telling you about my trip to Asda and the argument with the shop assistant about the price of Whiskas? I'll tell you now, love, halfway through that story I could sense you'd stopped listening, and I realized what a sad old sod I'd become. If I think back to when we were younger, to all the things we thought we'd achieve with our lives, and now look at us: two old fogies talking about the price of cat food.

5

"Libs, wake up!"

Something warm and sticky prodded Libby's face, jolting her out of her dream. She groaned and buried her head under the pillow. "What time is it?"

"Late o'clock, lazybones. Granny and Grandpa are here, and they want to know where you are," Hector said, prodding her again, this time in the back.

"Tell them I'm coming," she mumbled, and waited for the sound of his feet padding out of the room.

Libby had slept badly again. It had been a fortnight now and she'd still not heard a word from Simon, but every night he turned up around two a.m. to haunt her dreams. Last night, he'd been running and Libby had been trying to catch him, but for some reason, she was dressed in a chicken outfit and she kept falling over her giant bird feet. Now all she wanted to do was go back to sleep, but she had to face the torment of a family Sunday lunch.

Libby reached for her phone to check the time, and almost dropped it. On the lock screen was a missed-call notification from Simon.

She sat up, her mouth suddenly bone-dry. Was this it? After fourteen long days, and sleepless nights, of uncertainty and heartache and patronizing sympathy from Rebecca, was it finally coming to an end? Libby took a deep breath to steady herself, then pressed CALL.

"Libby."

The way he said her name made the skin on the back of her neck prickle. "Simon."

"I'm so glad you rang back."

Libby felt relief flood through her body, but she tried to keep her voice cool. He needed to do some serious groveling, after all. "How are you?"

"I'm okay. Work's been crazy busy, as you can imagine. I hear you're staying with Tom and the Gorgon."

Libby smiled, despite herself. In the early days of their relationship, Simon had given Rebecca that secret nickname, claiming that one look from her could turn anyone to stone.

"Yeah, it's been intense."

"You must be getting sick and tired of all the chia seeds. How's Hector?"

"He's good. I gave him a Percy Pig the other day and it was like he'd died and gone to heaven."

Simon laughed and Libby felt her heart lift. God, she'd missed that sound. She waited for the apologies to begin.

"Look, Libs, I'm sorry it's taken me so long to call you. And I'm sorry for the way I handled everything. I honestly thought I was doing the right thing taking you to that restaurant, but I realize it was a terrible idea. I'm so sorry."

There was a wobble in his voice, and Libby wanted to reach down the phone and hold him. This was the Simon she knew and loved, the Simon who brought her a cup of tea in bed every morning and left her little love notes stuck on the fridge. The Simon whom she'd planned her future with. So even though Libby knew she should have been yelling at him right now, forcing him to grovel and beg, all she really wanted to do was jump on a train and rush back to Surrey. If she left soon, she could be back home by midafternoon.

"You have every right to hate me after everything I said," Simon continued, interrupting her mental packing. "I know I've really hurt you, and I'm so sorry about that."

Libby took a deep breath. "The last two weeks have been hell, Si. And you're right—you handled it all really badly. But I don't hate you."

"Oh, Libs, thank god," he said, and she could hear the relief in his voice. "I'm so glad you said that, because there's something I want to ask you."

From downstairs, Libby heard the shrill ring of her mum's laughter, and she pictured her family's delighted faces when she told them that she and Simon were back together. She could almost hear her sister's satisfaction. *What did I tell you? Give him a few weeks and he'll come running back . . .*

"Libby?"

"Sorry. I'm listening."

"Okay, so . . ."

He sounded so nervous, Libby almost wanted to laugh.

"I really miss you . . ."

A smile spread across her face.

". . . at work. So I was wondering if you'd consider coming back and helping out again?"

Libby felt her whole body deflate, as if someone had pricked her like a balloon. She opened her mouth to speak, but no words came out.

"I realize this might seem a weird thing to ask, given I'm the one who wants this time apart. But things have been crazy in the past few weeks and I'm so behind on e-mails and invoices and the diary is all over the place without you here to organize things. I feel like I'm drowning."

Libby was listening to him, but Simon's words made no sense; it was like he was speaking another language.

"I've thought it all through," Simon continued, oblivious to Libby spiraling on the other end of the phone. "I can set you up with remote access to the server and divert the office phone to your mobile. That way you can work from your sister's place, and we won't have to physically see each other."

He stopped talking, waiting for her to reply, but Libby still couldn't formulate any proper thoughts, let alone sentences.

"Libs, are you still there?"

"Yeah."

"What do you think of the idea?"

"I don't know . . . I thought . . ." She trailed off.

"Oh, no," Simon said, and she heard the realization in his voice. "You thought that . . . Oh, shit, I'm so sorry. You thought . . . No, I'm sorry, Libs, but I still need more time apart. I feel like I'm only just starting to get to know myself again and—"

"I get it," Libby interrupted.

"You're amazing. You really are. But I feel like we were so young when we got together, and we rushed into a relationship so fast. I just really want to be sure what's right for me, because I think that maybe—"

"Good-bye, Simon." Libby tried to hang up, but her fingers were shaking too much, so she threw the phone onto the floor and pulled the duvet over her head as she let out a silent scream.

. . .

TWENTY minutes later, Libby came downstairs to find her family gathered in the kitchen, sipping champagne from long-stemmed flutes. She hadn't had time to shower, but she'd put on some mascara and the smartest top she'd brought with her. However, as she walked into the room and they all stopped talking and turned to stare at her, Libby had a sudden urge to run upstairs, slam the door shut, and hide in her bedroom.

"At last, there you are." Her mum, Pauline, looking as elegant as ever in skinny jeans and a silk blouse, stepped forward and kissed her on the cheek. As she did, Libby was overpowered by the smell of Chanel No. 5. "Are you all right, Elizabeth? You look unwell."

"I'm fine, thanks." Libby walked over to the kettle, but Pauline followed.

"How have you been finding things, darling?"

"All right."

"Any word from Simon?"

Here it was already. "Not yet, no."

"Really? What do your friends say? One of them must know what's going on with him."

Libby busied herself finding a tea bag. The truth was she still hadn't spoken to any of her friends back home. She'd hoped one of them might have reached out to her by now, checking in that she was okay, but she hadn't heard a thing. It seemed that everyone had already picked a side, and Simon had been the winner.

"Have you tried contacting him?" Pauline said.

"No, Mum."

"Well, I think maybe it's time you did. We all thought he'd

have come begging by now, but perhaps you'll need to give him a little nudge? You don't want him to get too comfortable without you."

"How have you and Dad been?" Libby said, keen to move the conversation on.

"Oh, you know . . ." Her mum let out an exaggerated sigh and then lowered her voice to a stage whisper. "I'm so busy with all my voluntary work, but your father's been at a loose end ever since he retired. I come home and find him sulking round the house like a teenager."

"He was a doctor for almost forty years, Mum. It's going to take him a while to get used to his new pace of life."

"I know that," Pauline snapped. "But he needs to hurry up and find a hobby before he drives me mad. I can't even convince him to play golf these days, and you know how he normally loves that. All this stress doesn't help."

"What stress?"

"You, of course. We really thought you and Simon were serious. You told us you were going to get engaged when you turned thirty."

"That's what we'd planned. I'm sorry, Mum."

"I'm not blaming you, darling. It's just so strange. I mean, your father and I have been together for thirty-six years and he's not grown bored with *me* yet."

Libby opened her mouth to respond, but her sister swept in. "Lunch is ready. Bring the salad, will you?"

They all sat round the kitchen table as Rebecca served up grilled salmon, quinoa, and salad. Libby saw her dad's nose wrinkle, but he knew better than to criticize Rebecca. Libby didn't blame him for his reaction, though. After two weeks of Rebecca's healthy cooking, Libby was dying for a Sunday roast.

She and Simon had had one religiously every week, always with Yorkshire puddings and a bottle of wine, before they'd collapse on the sofa to watch a film. Libby felt a physical pain at the memory.

"So, any news on when Rosalita's coming back?" Pauline asked Rebecca.

"No. I messaged her this morning and apparently her mum is sicker than they originally thought and she might have to have an operation."

"Poor thing," Libby said.

"I know. It's a bloody nightmare."

Libby looked at her sister. "I meant, poor Rosalita."

"Well, yes, her too, of course. It's just bad timing, that's all. I'm working on a big new deal and Tom's traveling lots, plus, we're starting another round of IVF. I could really do with knowing when she'll be back."

"Well, at least you've got Libby here to help for now," Pauline said. "It sounds like she's not going back to Simon anytime soon."

"Yes, what have you been doing with all your free time, Elizabeth?" her dad asked.

"Oh, this and that." In truth, when she wasn't with Hector, Libby spent most of her time huddled on the sofa rewatching *Titanic*. A couple of times she'd considered doing some drawing, but as soon as she picked up a pencil, she'd remember her excruciating humiliation at the hands of the stranger on the bus and drop it like it was red-hot.

"I keep telling her she should go to the gym," Rebecca said, skewering a piece of cucumber with her fork.

"I'm not really a gym person."

"Well, maybe you could give it a go, seeing as you've got

nothing else to do?" her mum said. "It would be good for your mental health. Plus, you do look like you've let yourself go a bit recently."

"Pauline!" Rebecca's husband gave an awkward laugh.

"I'm just saying, Tom, it might be time she started thinking about her appearance a bit more."

"I also suggested a haircut," Rebecca said.

"Ooh, now, that's a good idea," Pauline said. "You had shorter hair when you and Simon first met."

"My hairdresser, Antoni, is a miracle worker; if anyone can sort Libby's hair out, he can."

Libby focused on her salmon, but the texture was slimy and it was making her feel sick.

"Maybe you could do some shopping as well, spruce up your wardrobe," Pauline said, warming to the makeover theme.

"What's wrong with my clothes?" Libby asked, and then immediately regretted it when Rebecca smirked.

"Nothing's wrong per se," her mum said. "It's just . . . Well, you still dress like you did when you were a teenager, jeans and boring plain tops."

"You're turning thirty soon. It's time you learned to dress for your shape," Rebecca added.

"But I like these tops. They're comfortable."

"Comfortable is not the point," Rebecca said with the exasperated tone of a teacher talking to a particularly stupid student. "Do you think I'm comfy in the skirt suits I wear to work every day, the stiletto heels that kill my feet? Of course not. But I dress like that because I know that appearance matters."

"That's a bit anti-feminist, isn't it?" Tom said, and Libby nearly choked on a cherry tomato. She'd barely heard Tom speak since she'd been here, let alone challenge his wife.

"That's easy for you to say," Rebecca said, glaring at him. "You can swan into work in your jeans and trainers and no one bats an eyelid. But, as depressing as it is to admit this, what women wear *does* affect how people perceive us. If I dressed like you, no one would take me seriously at work."

"But still, are you suggesting Libby needs a haircut and new clothes in order to win Simon back? Because that sounds pretty outdated to me."

"We're not saying that, Tom, dear," Pauline said. "But I think Libby's lack of—how should I put it?—care in her appearance may send out a message that she doesn't care about herself. And who would want to be in a relationship with someone who doesn't love themselves?"

"Any chance of a top-up?" Libby's dad said, signaling his empty champagne flute.

"Plus, a bit of physical improvement can do wonders for your self-esteem," Pauline continued. "Remember when Hector was two weeks old and I gave Rebecca that size eight designer dress as an incentive to lose the baby weight? You were back to your old shape in four months, weren't you, darling?"

"I was," Rebecca said, although Libby thought she saw her wince slightly at the memory.

"And I can't help thinking Libby might also feel better about herself if she looked in the mirror and saw a nice haircut and a pair of jeans that actually fitted properly," Pauline added.

"I might feel better about myself if my family stopped talking about me as if I wasn't here," Libby mumbled, but no one was listening.

"Maybe I could come up one day and we could go to the big John Lewis on Oxford Street?" her mum said. "It's ages since we've had a girlie day together, and we could find you some nice new dresses."

"Sure," Libby said with a resigned shrug.

"I'll message Antoni and see if he can squeeze you in for an appointment this week," Rebecca said, reaching for her phone.

"Mum, I've had enough. Can I go and play with my train set?" Hector said.

"Fine," Rebecca said, not looking up from her screen.

"I'll come and help you," Libby said, standing up quickly.

"I don't need—" Hector started to say, but he must have seen the look in Libby's eyes, because he stopped, took her hand, and led her out of the room.

6

H ave you got your packed lunch?" Libby asked Hector as she opened the front door the next morning.

"Check."

"Wellies for forest school?"

"Check."

"Jet pack for mission to Mars?"

"Check!"

"Great, let's go."

They set off down the road, Hector leaping and skipping along the pavement with the enthusiasm of Tigger from *Winnie-the-Pooh*, with Libby following him, trying not to yawn. She'd thought she would have got used to Hector's energy levels by now, but two weeks in and she was more exhausted than ever. Since that fateful night when Simon had asked for a break, she had felt as though her battery had been drained and she was constantly shattered.

Once she'd dropped Hector at preschool, Libby made her way to the nearest bus stop. The traffic was heavy this morning, but after a ten-minute wait, an 88 pulled up and Libby boarded, climbed to the upper deck, and sat down in the front-right-hand seat, dumping her bag on the floor. She'd planned to spend the day at home job hunting, but this morning, Rebecca had announced with much fanfare that her hairdresser could squeeze Libby in. She'd tried to protest, but as usual Libby had been steamrollered by her sister. She cringed at the thought of what was to come. Libby had always hated getting her hair cut. As a child, she remembered countless hairdressers staring in dismay at her chaotic ginger curls, before telling her mother that there was *only so much that could be done with hair like this.* Matters weren't helped by the fact that Rebecca had long, silky brown hair that their mother had spent hours plaiting into elaborate styles, while the most Libby ever got was her mum swearing as she tried to drag a comb through the knots. Simon had always said he loved Libby's hair, although he sometimes teased her that she looked like Merida from *Brave.*

"It's you!"

Libby startled at a voice to her left. She spun round to see the elderly man in the faded velvet jacket sitting across the aisle.

"You *are* Libby, aren't you?" he said, looking suddenly concerned.

"I am. Hi, Frank."

"I'm so happy I remembered you!" He grinned. "The old memory's not so good these days, but I knew I wouldn't forget that beautiful hair."

"How are you?"

"Good, good. Have you been practicing drawing on the bus, like we discussed?"

Libby gave a wry laugh. "Funny you should say that. I did try once, but I'm afraid it didn't go well."

"What happened?"

"Well, I saw this striking-looking man and I remembered what you said, so I had a go at sketching him. But then I made the mistake of taking a photo so I could carry on with it later, and he caught me doing it."

"Oh, no!"

"Yeah, he wasn't impressed—I honestly thought he might kill me."

"Oh, dear, some people can be so grumpy on the bus. But I hope you've tried again?"

"Eh . . ." Libby looked down at her lap.

"Come on, now, you can't let one little incident put you off. What about the National Gallery? Have you been there yet?"

Libby shook her head. "Sorry. I've been busy looking after my nephew and . . ." She trailed off; he didn't need to hear about her tragic life. "It's so funny bumping into you again."

Frank didn't respond, and when Libby looked, he was staring out of the window, his attention fixed on the bus stop they were pulling up at. Libby could see his eyes scanning the passengers waiting to board. When the bus pulled off again, he turned back to her. "Sorry. What did you say?"

"I said I'm surprised to bump into you again."

"Oh, I'm always on this bus. It's practically my second home."

"Where are you headed today?"

"Nowhere in particular."

"Why are you on the bus, then?" Libby hoped she didn't sound nosy, but there was something about Frank that she found fascinating.

"Oh, it's silly, really." He ran a hand through his disheveled hair, looking faintly embarrassed.

"No, go on, tell me."

He studied Libby as if weighing something up. "I'm actually looking for someone."

"Who?"

"A woman."

Libby waited to see if he'd elaborate, but he didn't say anything else. "Who is she, Frank?"

He smiled. "Ah, now, that's a long story."

"I've got time." As she said it, Libby glanced out the window. They'd reached the bottom of Kentish Town and were turning right into Camden. She must have at least twenty minutes before she needed to get off the bus at the hairdresser's. "Please, I'd love to hear the story."

Frank wrinkled his nose. "Are you sure?"

"One hundred percent."

"Very well."

He took a deep breath and cleared his throat.

"It was a Sunday in April 1962 and I was on the 88 bus coming back from my aunt and uncle's house in Mitcham. I spotted her out of the front window as soon as the bus pulled up at Clapham Common Station . . ."

7

O h, wow, she sounds incredible!" Libby said when Frank had finished his story. "Did you really look like Rock Hudson back then? Do you still have her sketch?"

"I do. I keep it in pride of place at home," Frank said.

Libby sat back in her seat, exhaling. The girl really did sound remarkable, so cool and gutsy, plus, she'd stood up to her parents about going to art school. For a moment, Libby tried to imagine what her life might have been like if she'd been that brave, if she'd followed her dream of going to art school rather than giving in to her parents and studying medicine. Probably, she'd have graduated rather than dropping out in the second year, and maybe she'd have moved to London as opposed to returning to Surrey with her tail between her legs. But then she'd never have got a job at the local garden center, never have met Simon when he came in to buy some topsoil, never have accepted his offer to go out for a drink.

"So, tell me everything that happened next," Libby said, turning back to Frank. "Did you end up dating her?"

"I'm afraid it's not quite that simple," Frank said, and Libby waited for him to continue.

"As you can imagine, after she got off the bus, I spent the rest of the journey in a daze. I felt like a stick of dynamite had gone off in my life, blowing it to smithereens. I was already imagining marching into the shop and telling my parents that I wanted to quit and go to drama school. But mostly I was thinking about that extraordinary girl, her hair and those incredible green eyes. I'd never felt like this about anyone before, and I'd watched enough Hollywood romances to know what this meant: that she was the woman I was going to spend the rest of my life with. By the time I got off the bus, I'd planned it all: our engagement and the wedding, me working as an actor and her as an artist, the children we'd have. I walked home in a dream. I swear, Marilyn Monroe herself could have walked past me and I wouldn't have noticed her."

Libby laughed, but she was already dreading what was to come.

"When I got home, I went straight to my bedroom and emptied my jacket pockets. There was the picture she'd sketched of me, along with some loose change and my own bus ticket. But I couldn't find the ticket the girl had given me, the one she'd written her phone number on. I looked in my trouser pockets, but it wasn't there either, so I went downstairs to check if it had fallen out when I got my keys. But there was no sign of the ticket anywhere. I'd lost it."

"Oh, no, Frank! What did you do?"

"The first thing I did was retrace my footsteps back to the bus stop, picking up every discarded bus ticket I found in case it had her number on it. When that failed, I seriously considered catching the bus up to Oxford Circus, but then I realized I had no idea where she worked, or which art school she studied at. I didn't even know her name."

As he said this, Frank's face sagged, and Libby couldn't help but reach out and put her hand on his arm. He didn't speak for a moment, and Libby could see that he was still back there in the moment, sixty years ago.

"I was beside myself, Libby. In the space of one bus ride, I'd fallen head over heels in love, and now I had no way of finding her again. I sulked around the shop all week, moping and getting under my parents' feet. On my day off, the following Sunday, I went down to Clapham Common first thing in the morning and waited by the number 88 bus stop. It was a horrible day, pouring with rain, but I was certain that if I waited long enough I would see her. I'd brought a bunch of flowers for her, and I thought how she'd laugh when I told her what had happened, and how one day we'd tell our grandchildren this funny story about how we met . . ."

Frank trailed off, and Libby waited for him to speak again.

"I stood at that bus stop for twelve hours, soaked to the bone and freezing, but she never came. I caught a nasty cold, and by the time I got home that evening, I had to go straight to bed and stayed there for two days. I honestly believed that without her my life was over."

"Oh, Frank."

"Well, young people are prone to drama, aren't they? And of course, my life wasn't over, but it had changed forever. Everything that girl said had made a deep mark on my heart, and I knew I couldn't carry on my life as it was. A week later, I told my parents that I didn't want to work in the shop anymore, that I wanted to go to drama school."

"What did they say?"

"They were furious—I'd never heard my father shout or threaten the way he did that day. But I remembered what the girl had said about only getting one life, so I stayed resolute. After several weeks of hell, my father calmed down. I applied to drama school the following day."

"And?"

"I got in," Frank said with a proud smile. "It turned out all those trips to the pictures had taught me something. I got a place at Central School of Speech and Drama, with a full scholarship, and I started that autumn."

"So you're a famous actor?"

"Not famous, I'm afraid. But I did work as an actor for more than fifty years, mainly in the theater. I only stopped a few years ago when I started forgetting my lines."

"That's amazing. And what about the girl on the bus? Please tell me you found out what happened to her."

He shook his head slowly and Libby let out a gasp of realization.

"So that's why you ride the bus, Frank?"

"I've been looking for her for sixty years."

"Bloody hell." She slumped back in her seat, suddenly exhausted.

"I told you it was a long story," Frank said.

At his words, Libby looked out the window and saw they were driving past Hamleys toy shop. She must have missed her stop ages ago, and her hair appointment. Rebecca would kill her, but right now Libby couldn't have cared less.

"That's an extraordinary story, Frank."

"Makes me sound daft, doesn't it?"

"No! It makes you sound unbelievably romantic."

"You're being polite. And I haven't done it solidly—there have been periods of months, years even, when I haven't gone looking for her. But somehow I always end up coming back to this bus."

"But how do you know she's still in London?"

"I don't. For all I know, she might have left the city years ago or even have died. But something tells me she's still alive, here in the city, and as long as I have that feeling, I can't give up my search."

As he said that, Libby saw him look out the front window toward the approaching bus stop, as if suddenly remembering the purpose of his journey.

"That's why I always sit up here in the front seat," he said, nodding toward the window. "It gives me the best view looking down on the bus stop, so I can see who's getting on."

"I can't believe you've been searching all this time. That's such an extraordinary commitment."

"I wish everyone thought that. My daughter doesn't approve at all."

"You have a daughter?" From the way he'd told the story, Libby had got the impression that Frank had remained single, but he nodded.

"From an ill-fated affair in the seventies. Her mother and I worked together on a play, a terrible production of *Macbeth* in Sheffield. My daughter, Clara, was the only good thing to come out of it."

"So you never married?"

"I had a number of relationships over the years, but I'm afraid none of them ever lasted. Clara always blames my girl on the bus."

"Why?"

"She thinks I've never given any woman a proper chance,

because I'm always out here searching for the one that got away."

"And what do you think?"

Frank gave a small chuckle. "She's probably right, although I'd never tell her that. For a long time I did compare every woman I met to that redheaded artist who stole my heart."

"I'm not surprised. She sounds wonderful."

"But you know, over the years, that's changed. I'm not looking for her now because I want some grand love story. I'm far too old for that sort of thing. I'm looking for her because I want to thank her." He turned back to Libby. "That girl on the bus changed my life. If it wasn't for her, I'd have never had the confidence to stand up to my parents, never become an actor and lived the life I've had. So I want to say thank you."

"Well, I think it's the most romantic story I've ever heard." As Libby said this, Simon flashed into her mind. Would he have tried to track her down if they'd been in the same situation? Or would he have forgotten about her the second she'd got off the bus?

"Sadly, Clara hates me riding this bus route. And pretty soon she might stop me altogether," Frank said.

"Why?"

"My daughter wants me to move into a care home; she thinks I'm becoming a danger to myself. But if that happens, I won't be allowed to ride the 88 anymore, and then they might as well put me in a box and bury me."

"But why would you be a danger to yourself?"

"Well, I have been getting a little forgetful lately. And there was a small incident last year, when I forgot the grill was on and the fire service had to come out. But the nice firewoman was very sympathetic, said it happened all the time. And I've not had any issues like that since my carer started, but Clara still worries about me. She says I could get lost on the bus one day." He scoffed as he said this. "Imagine that. I know this bus route like the back of my hand."

"Have you tried telling your daughter you don't want to go into a care home?"

"Yes, but she won't listen. When Clara gets an idea in her head, she's like a dog with a bone."

"That sounds like my sister."

"She's threatening to set me up with some social services assessment where they decide whether you're fit to live alone. Can you believe it? I've lived in my house for fifty years, and now some busybody stranger gets to tell me whether I'm allowed to stay in my own home."

"Maybe the assessment will be fine, and you'll be able to stay?" Libby said, but Frank was frowning.

"I don't know what I'll do if I can't ride this bus, Libby. Time is running out for me to find her."

His shoulders sagged as he trailed off, and they rode on without speaking. Libby's mind was whirring with Frank's story. She couldn't imagine what that must have felt like, to have had such a strong connection with someone that you'd spend a lifetime trying to find them. How on earth would he cope if that purpose got taken away from him?

"Frank, have you ever tried any other ways of looking for her, aside from on the bus?"

"How do you mean?"

"Well, have you tried to find her on the electoral register or something like that?"

"The problem is, I never asked her name, a fact I kick myself about every single day. The only information I have is that she lived in Clapham and went to art school. I tried contacting all the London art schools back at the time, but understandably none of them would give me any information about their students. I even stood outside a few of them, hoping to see her arrive or leave, but to no avail."

"What about looking on the Internet?"

Frank shook his head. "I'm afraid I don't know the first thing about all of that. I've always been a terrible Luddite."

"Well, I'm no expert, but I could have a look for you if you like? Research red-haired female artists who'd be about the right age, that sort of thing."

"You'd do that for me?"

"Of course. I mean, it's a long shot but it has to be worth a go."

A smile spread across Frank's face, starting with his mouth and ending up in his eyes. "I don't know what to say. That's one of the kindest things anyone has ever offered to do for me."

"Well, I've got some time on my hands right now, so I'm happy to help. I'll have a dig around and see what I can find."

"Thank you, Libby," he said, and she thought she saw the glisten of a tear in his eye. "Thank you."

CHAPTER

8

PEGGY

Sometimes, my bus journey coincides with school chucking-out time.

Now, I know a lot of oldies don't like being on the bus at the same time as schoolkids. You remember Eileen from number eighteen? Terrible dress sense, drove her husband to an early grave with her moaning? She always complains if she ends up on the bus with a load of youths, says they're too noisy and disrespectful, not giving up their seats for her. But I love it. Nothing makes me happier than a bus full of youngsters, with their big voices and teenage swagger, brown and black and white skin all together in one sweaty, hormonal tin can on wheels. I sit in my seat behind the wheelchair spot and I watch them like I'm at the cinema. I love listening to their gossip, the schoolyard banter and insults, the tales of heartache and love.

Do you remember what it felt like to be that age? Because I do, better than I remember what it felt like to be forty or fifty. Everything felt so huge back then. There were no small emotions, no little pleasures or irritations—everything was either the biggest triumph or the end of the bleedin' world. I'm not sure if I've ever told you this, but I kept a diary all through my teenage years. I'd mostly fill it with sketches and doodles, but I also used to write these terrible poems about how hard it was being me, how no one understood me. Honestly, you'd have laughed if you read them, love. Thankfully, my father threw them all out when I left home, so you were spared.

You know, it's funny. I forget there was ever a time when we weren't in each other's lives. I assume you were there by my side when I was born, there when I started school or wrote my first awful poems. I wonder what you'd have thought of me if we'd met earlier. Because I wasn't always like that cocky nineteen-year-old you first laid eyes on, believe you me. By then I'd been through enough battles that I was already pretty tough, or at least I liked to think I was. But back when I was younger, I was much shyer and more nervous. I used to sit at the back of class, head down, sketching in my math book when I should have been do-ing arithmetic. The teachers all said I was stupid, but I wasn't; I just had no interest in algebra or Shakespeare's sonnets. All I wanted to do was draw.

Of course, it drove my parents mad, especially my father. And when I told him I wanted to go to art college, well, you should have seen how he went off. *People like us don't go to art school,* he shouted, loud enough that the neighbors banged on the wall. *You'll go to secretarial college like your sisters and then you'll damn well get married.*

Well, he got his way in the end, didn't he?

Do you remember my father's reaction when he found out I was pregnant? *I knew this would happen if you went off to that art school,* he screamed, like one of those fire-and-brimstone preachers. *Twenty-one, unmarried, and pregnant. You've brought shame on our family.*

I can laugh about it now, love, but at the time I thought he was going to murder me. Remember when I walked up the aisle, his face was so purple, he looked like he was going to explode? And my mother, holding her hankie like she was at a bloody funeral. Thankfully you caught my eye and made me smile; otherwise I'm not sure how I'd have got through it.

I find I've been thinking about those early days more and more lately. I'll be on the bus, minding my own business, when suddenly I'll see or hear something that takes me right back, fifty or sixty years. It's the strangest thing, all these memories floating up again. I suppose that's what happens when you get to our age, isn't it? And I'm not complaining, mind. The other day, watching all the schoolkids messing around on the 88, I could remember so clearly what it felt like to be their age, all the fear and the hopes and the longings.

They say youth is wasted on the young, but I'm not sure I agree. I think if you gave me those big emotions now—those feelings of triumph and disaster—I wouldn't know what to do with them. No, these days, finding a fresh copy of *Metro* on the bus is about as much excitement as I can handle.

CHAPTER

9

For the rest of the week, Libby spent every spare moment she had searching online for Frank's girl on the bus. He'd said he'd met her in April 1962 and she'd looked around eighteen or nineteen, so Libby started by looking for British female artists who were born in the early to mid-1940s. That produced a number of options, but none came up who had red hair and records of studying in London in the early sixties. Besides, Libby was aware that this woman might not have gone on to be a renowned artist, so she needed to broaden her search. Next, she tried finding alumni lists of London art colleges from the 1960s. A number of them had Facebook groups, so she posted on those, which led to several leads, but they all came to nothing. After four days of hunting, Libby had an elaborate color-coded spreadsheet and a cricked neck from sitting slumped over her laptop screen, but she was still no closer to finding Frank's woman.

On Saturday morning, Libby skipped Rebecca's oat milk porridge—and another lecture on missing the hairdresser's appointment—by heading down to her now-favorite café for breakfast. She'd promised Frank an update on her search today, but she was dreading having to tell him that it might be impossible to trace this woman online. He'd looked so excited when she'd offered to help on Monday, so desperately grateful that someone was taking him seriously, and now she had to tell him she'd failed.

Libby ordered a cappuccino and a chocolate croissant, then took a seat at one of the small tables outside the café. There was a bus stop on the other side of the pavement, and as Libby drank her coffee, she scanned the passengers waiting for buses. How many thousands of hours must Frank have spent doing this over the past sixty years? And all for nothing if he ended up in a care home without ever having found his woman. Libby might have been overtired, but the thought made her want to cry.

Once she'd finished her breakfast, Libby got up to leave. She was going to try another few hours of online hunting, and then she'd have to admit defeat and call Frank. But as she walked past the bus stop, her eye was caught by a piece of paper taped up next to the bus timetables. Libby stopped to read it.

MISSING DOG, the poster read, with a black-and-white photo of a small, wiry-looking dog. *Scamp has been missing since Tuesday. He's a black terrier with a white patch on his chest. Last seen on Alma Road. Reward if found.* Underneath were an e-mail address and a phone number. Libby stared at the poster, then reached into her bag for her phone and dialed the number Frank had given her on Monday. It rang seven or eight times and Libby was about to hang up when she heard a click.

"HELLO?" Frank's voice came bellowing down the line. "HELLO?"

"Frank, it's me, Libby."

"WHO?"

"Libby, from the bus."

"AH, LIBBY, HELLO!"

"Frank, you don't need to shout. I can hear you fine."

"Oh, sorry. I'm not really used to this thing. No one ever rings me on it. How are you?"

"I'm fine. I was wondering if you're free to meet up today? I've had a new idea I'd like to run past you."

"Of course. I'm just heading out for a walk up Parliament Hill, but why don't you come over later for tea?"

THE address Frank had given Libby wasn't too far from her sister's house. But as she left that afternoon, ominous gray clouds were gathering overhead, so she made her way to the bus stop rather than walk. After a short wait, an 88 pulled up, and Libby jumped on board and headed straight for the stairs.

She saw him as soon as she reached the top deck, and her stomach dropped. The angry punk. He was sitting in the seat directly opposite the steps, and he glanced up and spotted Libby at the exact same moment she saw him. His face didn't move, but she saw a flash of recognition in his eyes and felt her face glow with embarrassment at the memory of their last encounter. She averted her eyes and hurried down the aisle to the back of the bus, as far away from him as possible, but even at that distance, Libby could feel the contempt radiating off him. He was wearing the same beaten-up leather jacket as last time, but his spiked black hair now had bright red tips. Why would someone give themselves such a flamboyant hairstyle, and then complain when people stared at them? She felt a flash of anger that combined with her embarrassment to make her even hotter.

The bus moved slowly up Kentish Town Road and onto Highgate Road. At every stop Libby held her breath, hoping the man would get off, but he didn't budge. Finally the bus announcement signaled their approach to Parliament Hill Fields, and she hit the bell and made her way along the aisle. But as she reached the top of the stairs, two things happened at once: the punk stood up and the bus braked suddenly. Libby was thrown sideways, her face crashing into his chest. She was hit by the scent of leather and soap, and pushed herself away from him, aghast.

"I'm sorry," she muttered, even though it hadn't been her fault.

The man didn't say anything, but Libby saw his right hand flex by his side. She turned and hurried down the stairs two at a time. When she reached the lower doors, she almost banged on them in her impatience to get off. After what seemed like an eternity, the doors opened and she jumped onto the pavement beside Hampstead Heath.

Frank's address was a five-minute walk away, so Libby checked the map on her phone, then crossed Highgate Road and set off up Swain's Lane. But she'd not gone more than one hundred meters when she had the strange feeling she was being followed. She glanced back over her shoulder. Shit, it was him. Libby told herself it was a coincidence, but she still picked up her pace. When she reached the corner of Frank's road, she glanced back again, but he was still there, steadily following her. Libby felt her heart rate start to climb. Maybe he was still furious about her photographing him and was coming to exact his revenge? She was practically jogging now as she passed large houses numbered four and six. Frank had said he was number twenty-two, but would Libby get there in time before the man caught up with her? She didn't turn around again but she could sense he was still behind her, gaining ground.

Fourteen . . . Sixteen . . .

Libby was panting now, sweat forming on her lip.

Eighteen . . . Twenty . . .

Finally, there it was, Frank's house. Libby turned in through his gate and hurried toward the front door. As she did, she saw the man stop on the pavement in front of the house, watching her. Libby felt a surge of rage flood her body.

"Why the hell are you following me?"

The words were out of her mouth before she realized what she was doing. He was still staring at her, his face expressionless.

"Is this how you get your kicks, following women and scaring the hell out of them? Because if it is, you're sick."

"I'm not following you," the man said, but then he started to walk toward her.

"Stay back!" Libby shouted. "My friend lives here and he'll call the police."

The man tilted his head to one side. "Frank?"

"Yes!" Libby paused, suddenly confused. "What? You know Frank?"

"I do."

He reached into his pocket and she lurched backward in case he was about to pull out a weapon. But instead his hand emerged holding a key.

"Excuse me," he said, and it took Libby a moment to realize what he wanted. She stepped sideways, out of his way, and the man slid the key into the lock and opened the door. He walked in without so much as looking at her, leaving the door hanging open.

Libby hovered on the front step, still out of breath from racing here. She peered into the house, but all she could see was a dim hallway with several doors leading off it. She was about to call out for Frank when one of the doors opened, and he stepped into the hallway.

"Libby! What are you doing standing out there? Come on in."

Libby was unsure if she wanted to walk into the same building as that horrible man. But Frank was watching her expectantly, so she stepped in and pulled the front door closed behind her. There was a musty smell in the hallway, combined with a slight burned aroma.

"Come on through," Frank said, and Libby followed him as he shuffled into the front room.

It was a large space, crammed to the rafters with furniture, ornaments, and pictures. As Libby looked around, she saw a full suit of armor leaning up against a grandfather clock, and a giant stuffed bear, and the head of someone who looked like Henry VIII. It was like the strangest, most chaotic museum she'd ever seen.

"Souvenirs from my acting days," Frank said with a proud nod. "I always make friends with the props and costume departments on a play, and they often let me take a little souvenir home at the end of a production. I've gathered quite a collection over the years."

"It's incredible, Frank."

"Here, look at this one." Frank reached across to a tall coat stand and lifted down a dusty black bowler hat. "This was worn by Sir Laurence Olivier in a production of *The Entertainer* we were in together in 1963."

"You worked with Olivier?"

"Mine was only a small part, of course; he was the star. And what do you think of this?"

Frank picked up an ornate hand mirror and passed it to Libby. "That was a prop used by Jean Simmons in *A Little Night Music*. She was a wonderful actress, I tell you, and very beautiful. Although not as beautiful as my girl on the bus, of course."

Libby handed the mirror back to Frank and he stared at it for a moment. "You know, when I was onstage all those years ago, I used to look out into the audience and wonder if she was out there. I could never see her, of course; with all the bright stage lights, the audience are mere shadows to us actors. But I used to imagine that she'd be sitting out there, watching the play, and that maybe she'd remember me as the boy on the bus."

"Maybe she was, Frank," Libby said gently.

He put the mirror down and moved toward the far wall. "This is what I really want to show you. My favorite thing in the whole house."

He lifted down a small picture frame, carefully brushing some dust off the glass before he handed it to Libby.

It was a pencil sketch on a piece of paper yellowed with age. The lines must have faded over the years, but Libby could still make out a young man with a tall quiff of hair, a long Roman nose, and almond-shaped eyes. It was a beautiful sketch and unmistakably Frank.

"Is this hers?" Libby asked.

"The very one. It's good, isn't it?"

"It really is. I can't believe she did this on the bus."

"It must have only taken her about ten minutes."

"Wow," Libby said, remembering her own terrible attempt at drawing on the bus.

Frank sat down in a battered old armchair and signaled Libby toward what looked like a throne.

"From a production of *King Lear* with dear old Michael Gambon," he said as she perched cautiously on the edge. "Now, where is that tea of ours? I hear you met Dylan on the way in."

Libby didn't answer, worried she might say something rude. Was that man a relation? Frank had mentioned only a daughter, but perhaps he had a grandson or a serial-killer nephew. Through the wall, Libby could hear sounds coming from what must have been the kitchen.

"I know he looks alarming, but he's a pussycat really," Frank continued when Libby didn't say anything. "I don't know what I'd do without him."

"Is he a relative?"

"No. He's my carer."

"Carer!" Libby hadn't meant the word to come out with quite such incredulity, but she couldn't help herself. That man looked after people for a living?

"Not what you were expecting?" Frank said with a chuckle. "I'll admit I had the same reaction the first time I saw him. He rang the doorbell and I thought he was here to murder me."

"No, it's just—" Libby stopped as she remembered the awful way he'd shouted at her on the bus.

"Ah, here's the tea," Frank said as the door opened and the punk walked in. He was carrying a tray that held a teapot under a knitted cozy and two floral teacups. The whole sight was utterly bizarre. "I was just telling Libby here what a sweetheart you are, Dylan."

The man didn't say anything as he placed the tray down on a table between them and retreated toward the door.

"Only two cups?" Frank said. "Come on, don't be so antisocial. Join us."

"I can't hang about," he said, his voice deep and gravelly. "I've got to get to my next job."

"Oh, come on, you have time for a quick cuppa. And I'd like you to meet my friend."

Dylan looked as if meeting Libby was absolutely the last thing he wanted to do, and he turned and left the room.

"Bring a chair from the kitchen too," Frank called after him, and then sat back with satisfaction. "Now, when he comes back, you can tell us about this new idea you've come up with."

Oh, bugger. It had felt like a good idea this morning, but now Libby was here it seemed ridiculous. Plus, Dylan would probably stab her with a teaspoon. He came back in, carrying a teacup and a kitchen chair.

"Right, I'll be Mum, shall I?" Frank turned in his seat and picked up the teapot.

As he started to pour, Libby saw that his hand was shaking, sending half of the tea spilling onto the tray rather than into the cup. He seemed oblivious and carried on pouring. Libby glanced over at Dylan, who was watching Frank.

"Need a hand with that, boss?"

"I'm fine, thank you," Frank said, and there was a firm edge to his voice. He carried on until all three cups had some tea in, although there was more on the tray than anywhere else. "Milk, Libby?"

"Eh, no, thanks," she said, not wanting to see that added to the mess.

Frank picked up a teacup, the china rattling as his hand shook. Libby held her breath as she watched his arm reach out toward her, but miraculously none of the hot tea spilled. She took the cup from him as quickly as she could.

"Oh, silly me, I forgot the cake," Frank said.

"I'll get it," Dylan said, but Frank was already pushing himself up.

"No, Dylan, you're a guest now. Sit down and I'll fetch it."

Libby saw Dylan open his mouth to argue, but Frank had started to move. She watched as he made his way slowly toward the door, the only sound the shuffle of his feet on the carpet. Once he was gone, the silence in the room was deafening. Libby glanced at Dylan but he was staring at the floor, clearly finding this as agonizing as she was. Her face felt hot again, and she closed her eyes, wishing Frank would hurry up.

"I'm—"

"I—"

They both spoke at the same time, a collision of sounds interrupting the quiet.

"You go first," Dylan said, still studying the carpet.

"I wanted to say . . ." Damn, what did she want to say? Her mind was suddenly blank. "I wanted to say sorry about taking your photo on the bus. It was completely out of order."

"Ah . . . Well, I was going to say sorry for being such an arsehole. I'd had a crap morning and I was in a foul mood."

Libby looked at him in astonishment; an apology was the last thing she was expecting. "You were pretty rude, as a matter of fact."

"I'd had a fight with my old man and I was in a right hump, but I shouldn't have taken it out on you."

"Okay. Well, I'm sorry too."

They both fell back into silence. Libby could hear sounds from the kitchen, the scraping of drawers being opened and the rattle of cutlery. She could see Dylan's foot tapping on the floor.

"So, you're an artist, are you?" he said eventually.

"Are you kidding me? You saw my drawing. I'm terrible."

Dylan wrinkled his nose. "I wouldn't say it was terrible . . ."

"It was."

"You did make my hair look a little . . ." He stopped, searching for the right word.

"Like a child's drawing?" she offered.

"I was going to say phallic."

Libby let out a snort of surprise. "Phallic?"

"Yeah. It looked like I had a load of knobs on my head."

"Oh my god!" She buried her face in her hands. "No wonder you looked so horrified. I'm so sorry."

"Nah, that's all right. But you did make me check my hair in the mirror when I got home."

Libby looked at him through her fingers and thought she saw the corner of his mouth twitch.

"Well, you'll be relieved to know I haven't subjected anyone else to my terrible drawing since," she said. "My sketching days are well and truly over."

"Not because of—" Dylan started, but at that moment, Frank reappeared in the doorway.

"Right, where were we?" he said as he carefully crossed the room. Libby realized he wasn't carrying any cake, but Dylan didn't say anything, so neither did she. "Oh, yes. Libby, you were going to update us on your efforts to find my girl on the bus. Have you tracked her down yet?"

"I'm afraid not," Libby said, and she watched his face fall.

"I tried everything I could think of to trace her online—art colleges from the sixties, alumni groups on Facebook, records of London art exhibitions in that period—but nothing came up that could link me to a redhead. I'm afraid it was a bit like looking for a needle in a haystack."

"Oh, well, thank you for trying anyway," Frank said, and she could tell he was attempting to put on a bright voice.

"But then I had another idea," Libby said. "It might be a terrible one, but I wanted to share it with you."

"Go on."

"So, this morning I was on Kentish Town Road and I saw a poster on a bus stop about a missing dog."

"Yes, I see posters like that all the time," Frank said. "There's one particular cat round here that seems to go missing once a week. He's called Houdini, and I've always wondered which came first, the name or the behavior."

"Right. So I was wondering if . . ." Libby faltered, acutely aware of Dylan staring at her with those dark, suspicious eyes. "It occurred to me that I could do something similar to the missing-dog poster, but for your woman. So I could put posters up at bus stops along the 88 route with information about your story, in the hope that she might see one."

"Oh," Frank said, and Libby could tell he hadn't been expecting that. "What do you think, Dylan?"

She watched Dylan take a deep breath and prepared herself for his inevitable derision. "I think it's an interesting idea," he said in a voice that suggested he thought anything but. "You just know my concerns, boss. The chances of your woman still being in London, let alone riding the 88, are pretty small. It seems like a hell of a lot of work for the tiny chance she might ride the bus, spot the poster, and bother to read it."

"I agree," Libby said, hoping she sounded more confident than she felt. "But I had another idea too. As well as putting an e-mail and phone number on the poster, I could also put a hashtag on it to encourage people to share photos of the poster on social media."

"I'm sorry, but I have no idea what that means," Frank said.

"A hashtag is a way of identifying certain words," Libby said. "So people can go on Twitter or Instagram and type in 'hashtag missing dog' and then they'll find all the messages ever tweeted saying 'hashtag missing dog.'"

"I see. So you'd put 'hashtag missing dog' on this poster, and you think that might help find her?"

"No, I'd find a different hashtag just for you. But if we can encourage people to talk about your search on Twitter, then there's a much better chance of word spreading about it," Libby said. "And that way, I figure there's a much greater chance of your woman finding out about it too."

For a few seconds, no one said anything, and Libby watched Frank to see how he'd respond. Then he beamed.

"I think it's a wonderful idea!"

"Really?"

"Yes! Even if she doesn't see the poster herself, all it will take is for one person to mention it to their mother or grand-mother, and it could be her." Frank's eyes were bright. "Thank you, Libby. You're a genius."

"You're welcome," she said, smiling too.

"This is so exciting! I can't believe I never thought of doing something like this myself."

"So you're gonna put posters up at every bus stop along the whole 88 bus route?" Dylan said in a tone that immediately killed the buzz in the room. "How long do you reckon that will take?"

"I haven't worked it out yet. A day or two?"

He made a scoffing noise. "And the rest."

"Well, maybe a week, then."

"That route must be nine miles in each direction, with a hundred odd stops. Plus, as soon as you put a poster up, someone'll rip it down."

"So I'll put posters up on every lamppost and shopwindow as well," Libby snapped. There was something in this man's know-it-all tone that was really winding her up.

"Dylan has a point. It is a lot of work for one person," Frank said. "I wish I could offer to help, but with these damn feet, it can take me an hour just to get off the bus."

"That's all right. I'll be fine on my own."

Frank smiled as an idea occurred to him. "What about Dylan? You could help, couldn't you?"

Libby saw her own horror reflected in Dylan's face. "Oh, there's no need," she said quickly. "I'll be fine doing it on my own."

"Nonsense. Dylan rides that 88 back and forth between his clients anyway, and as he's just proven, he's got lots of helpful input. I'm sure you wouldn't mind giving Libby a hand, would you, Dylan?"

"Eh, I dunno . . ."

"And you've got a bit more spare time now Mrs. Higgins has popped her clogs. This will be a good way of filling it."

"Really, I don't need any help," Libby said.

"If the two of you work together, then the whole thing can be done in half the time."

Libby didn't say anything, and she could see Dylan searching for an excuse. Then his shoulders dropped an inch.

"Fine, I'll help her, but only the once," he said, doing an excellent impression of a surly teenager.

"Fantastic," Frank said, clapping his hands together. "Let the hunt for my girl begin!"

10

Libby woke up on Monday and immediately looked out the window to check the weather. She and Dylan had agreed to meet at nine fifteen unless it was raining, in which case they'd cancel. Sadly, the sky was clear and bright, and Libby let out a groan. Why on earth had she let Frank talk her into Dylan helping? The last thing she wanted was to spend another minute with that rude, grumpy man, and he clearly felt the same way about her. She just needed to get today over and done with; then she'd never have to see him again.

They'd arranged to meet at the bus stop outside Kentish Town Station, so once Libby had dropped Hector at preschool, she made her way there. While she waited for Dylan, she pulled out her phone and clicked open Instagram. She'd been keeping an eye on Simon's feed, although less so this last week, as she'd been so busy with her online search for Frank. Now Libby clicked on Simon's name and waited while the photos loaded. There were two new images since she'd last checked, both shots taken while he was running. In the most recent one, posted yesterday, he was standing back from the camera, smiling at whoever was taking the photo. The sight of Simon's bright blue eyes sent a flush of adrenaline through Libby's body.

Then she remembered their phone call the other week, Simon's heartless request that she go back to work with him, and his radio silence ever since, and she stuffed the phone back in her bag. As she did, she saw Dylan coming round the corner of the underground station.

Libby was struck, once again, by just how menacing he looked. It wasn't only the hair and the tattoos and the piercings; it was his whole demeanor: his height, the leather jacket and heavy black boots, the way he walked as if he owned the pavement. She watched people physically moving out of his way as he approached.

"All right?" he said when he reached her.

"Hi."

Libby looked up the road, willing the 88 to appear. "Did you come from Frank's?"

"Yup."

"How is he?"

"Fine."

Great, a man only capable of one-syllable answers. Libby gave up trying to make small talk and turned to look for the bus.

After what seemed like forever, an 88 pulled up and they boarded. It was busy with grim-faced morning commuters, but Libby found a seat at the back of the lower deck, hoping Dylan would choose somewhere else to sit. But to her irritation, he slid into the seat next to her, his long legs immediately taking up half her space. Libby squeezed against the window so they weren't touching.

"So, what are we actually doing today?" Dylan said as the bus pulled off.

"Right." Libby reached into her rucksack and pulled out a

plastic folder containing several sheets of paper. "I studied the bus route yesterday and I've come up with a plan."

She handed him a highlighted map, and then took out a second page for herself.

"There are ninety-six stops on the 88 bus route, forty-eight in each direction. So I've broken down the route into nine stages—marked here with the different colors." She pointed at the map in Dylan's hands. "Each stage is approximately a mile long, but obviously I need to cover both the north and south routes, so it's two miles in total. My plan is to go out three times a week and cover a different stage of the route each time; that's ten or eleven bus stops per stage. I'll put posters up on lampposts as well as at the stops themselves."

She looked at Dylan to see if he was following, but his face was scrunched up in confusion. As she'd suspected, he clearly wasn't the sharpest tool in the box.

"Do you need me to explain it again?" she said. "There are—"

"What's this?" Dylan interrupted.

"What?"

"This." He pointed at the piece of paper in her hand.

"It's an Excel spreadsheet. I've listed all the bus stops in this column, and then here is the distance between each stop, to the nearest ten meters. In this column I've marked where the north- and southbound routes diverge and . . ." Libby trailed off as she realized Dylan was staring at her.

"Did you seriously spend your weekend doing a spreadsheet for fly-posting?" The incredulity in his voice made Libby bristle.

"Do you have a problem with that?"

"Nah. It's just a bit . . . odd."

"It's not odd; it's organized. This way I can make sure each outing is as time and energy efficient as possible."

Dylan didn't say anything but she saw him raise an eyebrow.

"What would you suggest, then?" she snapped. "That I wander round randomly sticking posters up wherever takes my fancy, with no plan or process?"

"Maybe. I mean, you're putting up posters, not organizing a military occupation."

Our life has become so organized and predictable . . . I miss spontaneity.

Libby snatched the map back off Dylan. "I like to have a plan. That way there are no unpleasant surprises."

Dylan frowned. "Do you live your whole life like that?"

You used to be such fun, but things have grown stale . . . You've become boring, Libs.

Libby felt heat behind her eyes. Oh god, she was not going to cry in front of this awful man.

"If you don't like the way I'm doing it, then you can piss off!"

Libby spun round so her back was to Dylan, which was easier said than done when she was wedged into a cramped bus seat. Biting her lip, she stared out of the window as London rumbled past. Dylan made no attempt to talk to her, which Libby was glad of. She'd planned for them to go all the way down to Clapham today, as that was stage one on her map. But as the bus crawled slowly through traffic, the thought of having to sit next to this rude, insensitive, long-legged monster for the next ninety minutes was too much. Libby leaned past Dylan, almost knocking him off the seat, and hit the stop button.

"What are you doing?" he said.

"I'm getting off here."

"But according to your spreadsheet, aren't we meant to start at stage one, at the south end of the line?"

"Change of plan. We're starting here instead."

The bus stopped and Libby pushed past Dylan to get off. It was only when she stepped onto the pavement that she realized she had absolutely no idea where they were. She was aware of Dylan waiting behind her.

"This is Albany Street," he said as if reading her mind. "I think it was about halfway through stage seven of your plan."

"Let's get on with it, then." Libby reached into her rucksack and pulled out one of the yellow posters she'd made, plus a roll of Sellotape. Marching over to the bus shelter, she started to search for the end of the tape, the poster propped under her arm.

Dylan was standing back, watching her. "Need a hand?"

"No, thank you. I'm fine on my own." Libby managed to find the end of the tape and ripped off a long strip, then held up the poster against the bus shelter with one hand and tried to attach the tape with the other. Unfortunately, the tape kept sticking to either the bus shelter or her hand, but never to the poster. Libby gritted her teeth and gave her hand a shake to dislodge the tape, and then winced as it got stuck in her hair.

"Here, let me."

Dylan had suddenly moved in next to her. He leaned toward her face, and Libby stepped back, startled. But he just lifted his hand and gently removed the tape from her hair.

"How about I hold the poster in place and you attach it?" he said.

"Fine." Libby's voice came out as a squeak, and she coughed.

Dylan took the poster and held it up, then had to lower it when he realized he was holding it too high for Libby to reach. She pulled off a new strip of tape and stuck it along the side of

the poster, but as she did, she somehow managed to stick down
Dylan's thumb too. He pried it free, and then Libby attached
three more strips of tape to the sides of the poster, careful to
avoid all contact with Dylan. When she'd finished, they both
stepped back to read it.

HELP ME FIND THE GIRL ON THE 88 BUS

In 1962, I met a young woman on the 88 bus
between Clapham and Oxford Circus.

She was in her late teens or early twenties at the time,
had bright red hair, and was studying art.

I've spent the past sixty years trying to track her down
to say thank you. Please help me find her!

E-mail girlonthe88bus@gmail.com with any leads.

#girlonthe88bus

Libby smiled to herself. The bright yellow poster looked
eye-catching; it was bound to get people's attention.

"You really think people are gonna stop and read this?"
Dylan said, and the smile disappeared from Libby's face.

"I do, yes."

"And you think they're going to . . . what? Tell all their elderly female relatives about it? Tweet about it? Put their lives
on hold to help with your search?"

Libby took a deep breath. "It's not *my* search; it's for Frank.
Besides, not everyone is as miserable, mean-spirited, and mis-
anthropic as you. Some people are actually altruistic and want

to help strangers, rather than take the piss or shout at them on the bus."

She stopped, waiting for Dylan to snap something back at her, but he didn't say anything. When Libby turned to look at him, he was staring at his feet.

"Let's get on with it, shall we?" he mumbled.

They carried on without speaking. After a while they settled into a sort of rhythm, where Dylan would take out a poster and position it and Libby would tape it into place. They'd then walk on to the next lamppost or bus stop, never making eye contact or touching. After about forty-five minutes, they'd put up around fifteen posters and still not said a word to each other, and Libby was exhausted from the frosty tension.

"That's enough for today," she said when they reached the bus stop near the Euston Road.

"I thought you said you wanted to do a mile in each direction?"

"I can't today. I need to get back to Kentish Town."

"Well, I'm going the other way."

Libby felt a wave of relief that she wouldn't have to spend another minute with Dylan. His height might make him useful for holding up the posters, but she'd much rather do the rest alone, even if it took three times as long. She turned and hurried toward the zebra crossing.

"Bye, then," Dylan called after her, but she didn't bother looking back.

11

"ibby, where are you?" Rebecca's voice came hollering up from downstairs.

"Coming."

Libby pulled on her jeans, wincing at how tight they'd become. She really needed to cut back on all the chocolate croissants from the café. She quickly checked Twitter, but there was still nothing with the "girl on the 88 bus" hashtag. Damn it.

Down in the kitchen, Libby found Hector eating his breakfast and watching something on the iPad. It turned out Rebecca's no-screens rule didn't apply when she was the one doing the childcare.

"I've had a text from Hector's preschool," Rebecca said, looking up from her phone. "Apparently there's been a suspected gas leak on the grounds, and they're having to close today while it's investigated."

"Oh, well, I'm sure he'll be delighted to have a day off."

"I have my Wednesday team meeting, which I can't cancel, and Tom's got a pitch, so you'll have to look after him." Having issued her command, Rebecca started to walk away.

"I'm afraid I can't," Libby said.

"Why not?"

"I'm busy. I have plans."

Rebecca turned back and arched an eyebrow. "Leonardo DiCaprio and a family-sized bar of Dairy Milk don't count as plans."

"Actually, I'm—" Libby stopped. She was going on her second trip to put up posters this morning, but she could hardly tell Rebecca that. Her sister would have a field day if she found out Libby was helping a random stranger on a London bus find his long-lost love.

"You're what?" Rebecca said.

"Nothing. I can look after Hex."

Rebecca nodded and marched out of the kitchen to get dressed. Hector looked up from his iPad. "Can we go to the zoo?"

"Sure." Libby went to switch the kettle on, then turned back to Hector. "Actually, how do you fancy going on a special adventure instead?"

"What is it?"

"I need to put up some posters, and you could help me by holding them. It will be our fun secret project—even your mum won't know about it." She tried to sound exciting, but Hector looked unconvinced. "We can go to the Lego shop when we're finished."

"Let's do it!" he said, jumping up from the table.

They left the house at nine and walked up to the bus stop, Hector firing off his usual list of questions. "What killed the dinosaurs? Why do we have belly buttons? Would you rather be eaten by a lion or a shark?"

"Lion, definitely," Libby said as they approached the bus stop.

"Why?"

"Because if a shark tried to eat you, then you'd also drown, and I hate the idea of drowning."

"But a lion has really sharp claws as well as teeth, so it would hurt a lot."

"Yes, but—" Libby stopped talking when she saw a man standing at the bus stop. A tall, cross-looking man with a Mohawk.

Dylan spotted her and she saw him blink, startled. For a moment, she thought he was going to turn around and pretend not to have seen her, but he must have realized that was impossible.

"All right?" he said.

"What are you doing here?" Libby realized how rude that sounded but she didn't care.

"I'm on my way back from Frank's."

"Who's this?" Hector had grabbed Libby's hand and was looking up at Dylan, his eyes wide.

"This is Dylan," Libby said with a sigh.

She saw a flicker of surprise on Dylan's face when he looked down and saw the small boy.

"Hello. I'm Hector and I'm four and three-quarters," Hector said, peering up at Dylan. "You're tall."

An 88 bus pulled up and Libby stood back to let Dylan get on first. The bus was packed this morning, every seat on the lower deck taken. Dylan headed toward the stairs, so Libby moved to stand in the wheelchair area downstairs. But Hector seemed to have other ideas.

"Hector, come back!" Libby called after him, but the boy had either not heard or pretended not to, as he was already climbing the stairs after Dylan. Libby followed him up. The top deck was a bit quieter, and she saw that Dylan had sat halfway down the bus and Hector had moved into the row directly behind him. Great.

Libby sat down next to Hector, conscious of Dylan's tall, straight back in front of her, the tattoos crawling up his neck. She could sense he was as irritated by this proximity as she was. With any luck he'd be getting off soon, and until then they could ignore each other.

But Hector was having none of it. He gave Dylan a sharp poke on the shoulder.

"Why is your hair so strange?"

"Hector!" Libby said. "Don't be so rude."

She waited for Dylan to explode in anger, but to her surprise he glanced back.

"It's called a Mohawk."

Hector wrinkled his nose. "Why do you have it?"

"I'm a punk."

"What does that mean?"

"Hey, stop being so nosy," Libby pleaded, but Dylan was turning round in his seat to face the boy.

"Punk is a subculture that started in the seventies. We reject authoritarianism, corporatism, and consumerist culture. Plus, we like really loud music."

Hector's eyes lit up. "I like loud music too. Sometimes, I play it so loud that the lady next door bangs on the wall to complain."

"That is very punk," Dylan said, and Libby saw a flash of amusement in his eyes.

Hector beamed with pride. "Will you come to my house and play me your loud music? I always have to listen to Libby's music, which is so soppy and boring."

"No, it isn't," Libby said.

"Yes, it is. It's all moany and sad."

"I'm sure your mum's music taste isn't that bad," Dylan said.

"Libby isn't my mum!" Hector threw his head back in laughter. "She's my auntie."

"Oh, I thought . . ." Dylan looked between Hector and Libby.

"I'm looking after him today because his preschool's closed," Libby explained.

"She's staying at my house," Hector said. "Uncle Simon broke up with her and she doesn't have anywhere else to live."

"Hector!" Libby gasped.

Dylan looked out of the window, clearly horrified at having that personal information shared with him.

"I want to be a plunk like you," Hector said, oblivious to the embarrassment he'd caused. "How do I become one?"

"Anyone can be a punk if they want to," Dylan said. "You don't even have to have strange hair like me."

"What job would I have to do?"

"Any job you like."

"What job do you do?"

"I'm a carer."

Hector squinted at him. "What's a carer?"

"I look after people who need a bit of extra help at home."

"What, like my nanny, Rosalita?"

"A bit like that, yeah," Dylan said. "I usually help older people, though not always."

"Do you have to wipe their bums?"

Dylan smiled then, and it was so extraordinary that Libby did a double take. His whole face had transformed, his eyes sparkling and laughter creases round his mouth.

"I don't usually wipe bums, but I would if someone needed me to," Dylan said, and Hector groaned.

"That sounds like a rubbish job. Why would you do that when you could be an astronaut or a racing car driver?"

"Because I enjoy it. I like meeting different people and hearing their stories."

"But old people are really boring."

"Hector, don't say that," Libby said, glancing round to check there were no older passengers nearby who might have heard this.

"You know, I used to think that too. But let me tell you a secret . . ." Dylan lowered his head and Hector leaned forward to listen to him. "Old people might seem boring, but that's 'cos you're not listening to them properly. Take my mate Frank. He's really old, but he told Libby an amazing story, and now because of that, she's on a mission to help him. That's not boring, is it?"

"I suppose." Hector looked unconvinced. "Does your job make you rich?"

"Nah, but it does make me happy, and I think that's more important."

The boy's brow furrowed as it always did when he was thinking hard. "My mummy's job makes her angry, not happy."

"Oh, Hexy," Libby said, and she reached out to ruffle his hair. "I think your mum loves her job too, but it can be quite stressful."

"Some people like having stressful jobs," Dylan said to Hector. "And some people like jobs that are really creative or mean they can be outdoors all day. Everyone's different. I like working with people and helping them—I think it's the best feeling in the whole world."

"Hmm . . ." Hector was still looking thoughtful.

"What about you? What do you want to be when you grow up?" Dylan asked him.

"An astronaut and a footballer," Hector said quickly. Then he paused. "Do either of those jobs help people?"

"'Course they could, if you want them to. You could be a helpful astronaut or a helpful footballer."

Hector looked pleased with that and sat back in his seat, satisfied. Dylan turned round to face the front again and Libby stared at the back of his head, utterly confused. Of all the things she would have predicted about this man, being great with four-year-old boys was definitely not one of them.

12

"Dylan, which football team do you support? Have you ever been to London Zoo? Do you sleep with your hair like that?"

For the past ten minutes, Hector had been grilling Dylan, and now Libby knew he liked pasta more than pizza, had never seen *Cars* but had seen *Toy Story 2*, and would rather be eaten by a lion than a shark. Hector had even moved forward to sit next to Dylan, leaving Libby to ride in relative peace.

"Do you like Lego?" Hector asked.

"I love it," Dylan said. "I still have the original Lego X-Wing Starfighter I was given for my twelfth birthday."

Libby rolled her eyes. Of course Dylan was a grown man who still had Lego.

"Cumberland Terrace," the electronic bus announcement said.

Libby looked out the window and saw they were pulling up at a stop on Albany Street, the road where she and Dylan had put the posters up on Monday. She leaned forward to see her poster, but the one on the bus stop had disappeared. Libby kept looking as the bus moved off down the road, but there wasn't one on the lamppost either or on the next bus stop. They'd all gone.

Dylan must have been looking too, because he turned back to face her. "I see not many of your posters survived."

There he was, the Dylan she knew: not the sweet, child-entertaining one, but the know-it-all, thought he was better than everyone else, delighted to point out her failure one.

"Are you going to say 'I told you so'?" Libby said, crossing her arms.

"No, I—"

"I know you think this is a terrible idea, but I'm not going to give up at the first hurdle."

"I never said you were," he said, although Libby was pretty sure that was exactly what he was thinking.

"You may be completely unmoved by Frank's search, but I happen to think it's an amazing story. And I want to help him try and find this woman, before his daughter locks him up in some old people's home."

Dylan scowled. "I'm not unmoved by his story."

"Then why are you so against what I'm doing? Surely, if you care for Frank, you'd want to help him too?"

"Of course I care about Frank," he said, and there was a sharpness to his voice. "It's just more complicated than you realize."

"Why?"

Dylan paused and ran a hand over the shaved part of his head.

"The thing is . . . Frank's got dementia."

Libby's eyes went wide. "What?"

"He was diagnosed last year but he refuses to admit it. That's why his daughter employed me, so there's someone to check in on him twice a day, make sure he's taking his meds and eating properly. But recently he's been having these episodes where he blanks out."

"Oh my god."

"And that's why Clara wants to get him assessed, 'cos she's worried he might have one of these episodes when he's at home alone or out on the bus, and then who knows what could happen to him?"

Libby had realized Frank was a bit forgetful, but she'd had no idea it was as bad as dementia. "Surely that's all the more reason to try and find this woman, before his dementia gets much worse."

"Do you really, honestly believe that a couple of posters are gonna help track down one eighty-year-old woman in a city of nine million people?"

Libby felt a prickle of anger at his defeatist tone. "But isn't it better to try than give up? I mean, even if there's only the tiniest chance of me finding her, surely that hope is better than nothing."

Dylan sighed. "I'm just worried about Frank's expectations. He's convinced himself that you're going to find his woman and that will solve all his problems and they'll live happily ever after. You should have heard him this morning, talking like it was a matter of days before they were reunited. And I'm worried that when that doesn't happen, he won't be able to cope with the disappointment. His mental health is fragile enough as it is."

Libby felt a sinking sensation. "So are you saying I should stop looking for her?"

"No, I'm not saying that," Dylan said in a gentle tone she'd not heard him use before. "I know you want to help Frank, and that's brilliant—he's been more cheerful this week than I've seen him in months. I'm just saying we need to be careful to manage his expectations so that when you inevitably don't find his girl on the 88, the disappointment doesn't crush him."

Libby didn't say anything as Dylan's words sank in. Frank had been so excited when she'd offered to help him. But what if Dylan was right and she didn't trace Frank's woman? She'd had no idea he was unwell; what if her search failed and made him worse? Libby took a deep breath. She would have to make sure her search wasn't a failure, then; the alternative was too awful to consider.

"Hector, the next stop is ours," Libby said as the announcement came over the loudspeaker that they were approaching Oxford Circus.

"Isn't Dylan coming too?"

"No, he isn't."

"Oh, please!" Hector grabbed Dylan's arm. "Libby says once we finish putting up posters, then we can go to the Lego store. We could look at the *Star Wars* Lego together and I could show you the *Ninjago* one I want for my birthday?"

"Hector, Dylan has somewhere he needs to be," Libby said firmly.

"Actually, I don't," Dylan said.

Libby looked at him, aghast. "It's fine, honestly; you don't have to humor Hector."

"Yay, come! Come!" Hector said, bouncing up and down in his seat.

"I don't have to be at my next job for a couple of hours," Dylan said. "I don't mind helping you for a bit. If you want?"

Libby frowned. The last thing she wanted was to spend more time with Dylan, when their first effort at putting up posters had been so awkward and hostile and—

"Okay, fine."

Libby thought she saw the tiniest hint of a smile on Dylan's face, but he stood up too fast for her to be sure and rang the bell to stop the bus.

IT took them almost two hours to walk from Oxford Circus to Piccadilly Circus. Dylan completely ignored Libby's spreadsheet, and rather than doing one side of the road and then the other, he zigzagged them back and forth across Regent Street to post up posters on either side. They were also slowed down by Hector, who insisted on taking them on a detour to Carnaby Street and then into Hamleys toy shop. Libby was impatient to hurry up so they could finish today's section of the route and get home for lunch, but once Hector had found the Lego floor, he and Dylan spent half an hour exclaiming over the different sets. Eventually they made it out of the shop, but then two separate sets of tourists stopped Dylan and asked if they could have their photo taken with him. Libby waited for him to roar at them, but to her bewilderment, he obliged. By the time they made it down to Piccadilly Circus, it was well past twelve.

"Auntie Libs, I'm hungry," Hector said. "Did you bring me any food?"

"Sorry. I didn't think we'd be this long. I'm sure we can find something round here."

She pulled out her phone to search for a health food shop, but Hector was pointing up at the gigantic yellow "M" illuminated on the billboard above their heads.

"Can I have a McDonald's?"

"Come on, buddy, you know Mummy doesn't like us eating fast food."

"No fast food?" Dylan scrunched up his nose. "What, never?"

"My sister has very strict rules on healthy living."

"But Mummy's not here."

"Hex . . ."

"I won't tell her you let me have one, I swear. Please, Auntie Libby, *pleeeease* . . ."

She looked at the boy's pleading face. "All right, just this once."

"Yes!" Hector leaped up in the air. "Are you coming too, Dylan?"

Libby opened her mouth to say he wasn't, but Dylan was already nodding at Hector. The three of them walked down to McDonald's, where Libby ordered a Happy Meal for Hector and a Chicken McNuggets meal for herself. Dylan bought a coffee, and they found a table upstairs looking out over the bustling traffic on Shaftesbury Avenue.

Hector stuffed chips into his mouth, moaning with pleasure. "This is amazing plunk food, isn't it?" he said to Dylan.

"Careful or you'll make yourself sick, mate."

"But it's *sooo* good."

"My sister's going to kill me," Libby said, but she couldn't help smiling at Hector's delighted face.

"Surely she won't mind him having it once?" Dylan said.

"Oh, believe me, she will. But it's fine; I feel it's my duty as the wayward auntie to occasionally break the rules."

"I imagine you're a pretty cool aunt."

Libby almost choked on a chip. She glanced at Dylan, but he was looking out the window.

"I'm not sure my sister thinks so," she said, "especially now we're living under the same roof."

"Tell me about it," Dylan said darkly. Libby waited for him to elaborate, but he took a sip of coffee. "So, what do you do for a living, then, when you're not illegally feeding junk food to small children?"

Libby ate a bite of a nugget to give herself time to prepare an answer. Somehow saying *I run the business side of my partner's gardening firm, but at the moment he's weighing up whether he wants to be with me, so I'm currently unemployed* seemed overly complicated.

"I'm taking a temporary career break," she said, feeling pleased with her concise answer.

"Libby sells tacky gardens to people with more money than sense," Hector said to Dylan. "That's what my mummy says."

"Does she, now?" Libby said. "What else does Mummy say about my work?"

"That you never should have given up doctoring school. She and Granny talk about it sometimes, and Granny gets all red in the face and cross."

Libby felt as if she'd been stung. Dylan must have sensed it, because he turned to Hector.

"Did you get a toy with your meal?"

Hector started showing him some small plastic thing, and Libby slumped back in her seat. Did her family really still talk about her dropping out of medical school all these years later? It had been a huge drama at the time, full of anger and recriminations. Never mind that Libby had never wanted to study medicine in the first place and hated every minute of the two and a half years she'd done. In her parents' eyes, it had been a personal rejection, a repudiation of everything they'd ever dreamed of for their daughter. But still, Libby had assumed that those wounds had healed over the past decade, that her family now realized that quitting a degree she hated was ultimately in Libby's best interest. Apparently not.

"Are you okay?"

She looked up to see Dylan watching her.

"Yeah, fine. Come on, Hex, we'd better head home."

They finished their meals and left the restaurant, walking back toward Piccadilly Circus.

"This is my stop. I'm heading in the other direction," Dylan said as they reached the bottom of Regent Street.

"Can't you come back with us?" Hector said. "I want to hear your loud music."

"Not today. I'm afraid I've got to get to another client."

Libby nodded good-bye. Dylan had been less hostile than she'd expected today, and weirdly great with Hector, but she was still glad they didn't have to ride all the way back together.

"Bye, Dylan!" Hector said as Libby took his hand and led him across the road.

"Libby!"

She heard her name being shouted as she reached the far pavement, and turned back to see Dylan watching her through the traffic.

"Same time, same place on Friday?"

Before Libby could answer, an 88 drew up at the stop and Dylan disappeared from view.

CHAPTER

13

PEGGY

David came to see me on Sunday.

It's been a while since he's visited. Not that I blame him, of course. He's been under so much pressure with work, and you know how Emma keeps him on such a tight rein; it's remarkable she let him out the house. Honestly, I know I shouldn't speak ill of my own daughter-in-law, but I don't know how he's put up with her all these years, I really don't. I was a bit worried he was going to bring her too, but thankfully he called on Friday to say she had a cold and couldn't come.

He was coming for lunch, so I went shopping to get all his favorites in. I decided to do lamb chops with mashed potatoes (creamy, the way he likes them), followed by sherry trifle. It's a while since I've made a trifle and I had to go to three different shops to try to find those sponge fingers; nobody seems to sell them anymore. I was going to use tinned fruit, like I always have for us, but then I remembered that last time I made it Emma made a comment, so I bought fresh fruit instead. Cost me a bleedin' fortune, but you know me, only the best for my boy.

I tidied the flat from top to bottom—not that it was dirty in the first place, but I wanted to make sure it was spotless. I even dusted the old pictures, which, between you and me, I usually skip over. It was strange looking at mine up close again. I walk past them every day but never pay them any attention when there are much better ones in the flat. But today I did stop and look at them while I cleaned, and honestly, Percy, they weren't half bad. Some of the portraits I did in the bus series were pretty decent, and there's that one, *The Dreamer*, which wouldn't have looked totally out of place in the corner of some small art gallery somewhere.

And I know you'll say "I told you so," because to be fair, love, you always did say I had talent; I could just never see it myself. I suppose that's partly my dad's fault; when you've grown up with someone telling you you're wasting your time, it's hard to see past that. But also, I think perhaps it was easier for me to think I wasn't any good, so it made the decision to give up a little less painful. Because if I'd truly believed I was talented, that I could have achieved things in my life, then it would have been so much harder to walk away from it all when I had to. Does that make sense?

Besides, it's not like I had a choice. Once I was pregnant with David, there was no way I could have carried on chasing silly dreams of being an artist. It's different nowadays: women have all sorts of careers while having children—just look at our Maisie—but you have to remember what it was like back then. Anyway, I loved being a mum, as you know better than anyone. And I love being a grandmother and great-grandmother too, even if they are on the other side of the world.

Which reminds me: did I tell you that David said Maisie and the kids might come back for Christmas? I immediately started getting excited, thinking about what presents to get the boys—it's two years since I've seen them, so I have no idea what they're into these days—and then David told me off for getting carried away and said it might not happen. Still, I thought I might pop down to Argos next week and have a little look at their catalog. I know it's seven months early, but there's no harm doing a bit of research, is there?

Anyway, it was lovely to see David yesterday. He told me all his news. Apparently, he was up for some promotion at work, but they passed him over for someone half his age, which seems crazy to me. He said he might retire in a few years' time, but Emma isn't keen. And he gave me a gorgeous scarf for my birthday. It's very similar to the one he got me last year, but I love it and you can never have too many scarves. I put it straight in the drawer with the others, to keep it safe.

David didn't stay for lunch in the end. He said he'd love to, but he had to get back because they had friends coming over for dinner. So it looks like I'm going to be eating sherry trifle on my own for a while.

On Friday evening, Rebecca and Tom went out for dinner, leaving Libby to babysit Hector. She ordered herself an Indian takeaway and collapsed in front of the TV while she waited for it to arrive. It had been a busy day: she and Dylan had started at Piccadilly Circus, where they'd finished with Hector on Wednesday, then put up posters from Leicester Square, along Haymarket to Trafalgar Square, then down Whitehall to the Houses of Parliament. As they worked, they chatted about books, music, and films, and while they had quite different tastes, Libby was surprised that Dylan didn't mock her choices as she'd expected him to. He even promised to watch *Titanic* after Libby spent ten minutes giving an impassioned speech about why it was so good. They parted ways under Big Ben, Libby to head back north and Dylan to go to his next job south. And as they said good-bye, Dylan gave Libby his number and said he'd see her at the usual bus stop on Monday morning. Libby was bewildered as to why, but there was no doubt it was much quicker with Dylan's help. And whilst he was a bit unpredictable, she'd enjoyed his easy chat.

The takeaway arrived, and Libby carried it through to the kitchen and served it on a plate. As she was loading up her first forkful, savoring the delicious smell after weeks of steamed fish and vegetables, she saw her phone screen light up. For a second Libby wondered if it was someone messaging about Frank's girl, but when she picked up the phone, her heart leaped.

Simon.

It was exactly four weeks since that awful dinner, and two weeks since the phone call where he'd asked her to go back to work. What could he want now, at eight o'clock on a Friday night? Libby took a deep breath before she answered.

"Hi, Libs. How are you?" His voice sounded thin and edgy.

"Simon."

"You okay?"

"Fine, thanks. You?"

"Yeah, okay, okay."

He's not okay, Libby realized, and that gave her a flush of triumph. Good, let him suffer like he'd made her suffer.

"How's things with the family? Hex okay?"

"Simon, I'm eating dinner. What do you want?"

"Oh." She could hear his confusion at her sharp tone. "Well, I need to tell you something."

This is it, Libby thought with a lurch. This is the moment he either asks me to move back or says he wants to break up for good.

"What is it?"

"Well, the thing is . . . I wanted to tell you before you heard it from anyone else . . ."

"Tell me what?"

She heard Simon inhale at the other end of the phone line.

"What, Simon?"

"Ivemetsomeoneelse."

The words came tumbling out so fast that it took Libby a moment to decipher what he'd said.

"She's called Olivia," Simon continued. "We met running."

Libby realized she was still holding her forkful of curry, and she put it down with a clatter. Another woman. Running. She thought of the Instagram photos of Simon, his eyes glowing as he looked at whoever had been taking the shots. Of course. How could she have been so stupid?

"I'm sorry to tell you like this over the phone," Simon continued. "But we're going to the Lamb tomorrow and people are bound to see us and—well—I didn't want word getting back to you from someone else."

Libby and Simon used to go sometimes to the Lamb on a Saturday—his family had been drinking there for years and they knew most of the regulars. If Simon was taking this woman there, it meant they were meeting his parents, which meant things were getting serious.

"How long have you been seeing her, Simon?"

"What? Oh, not long. It's nothing serious, Libs; it's very casual."

But she could hear it in his voice. It was the same one he used when he'd double booked a gardening job and tried to pretend it wasn't his fault, or when Libby had caught him watching porn and he'd claimed it came on by accident.

There were so many things Libby wanted to say right now, angry, hurtful words she wanted to scream at Simon. But instead she took a deep breath and hung up the phone.

WHEN Rebecca and Tom got home later, they found Libby sitting in the dark at the kitchen table, an uneaten curry in front of her.

"What on earth are you doing?" Rebecca said as she switched on the kitchen lights.

Libby looked around her as if waking from a daze. She had no idea what time it was or how long she'd been sitting there. All she knew was that she'd wanted to cry, but no tears had come.

"What's happened?" Rebecca said.

"Simon called." Libby's voice was a croak.

"Did he tell you about his girlfriend?"

"What?" Libby looked up at her sister. "How did you know about her?"

"Mum called me earlier. Simon's mum rang her this afternoon to tell her they were meeting Simon's new girlfriend, as a courtesy or something."

Libby blinked. "Mum knew Simon was seeing someone else, and she didn't tell me?"

"Well, I imagine she wanted to let Simon tell you himself."

"When did you find out?"

"Oh, I don't know, sometime earlier. Why are you interrogating me? I'm not the one who left you for another woman."

"I'm going to bed," Libby said, standing up so quickly, she felt dizzy.

"Before you go, one quick thing." Rebecca sat down and waited until Libby had dropped into her seat again. "I wanted to tell you some good news."

"Good news?"

"Well, it's not good news per se. Rosalita's mum has apparently had some complications from her surgery, nothing critical but she's going to be bedbound for the next eight weeks, so Rosalita won't be back until August."

"How is that good news?"

"Well, it means you can stay here until then. I know how stressed you must be right now, so I wanted to reassure you that you've got somewhere to stay for a bit longer."

"Right." Libby knew she should make an effort to sound vaguely grateful, but a huge wave of exhaustion had suddenly crashed over her. "Thanks, Bex. I'm going to bed."

15

Libby had arranged to meet Frank for a walk on Hampstead Heath the following morning. She considered canceling it and staying in bed, but she didn't want to let Frank down, and besides, some fresh air would probably do her good. They'd agreed to meet at the café by the bandstand, and when Libby arrived she saw Frank sitting at one of the tables outside, drinking from a takeaway cup.

"Hi, Frank."

He startled at the sound of his name, spilling some coffee.

"Oh, sorry to make you jump."

Frank looked up at her, his brow furrowed. "Clara?"

"No, it's me, Libby."

"Libby?"

"Yes, from the bus. Remember, I'm helping you look for your girl on the 88."

"Oh, yes, Libby." Frank smiled, but his forehead was creased. "Sorry, forgive me. I woke up with a terrible headache this morning, so I'm a little out of sorts."

"Would you like to cancel our walk? We can go another time if you'd prefer."

"No, a walk is just what I need." Frank picked up his satchel and pushed himself up from the table. He wobbled a little as he stood, and Libby stepped forward and took his arm. "I'm fine," he said, but he didn't shake her off.

"Which way shall we go?"

"Have you ever been up Parliament Hill?" he asked, and Libby shook her head. "In that case, let's go this way."

He led her out of the café and toward a wide path that climbed slowly toward some trees. Frank's steps were slow and careful, but Libby didn't mind taking their time.

"So, how have your first few poster outings been?" Frank said. "I was out on the 88 on Thursday and saw a couple of them around Oxford Street."

"They've gone okay," Libby said. "It was a bit slow to start with, but I think I've got the hang of it now. The key is to use electrical tape; I think that stops them being pulled down so quickly."

"And Dylan's carried on helping you, I hear?"

"He has."

Libby could sense Frank waiting for more, but she moved the conversation on by telling him about her spreadsheet and color-coded map. After about twenty minutes, they reached the brow of the hill, both of them out of breath from the climb. Libby started to move toward the first bench, but Frank steered her to one a little farther along.

"My favorite," he said as they sat down. "Now, be still for a moment and take in this view."

Libby looked up and drew a deep breath in delight. London stretched out in front of them, shimmering in the morning sunshine. She immediately spotted the Shard, the tallest building on the horizon, and she could see St. Paul's Cathedral nestled beneath it. To its left was a cluster of skyscrapers that must be the City of London; Libby could make out the Gherkin and several others she recognized from the TV. And on the far-right-hand side, she could see the BT Tower, which she recognized from the 88 bus route.

"What an incredible view."

"It's like sitting on the rooftop of London, isn't it?" Frank said. "Now here, I brought you a little something."

He reached into his satchel and pulled out a thin parcel wrapped in brown paper. Libby opened it and let out a small gasp when she saw a sketch pad and a tin of pencils.

"For your sketching practice," Frank said. "I know you're not keen on drawing on the bus, but I thought you might like to practice landscapes instead."

"I don't know what to say, Frank. Thank you."

"You don't need to say anything; just get out a pencil and start sketching."

"Here?" Libby said. "I can't draw this view. I wouldn't know where to start!"

"Pick a small detail to begin with," Frank said. "How about the Shard?"

Libby hesitated, feeling self-conscious. But Frank was watching her, so she swallowed her embarrassment and opened the sketchbook.

"Do you walk up here a lot?" she said as she selected a pencil.

"I come up here several times a week, have done since I moved to the area. My best friend, William, and I used to swim in the Men's Pond, but I gave that up a few years ago, when he passed away."

Frank pointed behind them, and Libby turned around to see several small lakes at the bottom of the hill.

"These days, I like to sit up here and watch the city," Frank continued. "You wouldn't believe how much it's changed since I started coming."

Libby stared out at the Shard, trying to work out where to begin. "Have you always lived in London?"

"Born and bred. My parents ran a grocery shop in Shepherd's Bush and we lived in the flat upstairs. I moved out in my second year of drama school and rented with some fellow students in Notting Hill. And then I bought my place here in the early seventies so I could be near Clara and her mum."

"Does Clara still live nearby?"

"No, she went to university in Edinburgh and never came back." He said it matter-of-factly, but Libby could hear a tinge of sadness in his voice.

"Do you have grandkids in Scotland?"

Frank shook his head. "Clara has always been married to her job. Although she seems happy enough with her life." He turned to Libby. "What about you? I take it you're not a Londoner?"

"No, I was born near Guildford, in Surrey. Apart from a brief period at university in Bristol, I've lived there my whole life."

"And can I ask what brings you to London?"

Libby exhaled and put down her pencil. She might as well tell Frank the truth. "My boyfriend broke up with me. We've been together for eight years and I thought we were going to get married, but he got bored of me and now he's seeing someone else."

"Oh, my dear, I'm so sorry to hear that," Frank said, and he reached out and squeezed her hand. "You must be devastated."

"I'm fi—" Libby stopped as she felt a knot in her throat.

"Are you all right?"

"Yes, I'm fine," she said, although her voice wobbled as she said it. Libby could feel heat behind her eyes, and she pressed her hands against them. "I'm so sorry."

"Please don't apologize," Frank said. "You're allowed to cry, Libby."

And that was it. With five simple words, the tears that Libby had been holding back for the past four weeks burst forth like a tsunami. Within seconds, she was sobbing, her whole body shaking with the effort. Frank didn't say anything, just rested a hand on her back and gently rubbed it as she cried and cried and cried.

When she finally stopped, Frank passed her his clean handkerchief.

"I'm so sorry about that," she sniffed.

"Don't be silly."

"I never normally cry. It's just . . . I think you're the first person who's said that to me."

"Said what?"

"That they're sorry for me."

"Oh, Libby."

"I'm okay," she said as she wiped her eyes. "My family just aren't big on emotions or sympathy."

"I'm a big crier, always have been," Frank said. "Anything with animals or babies and I'm a goner. Dylan's the same; you should see the two of us sobbing our eyes out over a David Attenborough documentary."

Libby glanced at Frank to see if he was joking; Dylan did not strike her as the kind of man who'd cry in front of other people.

"Oh, Dylan's a massive softie," Frank said, chuckling. "You

know, this morning he told me he'd watched *Titanic* last night and cried for most of the second half."

For some reason, this fact gave Libby a flush of warmth, and she looked away so Frank wouldn't see her reaction.

"So, how long do you think it will take the two of you to finish the route?" Frank said.

"Well, if we stick to my plan and carry on doing three trips a week, then I reckon we should be able to finish in a fortnight or so."

"How exciting," Frank said. "Just think. Right now, as we sit here chatting, my woman might be riding the 88 bus and see one of the posters. She might be composing a message to you as we speak!"

Libby remembered what Dylan had said to her on Wednesday about managing Frank's expectations. "You know, she might never see the poster or find out about our search, Frank. You have to—"

"Oh, stop it, Clara. You sound like Dylan," Frank said, cutting her off. Libby wondered if she should point out his mistake, but Frank was midflow. "Dylan is a wonderful carer, but he worries too much. I may be eighty-two, but I'm as tough as old boots."

"I'm sure you are. I just don't want you to be too disappointed if we don't find her."

"I'm not a child. I wish people would stop treating me like one."

His tone was surprisingly sharp, and for a few minutes, neither of them spoke. Libby took in the view around them. It was busy up here at the top of the hill, dog walkers, joggers, and families with small children milling around. Libby looked behind them and saw several groups had set up picnics. One family had brought a kite with them and it was high in the air now, a flash of crimson against the blue sky.

She turned back to Frank. "You know, I might start by sketching that boy with the kite. What do you think?"

Frank didn't reply, still staring out at the panorama in front of them.

"Frank?"

He didn't move at the sound of his name, and Libby reached across and put her hand on his arm.

"Are you okay?"

Still nothing. Libby leaned closer and put her face in front of Frank's, but his eyes didn't move. It was like he was in some sort of trance. What had Dylan said the other day about Frank having episodes where he blanked out?

"Frank, can you hear me?" Libby gave his arm a gentle shake. His body moved, but he still didn't respond. She noticed a tiny line of dribble on his chin.

Libby felt her pulse quicken. What was she supposed to do now? She had no idea how long he'd stay like this, or if she should be getting him medical help. What if he was having a stroke? She pulled out her phone and dialed a number.

"Hello?" A man's voice, deep and gruff.

"Dylan, it's Libby."

"Libby? You all right?"

"I am, but I'm with Frank and I think he's having one of the episodes you mentioned. We were talking and then he drifted off and now he's staring into space, not reacting to anything."

"Are you on the bus?"

"No, we walked up to the top of Parliament Hill. We're sitting on a bench up here."

There was a rustling sound at the other end of the line. "How long has he been like this?"

"I don't know. At first I thought he was looking at the view. I didn't realize what had happened. Five minutes, maybe more."

"When he's had these before, they usually don't last too long. Are you all right to stay with him?"

"Of course. Should I do anything to try and get his attention back?"

"No, it's best to leave him be. When he does come round, he'll probably be a bit confused; he might not recognize you. Sometimes he can get a bit scared and aggressive." Libby heard what sounded like a door slamming. "Try and keep him calm and I'll be with you as soon as I can."

"You don't have to come. I'm sure I can handle this on my own," Libby said, but the phone line had already gone dead.

FOR the next half hour, Libby sat and watched people buzzing around them. The kite-flying family packed up their picnic and left. Two dog walkers got into an argument when one dog tried to mate with the other. An elderly woman came and sat on the bench next to Frank but moved to a different one when she realized something strange was going on with him. The whole time Frank didn't move, his eyes glazed over. Libby held his cool hand in hers, feeling its gentle tremor, and occasionally whispered reassuring words to him.

"Libby."

She spun round to see a tall man standing behind the bench, but it took Libby a moment to realize who it was. Dylan's Mohawk was nowhere to be seen, and instead he had dark hair framing his angular face. He looked so different; Libby was aware she was staring at him.

"How is he?" Dylan said.

"He's not moved since we spoke on the phone."

Dylan knelt down in front of Frank. "All right, boss?" he said in a soft voice.

Frank didn't move, but Libby saw a twitch of recognition in his face.

"You can go now; you don't have to hang around anymore," Dylan said to Libby, not taking his eyes off Frank.

"It's okay. I'm happy to stay."

"Honestly, it's fine. You don't want to waste your Saturday up here."

For a second, Libby considered telling Dylan that she didn't have anywhere else to be. Her boyfriend had dumped her, and her sister had friends over for lunch and had not so subtly made it clear that she'd like Libby out of the way. "Are you sure I can't do anything to help?"

"Nah." Dylan looked up at Libby. "Thank you for staying with him, though. I appreciate it."

He gave her a small smile and then turned his attention back to Frank. Libby watched for a moment as Frank blinked, his eyes focusing on the man in front of him.

"Dylan?" His voice was faint and croaky.

"It's all right, mate. I'm here."

Dylan reached out and stroked Frank's shoulder, a gesture so tender it made Libby's chest ache. With one last look at them both, she turned and hurried down the hill.

16

Hector, we're going to be late!" Libby shouted up the stairs. She glanced in the hall mirror, then bent down to pick up her rucksack, filled with posters.

Hector appeared at the top of the stairs. "Why are you wearing that?"

"What?"

"You never normally wear dresses."

"Oh, well . . . it's too hot for jeans today."

Hector wrinkled his nose. "You look weird."

"Thanks, buddy. Thanks a lot." Libby snatched up his bag and let them out of the house. It was the warmest day of the year so far, so it made perfect sense to wear a dress. There was no rule that said she could only wear jeans, was there?

"Do you have lipstick on as well?" Hector said as they set off down the road.

"Enough chatting. Hurry up or we'll be late for school."

Once Libby had dropped Hector off, she considered running back to the house to get changed, but it was already ten past nine, so Dylan would be there any minute.

As she reached the bus stop, Libby felt her phone vibrate. When she pulled it out, she saw a message from him.

Sorry, running 5 mins late

A moment later another text came through.

Am bringing Esme with me.

Libby slipped the phone back into her pocket. Dylan had mentioned his friend Esme a couple of times; she was a young woman with Down syndrome, and apparently she loved Frank's story and was keen to join them. Besides, Libby told herself as she smoothed out her yellow dress, the more people who helped, the quicker they could finish the route and get back to their lives.

She spotted Dylan walking down the pavement before he saw her. His hairstyle was back in place, but he'd abandoned his leather jacket in the heat and was wearing a tight black T-shirt, so for the first time, Libby could properly see the tattoos running up his toned arms. She usually hated tattoos, but somehow they suited him. Still not seeing Libby, Dylan turned and said something to the woman walking next to him. She was a good foot shorter than him and was dressed in a red-and-black polka dot dress with matching red sunglasses, like a colorful ladybird next to Dylan's long-legged black spider.

Dylan turned his head forward and spotted Libby for the first time. She saw him take in her dress, his eyes lingering for a moment too long on her breasts, and Libby felt her cheeks color.

"You all right?" he said when he reached her, and his voice sounded strange.

"Good, thanks."

"Cool. Eh . . . this is Esme. Ez, this is Libby."

"It's lovely to meet you," Libby said, extending her hand toward Esme, but the young woman stood there, unsmiling.

She was still wearing her sunglasses, but Libby got the distinct impression she was being stared at. There were an awkward few seconds as Libby held her arm out, feeling like an idiot.

"Here's the bus," Dylan said, signaling for the 88 to stop.

He boarded first and Libby went to follow, but Esme slipped in front of her. Dylan took a seat by the window and Esme promptly slid in next to him, leaving Libby to take an empty seat across the aisle. As the bus pulled off, Esme removed her sunglasses and turned to face Libby.

"I have some questions for you."

"Okay," Libby said.

"How old are you?"

"I'm twenty-nine. What about you?"

"I'm twenty-five. What is your star sign?"

"Well, I was born on twenty-third July, so a Leo."

Esme didn't say anything, but Libby saw her shake her head.

"Is that bad?" Libby glanced over at Dylan; he was looking forward, but she could tell he was trying not to smile.

"And what music do you like?" Esme said, ignoring Libby's question.

"Oh, all sorts of things. Nina Simone. Stevie Wonder."

Esme let out a small groan. "Do you like the Buzzcocks? The Vibrators? The Slits?" She was watching Libby, who felt herself getting hot.

"No, not really. Sorry."

Esme turned to Dylan. "This is never going to work."

He couldn't hide his amusement anymore. "All right, Katie Couric, go easy on her."

"You two have nothing in common, so she can't be your girlfriend."

The grin disappeared from Dylan's face, and he suddenly looked flustered. "Hang on a sec. Libby's not my—"

"What will you talk about?" Esme said, cutting him off. "Your star signs don't match and she doesn't like your music." She turned back to Libby, oblivious to Dylan's discomfort. "When I met my fiancé, I had a list of questions I asked him on our first date. You want a boyfriend who likes the same things as you."

Libby couldn't help but smile at the young woman's concerned expression. "I think that's excellent advice."

"I've told Dylan this, but he never listens. It's no surprise he can't find a girlfriend."

Libby saw Dylan wince and had to laugh. "He's lucky to have you to help him, Esme."

"He is." She smiled at Libby for the first time, her eyes sparkling. "But he needs a girlfriend so he doesn't get lonely when I'm married."

"I don't know how I'm going to manage," Dylan said, smiling as he shook his head.

"And you need new clothes," Esme said. "If you want a nice girlfriend, you need to wear some color. Not just black."

Esme looked at Libby expectantly, clearly confident she'd found an ally in her campaign.

"I think Dylan should dress however makes him happy," Libby said diplomatically. "But a little bit of color wouldn't do any harm now and then."

"See!" Esme said, turning to Dylan. "It's a shame about you and Libby. I like her."

Dylan chuckled. "What would I do without you, hey?"

Libby watched Dylan and Esme chatting away, the warmth and affection between them obvious.

"Libby only moved to London a few weeks ago," Dylan told Esme as they rode down Portland Place, at which point the young woman took it upon herself to be Libby's tour guide for the rest of the journey, pointing out important sights along the way.

"This is Piccadilly Circus. Dylan and I had lunch in the Rainforest Cafe here."

"This is Horse Guards Parade, where the soldiers practice marching."

"This is the River Thames. We took a boat along it to Greenwich."

Before Libby knew it, they were driving down Clapham High Street. This was the first time she'd been to the southern end of the 88 route, and as the common came into view, she remembered Frank's story.

"This is where he first saw her," she said to Dylan as they disembarked. "Do you think she might still live round here? Maybe she's going out on the bus today, and she'll see one of our posters?"

Libby looked at Dylan but he wouldn't meet her eye, and she felt suddenly stupid. Of course the woman wouldn't still live here sixty years later. How could she be so naive?

"What do we do now?" Esme said to Libby.

"Well, we usually put up a poster at the bus stop, and then we start walking the bus route, putting up posters on lampposts and—"

Libby didn't get to finish her sentence, as Esme had grabbed a pile of posters out of her hand and started crossing the road toward the common.

"Dylan!" she shouted, and he ran over to join her.

"We don't usually put them up on trees, Ez," Dylan said.

But Esme clearly had other ideas.

17

PEGGY

Oh my goodness—you won't believe the morning I've had! First off, I spilled tea on my good M&S blouse and had to go and get changed. Then, just as I was about to leave to come here, the phone rang—my landline, not the mobile— and I had to answer it because you know the only person who calls me on it is David and it might be important. Remember that time the phone rang in the middle of the night, and it was David saying Emma had gone into labor and his car had broken down, and we had to dash across London at two a.m. to drive her to the hospital? I thought we were going to get arrested, the speed you drove.

Anyway, I answered the phone, but it turns out it wasn't David; it was some woman telling me I'd recently been involved in a car accident and it wasn't my fault. Can you imagine? So I explained to her that I hadn't been in a car accident, and in fact I hadn't been in a car for ages, apart from that one time Barry from number six drove me to the hospital appointment to get my varicose veins done. And then she said, "Eh," so I felt I should explain to her what a varicose vein procedure involves in case she ever needs one. And then halfway through my explanation, she hung up on me. How rude!

Anyway, all of this meant I was late leaving the flat to catch the bus, and I knew that if I didn't hurry, then by the time I got here I'd basically have to leave straightaway in order to get back in time for bingo. And I know what you're going to say, Percy—I can miss bingo for one week—but Arpita has got back from visiting her grandkids in India and I don't want to miss seeing the photos. Besides, she always brings lovely fabrics back with her, and if I'm not there today, then Betty Fincher will pinch all the best ones.

So there I was, hurrying across the common toward the bus stop, and I notice that all these yellow pieces of paper have been stuck up along the path; they're literally on everything. Now, you know I can't stand littering, especially on the common. Remember that afternoon we were having a picnic with David, and I saw that family leaving their rubbish behind, and I chased after them and made them clear it up? Well, I also hate it when people put posters up all over the place; it makes it so ugly. So I look around and I see a young woman in a red-and-black polka dot dress taping one of these posters up to a tree, and I turn and march over toward her, getting ready to launch off on a rant, when I feel a hand on my shoulder. And when I turn around, guess who it is.

No? Give up?

It was Eileen Attwood, from number eighteen!

I don't mean to sound rude, but I have to tell you my heart sank. As you well know, Eileen is not someone who you can have a quick conversation with. I mean, why only use five words when you can use fifteen? That's Eileen's philosophy. And straightaway she launches into this story about her Jeremy, who's been made a partner in his law firm, and how they're going to Dubai to celebrate and they've invited her but she's not sure about the long flight. And she's telling me all this like she wants my opinion on whether she should go on the holiday, but really, I know she's just trying to show off about her son and his fancy job. She does this all the time, like when I had my fall and she called round to check I was okay, but really all she wanted was to tell me about her new Stannah Stairlift. So I'm nodding along, trying to pretend I'm interested when really inside my blood's boiling, and I want to tell her to take her first-class flight to Dubai and shove it up her . . .

And then the funniest thing happens. There's a big gust of wind, completely out of nowhere, and all of a sudden one of those yellow pieces of paper detaches itself from a post and comes flying across the path at great speed and hits Eileen straight in the face. I mean, you could actually hear it thwack her; it was like something out of a cartoon. And she's so shocked that she screams and starts pulling at her face like she's been attacked by a giant yellow bat, and then she steps backward and puts her foot in the biggest dog poo you've ever seen.

Now, I don't need to tell you my feelings on selfish owners not clearing up after their dogs, love. I know you feel exactly the same. But on this one occasion, I have to confess that I was secretly quite grateful for the inconsiderate bugger and this woman with her messy posters, because you should have seen Eileen's face. She went bright purple, and she starts howling about her new shoes and how she's on her way to have lunch with her Jeremy and she can't turn up smelling like this. And all the time she's using the yellow poster to clean the poo off her shoe, and I'm standing there, trying my hardest not to laugh. Thankfully, I saw an 88 bus coming, so I told Eileen I had to dash, and I left her cursing to herself as she hopped around, cleaning her shoe.

What a sight it was, love! Oh, you'd have laughed if you'd been there.

18

After an hour, Libby, Dylan, and Esme had barely made it thirty meters from the first bus stop, and every tree, lamppost, and railing had a yellow poster attached to it.

"I love how thorough Esme is, but we're going to run out soon if we're not careful," Libby whispered to Dylan as she watched the young woman tape one to a bike.

"Well, her approach is certainly getting us more attention than usual." Dylan indicated behind them, and Libby turned round to see several people stopping to read the sea of yellow paper.

"Can we go to the park?" Esme said, once she'd exhausted their pile of posters.

"Sure thing," Dylan said.

The three of them walked up to the playground, where Esme jumped on a swing and started to propel herself backward and forward. Dylan and Libby sat down on a bench opposite.

"Esme is great fun," Libby said as they watched the young woman fly higher and higher on the swing. "How did you two meet?"

"A couple of years back, her mum had a nasty fall and broke her hip, so the two of them needed some extra help at home for a couple of months. Ez and I have been mates ever since; we must have been to every tourist attraction and karaoke bar in London."

"And she's getting married soon?"

"Yeah, in November. Then she and Johnny are moving into an assisted-living flat together. I'm not sure she'll have much time for me after that; she's got the busiest social life of anyone I know."

Dylan gave a soft laugh as he said this. Libby watched him watching Esme on the swing, and remembered how gentle he'd been with Frank on Saturday. It was strange to think that little more than a week ago, she'd been so horrified when Frank had told her that Dylan was his carer.

"Did you always want to be a carer?"

"Nah, I wanted to be a musician. I've played in bands since I was a kid, still do a bit now. But sadly, music isn't going to put food on the table."

"So how did you get into caring?"

"I sort of fell into it. I dropped out of school at sixteen; me and the British education system were not a good match. I pissed around for a bit, playing in bands and getting into scrapes. And then about fifteen years ago, I took a temp job at a care agency. And the rest, as they say, is history."

"Well, you're clearly brilliant at it."

"I dunno about that. But I enjoy it and the hours suit me: I work a lot of night shifts, which I like, as it gives me free time in the day. I'd rather die than do some soul-sucking corporate nine-to-five."

"Have you ever thought about changing careers?"

Dylan paused for a moment, knocking an empty Coke can back and forth between his feet. "A few years ago I did have this crazy idea about going into nursing; I sometimes work with learning-disability nurses and they're amazing. But I looked into it, and you need A levels and a degree and loads of other stuff, so it's stupid to even say it." He gave the can a kick, sending it skidding out of the playground.

"I don't think it's stupid."

"I think your thirties are a bit late to be going back to school, aren't they? I'd look like a right twat, sitting there with a load of spotty teenagers."

"It's not too late, if it's what you really want." As she said it, Libby thought about her own teenage ambitions. She was hardly one to talk about following your dreams.

"What about you?" Dylan said. "Did you always want to work in the gardening industry?"

"God no. It was my boyfriend . . . ex-boyfriend's business, and I started working there because he needed another pair of hands." This was the first time she'd mentioned Simon to Dylan, although he was clearly aware of his existence, thanks to Hector.

"What did you dream of doing when you were younger?"

Libby bit her lip. Would he laugh if she told him the truth, given he'd seen her terrible attempt at drawing?

"I wanted to be an artist."

Dylan didn't laugh. Instead he looked at her, his eyes serious. "So what happened?"

"My parents refused to let me go to art school."

"Whoa. Like Frank's woman on the 88?"

"I know. Weird, right?"

"Why didn't they want you to go?"

"They said I'd end up spending three years smoking weed and have no job at the end of it. My parents are very goals oriented."

"And you didn't consider disobeying them?"

Libby shook her head. "I'm not as brave as Frank's girl. Besides, there was no way I could have paid the fees without their support."

"That really sucks. I'm sorry."

This was the second time someone had been kind to Libby in forty-eight hours, and she did not want to burst into tears again. "I probably wouldn't have got into art school anyway; I wasn't very good."

"You looked pretty talented, from what I saw."

"What, at drawing penis hair?"

Dylan laughed, an enchanting sound that made Libby smile.

"Your sketch was really good, though," he said. "The way you'd drawn my eyes, it's like you'd captured exactly what I was thinking."

"Was it 'I wish this stupid woman would stop drawing me'?"

"Nah. I was angry with my dad, and you'd caught that somehow. That's not something everyone can do when they draw; it's a talent."

"You're just being kind," Libby said, staring down at her flip-flops.

"No, I'm being serious, Libby."

The way he said her name sent a small shiver across Libby's skin.

"So, Hector said you did medicine at uni?" Dylan said.

"Yeah. My dad's a doctor and he always wanted one of his kids to follow him into the profession. My sister set her sights on law at a young age—she likes an argument—so it was medicine for me, whether I liked it or not. Unfortunately for everyone, I absolutely hated it and dropped out."

"That must have been full-on for you."

"It was. And my family are apparently still flipping out about it ten years later." And about my broken relationship and failed life, Libby thought with a shudder.

"You know, this is none of my business, but I think you need to stop caring so much what your family think," Dylan said.

Libby turned to him. "What do you mean?"

"Well, several times now you've mentioned them being disappointed in you. But you're a grown woman; why do you give a shit?"

"That's easy for you to say, Mr. Anarchist Punk."

"I'm not an anarchist. But I don't care what other people think about my life choices, and *definitely* not what my dad thinks."

"Maybe I wouldn't care so much if they weren't right," Libby said with a sigh. "I mean, I haven't exactly made a success of my life, have I? I dropped out of uni and fell in love with a man who's got bored of me, and I'm currently unemployed and soon to be homeless. This is hardly the life I planned for myself."

"Who says your life isn't a success? All that 'get a proper job, settle down, have two-point-four kids' stuff is bollocks anyway. The second I worked out I didn't want any of that, my life became so much easier."

"Lucky you." Libby knew she sounded bitter, but Dylan clearly didn't live in the real world.

"I know things must feel a bit crappy for you right now. But maybe it will all turn out for the best in the long run? Maybe you'll end up going to art school, after all, and becoming a world-famous artist who draws people with cocks on their heads."

Libby laughed out loud at this and elbowed Dylan in the ribs.

"Ouch," he said, but when she looked at him, he was laughing too. For a moment they held each other's gaze.

"What's so funny?" Esme said, coming over to join them.

"Nothing." Dylan stood up and rubbed his side. "Shall we get you home, miss?"

Esme took Libby's hand and the three of them began to make their way back toward the bus stop through the sea of yellow posters.

"You really did a great job with these," Libby said to Esme as she saw how many people were stopping to look at them.

"You have to get people's attention," Esme said. "If it's just one or two, people will ignore them."

They waited a few minutes for an 88 to arrive. This time, Esme didn't push Libby out of the way as they boarded, and instead made a great show of directing her to the seat next to Dylan. Esme sat down in the row in front of them, next to a lady reading a newspaper.

"Is that 'Rush Hour Crush'?" Esme said to the lady as the bus pulled off. "Can I read it too?"

The woman gave a disgruntled sniff but moved the paper a fraction so Esme could see it.

"What's 'Rush Hour Crush'?" Libby asked.

"It's where people try and find someone they saw on the bus or tube, because they fancy them. It's mine and Dylan's favorite bit."

"It is not," Dylan said with an embarrassed cough.

"I've never heard of it; can I see too?" Libby said, leaning forward.

"Oh, for goodness' sake, you two have it," the lady snapped, thrusting the paper toward Esme.

"Thank you," Esme said brightly, then held it up for Libby to read.

To the dark-haired guy with the red backpack on the Central line this morning. We caught each other's eye at Bond Street, but I was too embarrassed to say hello. Fancy a drink sometime?

Blond Girl with Green Satchel

"I wonder if any of these people actually find the person they're looking for," Libby said.

"That's it!" Esme shouted, startling Libby. "We should do one of these for Frank."

"Erm, that's a nice idea, Ez, but I think it's mainly for horny young people looking for a shag," Dylan said.

But Libby was sitting up in her seat. "No, Esme's right. How many thousands of commuters must read these each day? Like she said earlier, we need to catch people's attention."

"Exactly," Esme said, giving Dylan a satisfied smile.

For the rest of the bus journey home, Libby and Esme worked on the wording, and by the time they got back to Camden, Libby had e-mailed the newspaper their entry.

To the #girlonthe88bus. In April 1962 we met on the top deck of the 88 and talked from Clapham Common to Oxford Circus, and you changed my life. I have been looking for you ever since.

Young man reading *On the Road*

CHAPTER

19

"Peanut butter or Marmite?"

"Peanut butter, of course. Countryside or city?"

"City, every time. *The Simpsons* or *South Park*?"

"Erm . . . neither."

"What!" Dylan looked at Libby in mock horror. "How can you not like *The Simpsons*?"

"I don't know. I've just never really watched it."

"Seriously? Well, we have to remedy that. One day I'm gonna make you sit down and watch a *Simpsons* marathon with me."

Libby looked out of the bus window to hide her delight. They were at the end of their third week of putting up posters, and she found herself looking forward to each outing with a mixture of excitement and apprehension. It felt wonderful to have a purpose, a project she cared about; Libby couldn't remember the last time she'd felt so motivated. Her job working for Simon had never made her feel like this, she realized. It had been Simon's business, his dream, and whilst Libby had done everything she could to support him, it had never excited her in the way this project did.

Although it wasn't just helping Frank that made her feel like this, Libby was well aware. She glanced at Dylan, who was using two rolled-up posters as pretend drumsticks as he beat out a fast-paced rhythm on his knees. When she was with Dylan, Libby felt like a different version of herself. Funnier. Calmer. More spontaneous. She couldn't remember ever having laughed as much as she had done with him these past three weeks, or felt so at ease. And yet they were rapidly approaching the southern end of the 88 bus route. They had only the final section from Stockwell down to Clapham High Street and then they would have put up posters along the whole route, and their project would be complete. What would happen to this new version of Libby then? Would she still exist without this purpose? Without Dylan?

"Excuse me."

Libby heard a quiet voice behind her, and she and Dylan both turned round to see a young man sitting in the row behind them, dressed in a suit and tie, his dark hair neatly combed to one side.

"I'm . . . I'm so sorry to disturb you," he said with a slight stutter. "I did not mean to be rude. I just couldn't help noticing what you are holding."

"What, these?" Dylan said, holding up his poster drumsticks.

The man nodded. "Yes. I have seen them around London, and I have been wondering about them."

"We're trying to help a friend of ours find a woman he met on this bus a long time ago," Libby explained.

The man nodded again, more vigorously this time. "Yes, and that is what I was wondering about. Is this man called Frank, please?"

Libby looked at Dylan in astonishment, then back to the man. "Yes. How did you know that?"

He gave her a lopsided smile. "It is him! I thought it must be. It is a most unusual story, after all."

"How do you know Frank?" Dylan said. "Is he a friend of yours?"

"Not a friend, as such. But he did show me great kindness once, and I am forever in his debt."

The young man hesitated, and Libby waited, intrigued.

"I'm Libby and this is Dylan," she said, hoping that might encourage him.

"I am Sunil, but everyone calls me Sunny."

"And how did you meet Frank?"

"I met him here, on the 88 bus."

Libby laughed. "Frank does like to chat to strangers on the bus. That's how I met him too."

"He is a very good man." Sunny looked up at them both. "May I tell you about my encounter with Frank? I would like you to know what he did for me."

"We'd love that," Libby said, and she turned round fully in her seat to face him.

Sunny brushed an invisible speck of dust off his suit sleeve before he started. "This must have been 2014, so the year after I first came to England. I am from India, but I came here to study a master's in computer science at King's College London. Very prestigious course; my parents were very proud.

"For my first year, I was happy. I worked hard and I lived in a shared house with other international students. But then, at the start of my second year, my father died. It was such a shock; he was still young."

"I'm so sorry to hear that," Libby said.

Sunny blinked at her. "Thank you—that is very kind. I wanted to go home to support my mother and younger siblings, but my family wanted me to stay here and finish my studies. They said it is what my father would have wanted."

He looked out of the window before he spoke again.

"I vowed I would work even harder to graduate and get a good job, but it was difficult. I had a cleaning job but the rules are very strict on student visas. You can only work twenty hours a week, and I sent most of that money back home to my family. I cut down on all my expenses, even food, but it was still too much. By that Christmas, I could not pay my rent and my housemates asked me to move out."

For a moment, Sunny watched the city spooling past the bus window, and Libby waited for him to continue.

"That was a very difficult time," he said, his voice so quiet she could barely hear him. "London is a wonderful city, but not for a young Indian man with no money or place to stay. And I was too ashamed to tell my friends or worry my mother."

He stopped again, smoothing his hair with one hand.

"Is that when you met Frank?" Dylan asked gently.

Sunny nodded and looked back to them. "It was February or March, and I was staying in a homeless shelter run by the church. They provided a bed in the hall, but it was only open from nine o'clock at night until seven in the morning. I was okay during the week, when I could go to my lectures or the university buildings. But the weekends were much harder. I had nowhere warm or dry to go, except the library or the bus. I was so close to giving up and letting my father down."

Libby nodded as she listened. She'd seen a couple of people sleeping on the bus over the past month, their bags clutched tightly to their chests, and wondered about their stories.

"I was on the 88 that day, thinking about sending an e-mail to my mother telling her I was coming home, when Frank sat down across the aisle from me," Sunny said. "When he started talking to me, I was suspicious. Not everyone has good intentions, you see."

"I can imagine," Libby said.

"But Frank was so kind." Sunny smiled for the first time since the start of his story. "He asked me about India. No one had asked me about home in a long time, and it was wonderful to speak about my family. And he told me a little about his life too: his career as a great British actor, how he once worked with Laurence Olivier."

Libby smiled, remembering the bowler hat Frank had shown her.

"When we got to Clapham Common, I said good-bye, but Frank invited me to join him for lunch. I was so hungry, I couldn't say no, and he bought me a meal. While I ate, he told me his story about the woman on the 88 bus and how he was trying to find her. It reminded me of my father. He loved my mother very much. I think he would have done the same thing for her too."

"It is an extraordinarily romantic story," Libby said.

Sunny tilted his head to one side. "I think only a person with a good heart would still be looking for his love after all this time, no? To not give up is a very brave thing."

"It is," Libby said, feeling a dull ache in her chest. Despite all the posters they'd put up and the "Rush Hour Crush" advert, there was still no lead on finding the woman. She or Dylan checked the e-mail inbox every day, but there was never anything aside from junk mail, and hardly anyone was using the hashtag. And all the time, the clock was ticking for Frank.

"So, what happened with you and Frank after lunch?" Dylan said. "Did you see him again?"

Sunny shook his head. "We said good-bye and went our separate ways. But my time spent with him had deeply affected me. Frank had talked to me like a real human being, not some homeless person to be ignored or disapproved of. He had treated me with respect and kindness, like no one else had for months."

"That sounds just like him," Libby said.

"Riding back on the bus that afternoon, I decided not to e-mail my mother just yet. I had six months of my course left, and I would not give up on my dream, like Frank had not given up on his. So I stayed, and I graduated top of my class."

"That's wonderful," Libby said, grinning at him. "Are you a computer scientist now?"

"I am," Sunny said, nodding proudly. "I work for a company here in London. I met my wonderful wife there too, and we are expecting our first baby this summer. I am on my way to meet her for an ultrasound scan now."

"Oh my goodness, Frank will be so happy to hear this!"

"I'm sure he will not remember me," Sunny said shyly. "But I am so happy to be able to tell you my story, because for all these years I have thought about Frank and wondered how he is."

"He's very well," Libby said. "And he's still being kind to strangers on the bus, so nothing's changed there."

Sunny's face turned serious again. "Libby, Dylan, I must ask of you a favor, if I may?"

"Sure, what is it?" Dylan said.

Sunny nodded toward the posters in Dylan's hands. "I would like to help Frank, like he helped me. Perhaps I might be allowed to put up some posters for you?"

"Oh, that's very kind but we're almost finished," Libby said.

"We only have a short stretch to do, and then we've covered the whole route."

"Oh, okay. I understand." Sunny looked down at his lap.

"Of course you can help," Dylan said, giving Libby a discreet nudge. "Here, why don't you take half of these?"

"Really?" Sunny looked up at the pile of posters Dylan was offering him.

"We're going to put them up around Stockwell today, but maybe you could replace some missing ones along the route?"

"Of course, I will be most diligent," Sunny said, putting the posters carefully in his bag. "I will go out tomorrow with the posters and tape, and I will fill in missing spaces."

"If you're sure you have time?"

"It will be my absolute pleasure," Sunny said. "For a long time I have wished I could repay my debt of kindness to Frank. Now, in a small way, I can."

"WHAT an incredible story," Libby said when she and Dylan had said good-bye to Sunny and disembarked at Stockwell Station.

"It doesn't surprise me at all," Dylan said. "Frank's made friends with half the passengers on the 88 over the years. And he's always loved helping people."

"Which makes it all the more important that we help him now while there's still time."

Dylan didn't reply and just reached into his bag to get out a poster.

"What is it?" Libby said.

"Frank had another episode yesterday, the longest one yet. I had to call Clara."

"Oh, no, what did she say?"

"She's keen to get him assessed soon, for obvious reasons. But Frank is still refusing to go through with it, won't even hear the words 'care home.'"

"Poor Frank," Libby said. "I can't imagine what he'll do if he can't ride the bus."

"I know. His routines riding the 88 and walking up Parliament Hill are so important for his mental health, he's going to be lost without them. But there's no denying his dementia symptoms are getting worse."

"I wish there was more we could do to help," Libby said as she pulled off a piece of tape.

"I don't think there's much more we can do, aside from carrying on being his friend."

Dylan held the poster up against the side of the bus stop shelter and Libby attached the first strip of tape. As she did, he moved his thumb out of the way so she didn't stick that down too. They had their routine down to a fine art now, their hands moving round each other like dancers in a well-rehearsed ballet. But as Libby was attaching the last piece of tape, her hand brushed against Dylan's, sending a jolt of electricity through her body. Dylan must have felt it too, because for a moment he didn't move, his body so close behind her that Libby could almost feel his heart beating against her back. For a brief second she imagined turning round so she was facing Dylan, lifting her face up to his, and—

"Excuse me. What are you two doing?"

They swung round in unison at the sound of an unfamiliar voice. Two police officers were standing behind them.

"Is that poster yours?" the female officer said, pointing at the yellow sheet that Libby was very clearly taping to the bus stop.

What the hell should she say? "I'm so s—"

"No comment," Dylan interrupted, putting his hand on Libby's arm.

The police officer eyed Dylan up and down. "Are you aware that fly-posting is illegal?"

Shit. Libby had had no idea they were breaking the law. Dylan didn't say anything, staring back at the officer with his arms folded.

"Unless you have permission from the owners of this bus stop, then you're breaking the law and liable for a fine," the officer continued.

"I'm so sorry," Libby said. "We had no idea. We'll—"

"No comment," Dylan said again.

The police officer let out an audible sigh. "I'm going to have to ask you to remove this poster and any others you've put up."

Libby looked at Dylan to see if he'd agree, but he didn't move.

"Sir, did you hear what I said? What you're doing is illegal."

"This is fucking ridiculous," Dylan said, and it was the voice she remembered from the first time they met, laced with rage.

"Dylan, it's all right," Libby muttered.

"No, it's not." He glared at the two officers. "Are you telling me that every time someone puts up a poster for a missing cat, you stop them too? Or are you just harassing us today because of the way I look?"

The male officer stepped forward. "Look, mate, one or two posters we can turn a blind eye to, but yours are pasted up over half of Lambeth. It's remarkable the council haven't slapped a fine on you already."

"I'm not your mate." Dylan's arms were still folded, and

Libby could sense him pulling his body up to its full, intimidating height.

"I'm going to ask you again, please remove all your posters," the first officer said.

"No. They're not doing any harm; we're just trying to help a friend."

What was Dylan doing? At this rate he was going to get them both arrested.

The officers exchanged a glance. "Do you really want to get yourself fined over this, sir? Because if you continue to refuse our request, then we have the power to authorize a—"

But Libby didn't hear the rest of what the officer said, because at that moment Dylan grabbed her hand and yelled, "Run!"

n the split second it took for Libby to work out what was going on, Dylan had started pulling her along the pavement, away from the police officers. She almost tripped over her feet, but his strong arm held her and she started to sprint alongside him. What the hell were they doing, running away from the police? They were bound to get arrested for this, and with the fly-posting offense as well, maybe they'd even be prosecuted. Libby picked up her pace. Dylan was still holding her hand, and he suddenly swerved out into the busy road. Libby squealed as they dodged through traffic until they reached the far pavement. She had no idea if the police were following them, but she didn't want to slow down to look back.

"I need to stop. I've got a stitch," she panted as she felt a stab of pain in her right-hand side.

"Over here," Dylan said, and he pulled her right into a small alleyway between some shops, lined with industrial-sized green bins. At once they stopped running and released hands, and Libby bent forward, gasping for air.

"Oh . . my . . god," she wheezed.

Beside her, Dylan was leaning against one of the wheelie

bins, his body convulsing, and it occurred to Libby he might be having some sort of fit. "Are you okay? Should I call a . . ."

Dylan looked up and Libby could see that his whole body was shaking with laughter.

"Why are you laughing?" she shrieked.

"'Cos that was fun!"

"Are you kidding me?"

"Come on, you must have run away from the police before."

"What? No! I've never even been stopped by the police, let alone run away from them."

"Seriously? Not even when you were a teenager getting drunk with your mates?"

"Never! I swear, until today I'd never even been in trouble with a teacher at school, much less broken the law."

Dylan shook his head in disbelief. "Wow, I'm not sure I've ever met anyone like you, Libby."

"I've never met anyone like you either."

As she said this, Libby glanced up and caught Dylan looking at her. He didn't look away, and for a moment, neither of them spoke. Libby's heart was hammering, and she was pretty sure it wasn't from the running anymore.

"I really need to start doing some proper exercise," she said, pushing her hair out of her hot face.

"Do you want me to get you some water?"

"No, I'll be fine in a minute. Do you think the police will still be looking for us?"

"I doubt they even followed us in the first place; we're hardly Bonnie and Clyde. But we can stay here for a bit if you like, to be safe. Let me find you somewhere to sit." Dylan looked around, but the only objects in the alleyway were the bins and some abandoned crates. He picked up two crates and carried them over. "Your throne, madam."

"Why, thank you, sir." She sat down and Dylan took a seat next to her. After the excitement of their getaway, the alley suddenly seemed very quiet.

"What was going on back there with the police?" Libby asked.

"What do you mean?"

"You seemed so angry."

Dylan stretched his long legs out in front of them. "I dunno, I always get that way around the cops. They've given me so much trouble over the years, stopping and searching me and my mates just 'cos of the way we dress. I guess it's made me pretty suspicious of them."

"But those two seemed all right. I mean, it turns out we were breaking the law and all they asked was for us to take the posters down."

"But it's wrong. You know the only reason we can't post things is 'cos the big corporations don't want us covering their precious adverts, which con people into spending money they don't have on crap they don't need. And yet you and me, who are actually trying to do something good, are treated like the baddies. It's bollocks." He leaned back against the wall and sighed.

Libby stretched her legs out next to his, their shoes almost touching. "Do you reckon they'll rip all our posters down?"

"Maybe, but I can come back and replace them tomorrow."

"This could go on forever, you realize. You and me riding the 88, replacing posters that get pulled down."

"Like painting the Forth Bridge, a job that never finishes."

"We'll be like Frank, still doing it when we're eighty, out on the bus every day."

"Come on, Libby, dear." Dylan put on an exaggerated old person's voice. "Time to catch the 88, we've got more posters to put up."

"All right, Dylan, let me put my teeth in and I'm coming," Libby croaked, and Dylan threw back his head in laughter.

"Can you imagine?" she said when his laughter had died down.

"Yeah, that's probably not a good idea. I guess we should stop when we've done this last bit; otherwise we never will."

This was the first time either of them had mentioned the imminent end of their project, and for a moment neither of them spoke.

"So . . . I guess that means we'll be finished soon?" Libby said.

"Well, you're the one with the spreadsheet, but I reckon one more trip should do it."

They didn't look at each other, both studying the bins opposite. When would they see each other again once they'd finished? Libby wondered. They might bump into each other through Frank, but the chances of that were pretty slim. She thought of the electricity she'd felt a moment ago, the feeling of Dylan's body so close to hers, and she felt her face getting hot again.

"You must be looking forward to your life getting back to normal," Dylan said.

"I'm not sure my life will ever be normal again." As soon as Libby said it, she regretted her choice of words. "I mean, what with everything that's happened to me recently," she added quickly.

"Of course." Dylan was staring at his boots. "Have you got any thoughts about what you'll do next?"

"To be honest, I have no idea. I need to find somewhere to live and a new job. These past few weeks helping Frank have been a wonderful distraction, but I have to start making some decisions."

"Might you move back to Surrey?" Dylan said it innocently, but Libby could hear his question mark hanging in the air.

"That's *definitely* not happening."

"Oh, okay . . . Look, if you don't mind me asking, what happened between you and your ex?"

They'd skirted round this conversation before, but Libby had always found ways to change the subject. Now she paused, trying to work out how best to explain.

"Simon and I had been together for eight years and he got bored of me. We'd got stuck in a bit of a rut, and Simon said it was all too dull and predictable. He said he wanted more from his life than I could give him."

She heard Dylan inhale next to her, but he didn't say anything.

"We'd always been a bit of an unlikely couple," Libby continued. "Simon is this rugged, outdoorsy type; he's never happier than when he's playing rugby in the pouring rain on a Saturday morning. And I like spreadsheets and color-coded maps, as you well know." She laughed at this, but Dylan didn't join in.

"But were you happy?" he said.

Had she been happy? No one had ever asked her that question about their relationship before.

"At the time I thought I was, yes. I loved Simon, and I liked our routines and stability. We had our future all planned out: engaged at thirty, married at thirty-one, and then start trying for kids shortly after. I honestly thought we were going to spend the rest of our lives together."

As she said this, Libby remembered something Dylan had said last week, about not wanting marriage and 2.4 kids.

"I guess Simon and I were on the long-term relationship treadmill, and it never occurred to me that I might want anything else," she added.

"I get it. There's a lot of pressure in our society to live a certain way, to conform to the patriarchal-capitalist agenda of work, marry, procreate."

"I really thought that was what my life had to be like," Libby said. "A good daughter, a good girlfriend, one day a good wife and mother. But since spending these past few weeks in London, I'm beginning to realize that might not be the only way."

"How do you mean?" Dylan said.

"Well, look at Frank and his girl on the bus. She rebelled against her parents and went to art school, and Frank has spent his entire life looking for a woman he met once, even though his own daughter disapproves. They both had the confidence to chase their own dreams, but I've given all of mine up to make other people happy."

"It's not too late to change that; you could still go to art school. You're only, what—"

"About to turn thirty," Libby said. "And as you said yourself, thirties is a bit old to be going back to college. Besides, I've not drawn in years."

"What about that sketch pad Frank gave you?"

"Honestly? It's sitting beside my bed, gathering dust."

Next to her, Libby felt Dylan adjust his position. "You know, this might be a crazy idea but there's this pub in South

London that does a weekly life-drawing class. A mate told me about it—apparently it's very casual; people just turn up and have a few drinks and get to practice drawing a model. You could give that a go?"

"Thanks, but I'm not sure I'd ever have the confidence to walk into a room full of strangers and start drawing."

"I could come with you if you want?"

He said it quickly, and Libby was so surprised that for a moment she didn't know how to answer.

"I mean, I'm terrible at art," Dylan continued, sounding unusually flustered. "I once got a detention at school because we had to draw a classmate and mine looked like a pig and my teacher thought I was taking the piss. But I'm happy to give it a go with you."

"Oh. Well, that would be cool, thanks." Libby hoped Dylan couldn't sense the joy that was suddenly radiating out of her whole body.

"Cool," Dylan said, and when Libby glanced across at him, she could see he was trying to suppress a grin as well. "Shall we get on with it, then? These posters aren't gonna put themselves up."

CHAPTER

21

Libby! Don't you look radiant this morning," Frank said as Libby approached him at the bus stop. It was Saturday morning, but rather than their weekly walk up Parliament Hill, Frank had asked Libby to meet him at the stop near his house.

"Thanks, Frank. How are you today?"

"Very good. And here's our bus right on time."

Frank signaled to an 88 as it pulled up, its doors opening in front of them. He took hold of the side of the bus to steady himself as he stepped on board.

"Mr. Weiss!"

The bus driver, a middle-aged woman with black corkscrew curls, was beaming at Frank from behind the steering wheel.

"Patience!" Frank said. "How are you? How's your father?"

"Oh, you know him, still making trouble," Patience said. "When I visited him on Saturday, the nurse told me he's been entertaining them all with Jimmy Cliff songs."

Frank laughed. "Ah, well, please give him my love, and your dear mother."

"Of course." Patience pressed the button for the doors to

shut. Libby waited for Frank to move toward the stairs, but he stayed standing where he was, holding on to the nearest pole.

"This is my friend Libby," he said to the driver, and Libby heard something like pride in his voice. "She's been helping me with the search for my girl."

"Oh, is that right?" Patience said, her eyes on the road as she pulled the bus out into the traffic.

"Yes. She and Dylan, my carer, have been putting posters up along the 88 route. You must have seen them?"

"Are they the yellow ones that have been popping up over the past few weeks?"

Frank nodded. "They're the ones! We're hoping that either my woman will see it or someone will tell her about my search."

Patience chuckled. "Good on you. Dad will be pleased to know you've not given up your search."

"Never!" Frank said. "I have to say, your parents' marriage has always been something of an inspiration to me. To see how those two adore each other, even after everything they've been through. That's true love, I tell you."

Patience didn't say anything, focused on the road in front of them. But in the mirror, Libby thought she could see a flash of emotion in the woman's face.

"I tell you what, Mr. Weiss," Patience said after a moment. "I'm not supposed to do this, but how about you give me a few of your posters and I'll pin them up down at the bus depot? And I can put word out on our message boards too. Bus drivers love a gossip; perhaps one of them can help find your lady."

"Would you do that?" Frank said.

"Of course. After all you did for my dad over the years, it's the least I can do."

"Libby, did you hear that? How wonderful!"

Libby reached into her bag and pulled out a handful of posters, handing them over. "Thank you so much."

"I'll get the word out on the drivers' network," Patience said with a nod.

The bus pulled up at the next stop, where a small queue of passengers was waiting to board.

"We'll get out of your way, then," Frank said. "It was lovely seeing you, my dear. Tell your old man I'll pop in to see him soon."

"All right, Mr. Weiss. You take care now," Patience said as the bus doors opened and new passengers started to push on.

Libby followed Frank slowly up the stairs, where his usual seat was free.

"She seems lovely," Libby said as she slid in next to him.

"Oh, yes, I've known Patience since she was a baby," Frank said. "Her father was a bus driver too. I met him on here and we became good friends. He's in a home now. Parkinson's . . ."

Frank trailed off. Downstairs, Libby could hear Patience greeting new passengers. When she glanced at Frank, he was frowning.

"Did Dylan tell you about Sunny?" Libby said, suddenly remembering her and Dylan's encounter on the bus yesterday.

"Who's Sunny?"

Libby recounted the story the young man had told them. Frank listened with a growing smile.

"Of course I remember him!" he said, clapping his hands together. "He was such a charming young man. He told me all about India, which is a place I've never had the pleasure of visiting. Fascinating lad."

"Well, you clearly made an impression on him too. And

he took some posters to put up because he said he wanted to help you."

"How marvelous," Frank exclaimed. "Between you, Dylan, and Sunny putting up the posters and Patience spreading the word among bus drivers, we'll find my woman in no time."

"Frank, remember what Dylan said. She might have left London years ago or—"

"But I know she's still here in this city," Frank interrupted. "Even if I've never seen her, I sense her all the time: the laugh of a woman in a café, a flash of red hair on an underground escalator. I wouldn't have spent all this time looking for her if I wasn't certain she's somewhere nearby."

"I hope you're right."

"I know I am. And now all it will take is for her to see a poster or pick up a copy of the *Metro*, or someone to mention it to her, and we'll be reunited. Just in time . . ." Frank trailed off again, and when Libby looked at him, he was staring out of the window.

"What do you mean?" she said.

"What?" He looked round at her.

"You said you'll be reunited just in time."

"Did I?"

"Has something happened?"

Frank rubbed his forehead, and Libby could tell he was trying to remember. Then he shook his head and let out a sigh of frustration. "I'm sorry."

"That's okay, take your time."

"It scares me, Libby. I keep forgetting things, silly little things. I'm an actor, for god's sake. I used to be able to recite the whole of the Duke of Gloucester's soliloquy in *Henry VI*. But now . . ."

He stopped and turned to face her, and Libby could see his face was full of doubt.

"What if I wake up one day and I can't remember my girl on the bus?"

"Oh, Frank. I'm sure that won't happen."

"But my memory is getting worse every day. She might get lost in there, like so many other things. And then I'll never get her back."

"I'm sure you won't forget her. Not after all this time."

Frank shook his head. "My daughter has been preparing me for the worst. She says this dementia means that one day I won't even remember my own name."

This was the first time Libby had heard Frank use the word "dementia."

"I'm so sorry you're having to go through this, Frank. It's not fair."

"Clara's been on at me about the care assessment again. I've been having these funny turns and she wants to set one up for next month."

"And what do you think about that?"

Frank took a deep breath before he answered. "I think we need to find my girl, Libby. Time is running out."

"SO, do you want to know where we're going today?" Frank said as the bus reached the bottom of Haymarket.

"Yes, please."

"I decided it was about time you finally revisited the National Gallery. You've been in London for weeks now; it's crazy you've still not been."

"Oh, amazing, Frank, thank you!"

"I thought we could start with the Renaissance master-pieces on the second floor, visit my old friends Bacchus and Ariadne, and then stop for lunch in the café. After that we can pop down to see the Monets and Renoirs on the ground floor," Frank said as the bus turned left toward Trafalgar Square.

"You clearly know the place inside out, so I'm in your hands."

"Well, I've been visiting for sixty years, ever since my girl on the bus first told me about it, so I do know it pretty well. I was so intimidated to begin with; I didn't dare tell any of my friends in case they laughed at me. But now I've been to art galleries round the world, and this is one of the finest."

"I loved it the one time I went with school. I remember this one huge room with a domed roof, and there were so many paintings that I didn't know where to look. I'd never seen any-thing like it in my life."

Frank beamed. "Well, it's time to reunite you now."

He reached past Libby to hit the stop bell and then began to pull himself up. Libby stood up to help him and felt a sud-den rush of blood to her head.

"Everything all right?" Frank said as she grabbed the bar to steady herself.

"Yes, fine. I'm just a bit dizzy."

"Let's get you off this bus, then."

Libby followed Frank down the stairs, grateful for his slow pace. When they stepped onto the pavement, she took a deep lungful of air.

"That better?" Frank said.

"Yes, thanks. I didn't have any breakfast, so it's probably low blood sugar."

"Well, in that case, let's head to the café first and get you something to eat."

They began to make their way toward Trafalgar Square, Frank pointing out details of the statues. But Libby couldn't concentrate; her head felt like it was full of cotton wool, and small white dots were swimming in front of her eyes.

"The fourth plinth over there is now used for contemporary art installations," Frank said as they walked past the stone lions. "There have been some wonderful ones over the years and . . . Are you sure you're all right, Libby?"

"I think I might need to sit down," she said, feeling herself sway.

"Of course, let's get you to—" Frank started, but Libby didn't hear the rest of his sentence, because she felt her knees buckle and then everything went black.

CHAPTER

22

PEGGY

Excuse me if I don't stay long today, love, but I've had the strangest morning.

Have you ever woken up and known that something bad was going to happen? You don't know what it is, but you've got this feeling, deep in your bones, that trouble is on its way. My mother used to say it was like someone walking over your grave, that cold shiver that passes through your body.

Well, I woke up with one of them this morning.

My first thought was that something had happened to David or Maisie and the boys, but I checked my mobile phone and no one had been in touch. I wanted to call David to check, but you know what he's like; he'd have got annoyed and said I was fussing. So I told myself it was nothing and got up to make my cup of tea. But I couldn't shift this feeling; it followed me round the flat, whatever room I went in. I tried watching a bit of TV but I couldn't even concentrate on *This Morning*, and you know how much I love that Phillip Schofield.

Anyway, I had my breakfast, got dressed, and headed out to catch the bus. But the whole time I kept looking over my shoulder, like death himself was following me. And then I'm sitting on the 88, trying to distract myself by listening to the conversations around me, and I see a man and his young son get on board, carrying a kite. And that's when I suddenly remembered.

The last time I felt like this, the same sense of creeping dread.

It was the day you nearly died.

I'm not sure if I ever told you this, but I woke up that morning knowing something bad was going to happen. I thought it was about David, who was always getting into trouble in school at the time. And I remember fretting round the flat all day, waiting for the moment I got the call from the headmaster to summon me in again.

And then there was a knock at the front door, so faint I almost didn't hear it. So I pulled the door open and there you were, slumped against the frame, looking like you had only hours left for this world.

Do you remember it, Percy? You probably don't; you were so ill. I don't know how I managed to drag you to the bedroom, because you were a deadweight in my arms. And when I finally got you into bed, your skin was so cold and your lips were blue. And I remember saying I was going to call the doctor but you grabbed my hand, with surprising force for someone who looked as rough as you did, and refused to let me go.

So I lay in bed next to you, holding you in my arms, praying to a god I didn't believe in to save you.

I haven't thought about that day in years: maybe I blocked it out once you got better, or maybe it's because of what came next for us. But sitting on the bus this morning, filled with that same cold feeling of dread, I remembered it all so well. It was like I was back there, lying in bed with you shaking in my arms, wishing with every bone in my body that you'd survive.

And I was thinking about all of this when I heard a noise, a loud siren screaming up behind the bus, and this ambulance came tearing past and swerved to a halt in front of Trafalgar Square. And everyone on the bus craned forward to see what was going on, and as the bus inched through the traffic, I saw a body lying on the ground near one of the lions. It looked like a young woman with bright red hair, and an old man was kneeling next to her, fanning her with a piece of paper. And then the bus moved on, and I couldn't see her anymore.

Poor thing. That's no way to go, is it?

Anyway, I don't know what that funny feeling was about this morning, Percy, but I'm not going to lie; it's given me the heebie-jeebies. I think I'll head home soon and have a nice cup of tea. And maybe I'll call David tonight, just to make sure everything's all right.

23

L ibby, are you all right? Libby, can you hear me?"

Libby opened her eyes and squinted into the bright sunlight. She could see the shadow of a face looming over her and felt something cold and hard under her back.

"Frank?" She tried to pull herself up, but he squeezed her hand to stop her.

"Don't move yet. I don't want you blacking out again. There's an ambulance coming."

"What happened?"

"You passed out. But don't worry; the paramedics are nearly here."

"I'm fine, honestly. I just need to eat something." But as she said the words, Libby's vision started to swim again and she closed her eyes.

"Stay where you are; you'll be fine," Frank said.

Libby could hear other voices and sense people standing around them, watching. "I don't want to make a scene," she mumbled.

"You're not; stop worrying."

Libby stayed lying with her eyes closed while Frank knelt next to her, gently fanning her with a newspaper. A minute later, she heard the sound of sirens and, shortly after that, approaching footsteps. Frank started to explain what had happened and then Libby sensed someone else kneeling down next to her.

"Hi, Libby, I'm Jonathan, a paramedic. How are you feeling?"

"Just a bit dizzy."

"Okay, let's get you checked out, then. I'm going to start by taking your blood pressure, okay?"

Libby nodded as the paramedic attached a strap to her arm. When she glanced up, she saw a crowd of onlookers had gathered around, and someone was taking her photo.

"I'm sorry to cause such a fuss," Libby said as the strap squeezed her arm. "I forgot to eat breakfast, that's all."

The paramedic didn't reply, his eyes fixed on the blood pressure monitor. "Has this ever happened before, Libby?"

"Erm, I passed out once when I was eighteen and drank too much cider at a party."

"Okay. What about more recently? Any dizzy spells?"

Libby was about to say no but stopped herself. "I felt a bit dizzy yesterday, but I had been running."

"I'm going to check your blood oxygen levels now." He attached a clip to her index finger, looked at the number, then stood up to consult with his colleague.

While he was gone, Frank leaned over Libby. "Are you all right?"

"A bit embarrassed, to be honest," she said, although she was pleased to see the gawkers had mainly moved on now it was apparent that she wasn't about to die. "I'm sorry, Frank. This was meant to be a lovely day at the National Gallery."

"Don't be so silly. We can go to the gallery anytime—what matters is making sure you're okay."

"Maybe this is a sign I finally need to start looking after myself a bit better."

"And to eat breakfast. Most important meal of the day and all that."

The paramedic rejoined them. "Okay, Libby. Well, the good news is your oxygen levels are fine. But your blood pressure is low, and given you passed out, we'd like to take you into hospital to get you checked over by a doctor."

"Hospital? There's really no need. I—"

"Listen to the paramedic," Frank interrupted. "You don't want to take any chances with your health."

"But really, I just got a bit light-headed. I promise I'll go home and have a lie-down," Libby said, but both the paramedic and Frank were staring at her, and she knew she was wasting her breath. "Okay, fine. But there's nothing wrong with me, I swear."

TWO hours later, Libby was sitting on a bed in a bay in A&E, all dizziness gone. She'd been wired up for an ECG, had bloods taken, and peed in a small plastic pot. She'd also eaten a cheese sandwich and banana provided by one of the nurses and was feeling even more embarrassed at having wasted everyone's time. At least she'd managed to convince Frank that he didn't need to come to the hospital with her, although he'd made her promise she'd call him as soon as she had any news.

After what felt like an eternity, the blue curtain was pulled back and a young doctor walked in, carrying a clipboard.

"Elizabeth Nicholls? I'm Dr. Singh. How are you feeling?"

"I'm fine, thank you. I'm sorry for wasting everyone's time today."

"You're not wasting anyone's time." She perched on the edge of the bed and consulted her clipboard. "The good news is that your ECG was normal and there was nothing worrying in your bloods."

"That's great. I promise I won't skip breakfast again."

"There was one thing that came up, though." The doctor looked up at Libby. "Your urine sample and blood results both came back with very high levels of HCG. Do you know what that is?"

Libby shook her head.

"HCG is a hormone produced in pregnancy. So the tests indicate that you're pregnant."

"What?" Libby was so surprised she almost laughed. "That's impossible."

"Do you know when your last period was?"

Libby tried to scan her memory, but blood was beating in her ears and making it hard to concentrate. Why wasn't the doctor laughing right now and telling her it was a joke?

"But I've not had sex for months."

"I'm sorry to push, Libby, but it would be really helpful to know when your last period was."

Libby pulled out her phone. She usually tracked her periods in an app, because her sister had once told her it would be useful to have this information when she and Simon started trying to conceive. But now, as she clicked the app open, she saw the last period she'd logged was back in early March. Surely she'd had one since then? Libby desperately cast her mind back over the past few months, but in all the chaos of the breakup with Simon and coming to London, she'd lost all track of her body. She'd definitely had some bleeding at some point, but had that been a proper period?

She looked up at the doctor. "It's possible it was the fifth of March."

"Right. So that would mean . . ." Dr. Singh paused, doing the math. "It would mean you're fourteen weeks pregnant today."

"But that's impossible. Surely I'd have known if I was pregnant for the past three months. You must have mixed my results up with somebody else's."

"Have you had any other symptoms? Nausea or fatigue? Any weight gain?"

Libby froze. The feelings of sickness that she'd put down to stress. The extra pounds she'd attributed to all the chocolate croissants. The constant exhaustion that she'd blamed on Hector.

"Oh, crap," she said as dizziness washed over her again. She put her head in her hands. "I can't be pregnant. This can't be happening."

"I'm sorry this has come as such a shock to you," Dr. Singh said. "Is there anyone you'd like me to call? Your partner, maybe?"

"No!" Libby said it so loudly she saw the doctor start.

"Okay, I'll give you a minute alone to process this. Let me make a quick call and get you registered with the maternity unit; then you're free to go. Okay?" The doctor moved toward the curtain and then stopped. "Are you sure there's no one you want me to call? Anyone you live with?"

Libby thought of how her sister would react if she received a call saying Libby was pregnant and in hospital, and winced. "No, thank you. There's no one I want you to call."

The next week passed in a daze. Libby went through the motions around the house—sleeping and eating, looking after Hector—but she felt numb. Was it really possible that she was pregnant? She and Simon had always been so careful. But somehow it had gone horribly wrong, and now she was pregnant by a man who no longer wanted to be with her, a man who was seeing someone else. Plus, she didn't know the first thing about raising a baby, she was unemployed, soon to be homeless, and her savings were fast running out. Panic gnawed at Libby's insides and her head spun as the grim reality of the situation hit her again and again.

She avoided Rebecca as much as possible, too scared to tell her yet, and although Libby sent Frank a brief message to reassure him she was home from the hospital, she'd not gone into any details. As for Dylan, Libby had ignored his WhatsApp message on Monday morning telling her he was waiting for her at the bus stop, and the voice mail he'd left later that day checking she was okay and informing her he'd finished putting posters up along the route. Once or twice she'd considered calling him back and confessing why she'd failed to meet him as agreed, but every time she bottled out. Dylan was a lovely guy, but any chemistry they might have had would disappear the moment he knew she was pregnant, and Libby couldn't bear to see Dylan be awkward around her. Now their poster project was finished, it was easiest if Libby ignored his messages and let him forget about her.

And then there was Simon. Libby knew she had to tell him, but the thought made her feel physically sick. Simon had moved on with his new life and girlfriend, so how would he react when she told him she was pregnant? Would he be angry, thinking she was trying to trap him? Would he want her to get rid of the baby? Because as much as this pregnancy was unplanned, it definitely wasn't unwanted; Libby had dreamed of being a mother since she was a child. But in all those dreams, she'd been married, bringing up a baby as part of a family, not raising it alone. Libby had run this over and over in her mind all week, until her head ached and her eyes were sore from crying.

On Saturday morning, once she was sure that the others had left the house, Libby went down to the living room and pulled one of Rebecca's books off the shelf. She'd spotted it during the week but hadn't dared look at it. Now she carried it through to the kitchen and sat down at the counter. *The Pregnancy Planner for New Parents*, it read on the front, with a photo of a woman with a huge, distended belly and a man standing behind her, smiling smugly. Libby opened the book and flicked through until she came to the relevant page.

At fifteen weeks your baby is around 10cm long and approximately the size of an apple.

Libby put her hand on her stomach. There couldn't be something the size of an apple in there. Surely her tummy should have been properly bulging by now, not this small, slightly soft paunch. She read on.

> If this is your first pregnancy, you may not have a visible baby bump yet, although your weight gain is likely to have started speeding up. Every pregnancy is different, so if you feel concerned in any way, then speak to your doctor.

Yes, I feel bloody concerned. Libby scanned farther down the page.

> The baby's eyes are now sensitive to light and its fingernails are starting to grow.

For some reason, this fact made Libby gasp. She'd been amazed by Hector's tiny fingers when he'd been born, so small and wrinkled, like a little old man's.

> Around fifteen weeks, your baby will start hearing you, so you can talk to it whenever you like.

Libby put the book down.

"Hello, little one," she said, and then felt self-conscious at hearing her own voice in the empty house. "I'm your mummy."

She pressed her hands more firmly on her tummy, imaging the apple-sized baby underneath.

"I'm sorry I've been a bit crap so far. I realize it's not a great start, me not even knowing you were there. And sorry for all the crying this week. It's been a bit of a shock, that's all."

There was a muffled sound from a neighboring garden, and Libby paused.

"Look, this isn't exactly how I'd hoped it would happen, what with your father and me . . . Well, never mind about that now. But I've had a lot of time to think about things this week, and I want you to know that I'm excited about this . . . about *you*. I apologize now that I have absolutely no idea what to do and I'll probably make a shit ton of mistakes, like swearing in front of you. And right now I have no idea where we're going to live or how I'm going to support us. But I'll work it out, okay? I promise."

Libby held her breath, waiting to see if she'd feel anything under her hands, the tiniest sign that the baby had heard and was excited too. But instead, all she felt was a sudden, desperate urge to go for a wee.

As she was washing her hands in the bathroom sink, making a mental list of all the things she needed to do, Libby heard the sound of the front door clicking open downstairs. Rebecca, Tom, and Hector were usually out at football practice until lunchtime every Saturday. She dried her hands and stepped out into the hall.

"Hello?"

"Libby, where are you?" Rebecca's voice shouted up the stairs.

"Up here. What are you doing back so early?"

"Mum's here for brunch, remember?"

Bugger. Libby absolutely did not remember, and the last thing she needed was a meal with her family right now. Her mum would take one look at her and immediately know something was going on.

"I hope you're not still lazing in bed, Elizabeth," Pauline's voice called up.

"No, Mum," Libby replied, looking down at her scruffy pajamas.

"Good. Well, come down, then. I need your help preparing the smoked salmon and scrambled eggs."

Libby glanced in the bathroom mirror at her tired, pale face, then pulled her hair up into a ponytail, brushed on some mascara, and made her way downstairs.

"Are you ill?" her mum said as soon as Libby walked into the kitchen.

"No."

"Well, what's wrong with you, then?"

"Nothing's wrong. I'm just tired. Where are the eggs?"

"In one of those shopping bags." Pauline nodded at several large brown paper bags on the counter.

Libby took a step toward the counter and then froze. Poking out from underneath one of the shopping bags was the pregnancy book she'd been looking at earlier, still open at the fifteen-weeks page. It seemed neither her mum nor her sister had noticed it when they came in, but Libby had to get it out of the kitchen, and fast. She glanced across at them, and they both had their backs turned to her, arguing over something in the fridge. As quietly as possible, Libby lifted up the bag and slipped the book out from underneath it.

"Libby, can you pass me the smoked sa—"

Her mum had turned to face her, and her mouth fell open as she saw Libby clutching the book. For a moment she remained like that, as if someone had pressed PAUSE, and then her whole face lit up.

"Rebecca!" she squealed so loudly that Rebecca almost dropped the carton of orange juice she was lifting out of the fridge. "Why didn't you tell me?"

Libby could feel a crushing sensation against her ribs as she realized what was going on. She opened her mouth to explain, but Rebecca spoke first.

"What are you talking about, Mum?"

"Is that why you invited me today, to make a big announcement? Well, then, you for leaving the book lying around!"

Rebecca's face was blank. She turned to look at Libby for an explanation, and as she did, her eyes dropped to the book. For a moment nobody spoke, and Libby saw color rising up her sister's throat.

"How many weeks?" Rebecca said, and her voice sounded like something was twisting her windpipe.

"I don't know; you tell me, darling," Pauline said with a laugh. "You're not showing yet, so I'd guess less than twelve."

Rebecca was staring at Libby, her expression vacant. The only indication of emotion was the bright flush of pink that had now moved up to her cheeks.

"Fifteen weeks," Libby said quietly. "I'm sorry, Bex. I only found out—"

"Would someone tell me what's going on?" The laughter in her mum's voice had gone, and she was looking between her two daughters. "Rebecca?"

"I'm not pregnant," Rebecca said, her voice faltering. "We just found out that our last round of IVF failed."

"Oh. But then I don't understand. Why are you reading—"

"It's Libby. *She's* pregnant, not me."

A few seconds of agonizing silence.

"Elizabeth?" her mum said, her eyes wide. "But . . . how?"

"I got pregnant before Simon and I broke up," Libby said.

"It's Simon's, then?" Pauline's face brightened with relief. "Thank god for that! Well, in that case it's not terrible news at all." She walked across the kitchen toward Libby. "In fact, I think it's wonderful. Congratulations, darling!" She pulled her into a tight hug.

"Eh, thanks, Mum." Libby's eyes were on her sister, who hadn't moved.

Pauline lowered her voice as she stage-whispered into Libby's ear, "I have to admit, I'm a little relieved that at least one of my girls can get pregnant without any fuss."

Rebecca flinched as if she'd been slapped. She quickly regained her composure, but Libby had seen it, that flash of searing pain.

"Rebecca, have you got any champagne in the fridge?" Pauline called, not turning round to look at her. "We need to celebrate Libby's exciting news."

Rebecca walked silently toward the fridge, her movements stiff, and she pulled out a bottle.

"Simon must be over the moon; he always wanted to be a father. What did you say when you told him?"

Libby realized she was still clinging on to the book, and she put it down on the counter. "I . . . I haven't told him yet."

"Why not?"

"Well, it's all been a bit of a surprise."

"When did you find out?" Pauline took the champagne bottle off Rebecca and popped the cork.

"Only last week."

"Really? I knew I was pregnant with you girls the night you were conceived," Pauline said. "Both times I said to your father, 'Roger, we just created a baby.'"

Libby winced and tried to catch her sister's eye, but Rebecca was looking away from her, staring out of the window into the garden.

"At least this explains the weight gain," Pauline said, pouring champagne into a glass. "But I have to say, darling, in many ways this is very clever of you. Now Simon will have to forget about his silly little affair and take you back, and all this nonsense will finally be over with."

"I'm not so sure about that," Libby said.

"Oh, of course he will. Simon's an honorable young man; there's no way he'll leave you to have a baby on your own."

"But he's with someone else now, Mum. And to be honest, I'm not sure I want him back after everything that's happened."

"Oh, don't be ridiculous. As soon as you tell him you're carrying his baby, he'll forget all about this skinny Olivia woman. Just you wait and see."

"You *are* keeping the baby, aren't you?" It was the first time Rebecca had spoken in a while, and when Libby looked up at her, she saw a glint of something dangerous in her sister's eye.

"Of course I am."

"And you *are* going to tell Simon?"

Libby hesitated a second too long, and she saw her sister draw breath. "You have to tell him, Libby. He's the baby's father."

"Of course she's going to tell him," Pauline said, and tutted at her elder daughter. "Come on, Rebecca, can't you try and be happy for your sister?"

"I am happy for her," Rebecca said, but her voice was flat.

"A toast, then," Pauline said, thrusting a glass of champagne toward each of her daughters. "To Libby and her pregnancy."

"To Libby and her pregnancy," Rebecca said, and then promptly drained her glass in one.

25

Brunch was excruciating. Pauline spent the whole time talking at Libby about the pregnancy: how she should sign up for antenatal yoga classes to keep in shape, how she should register with a hospital in Surrey because they were better than London ones, how delighted Simon's parents would be when they found out. Libby tried to change the subject several times, but her mother barely paused for breath, and in the end, Libby gave up. Besides, she was much more concerned about her sister. Rebecca didn't say a word and her food sat untouched, the scrambled egg congealing as she drank glass after glass of champagne. And Libby couldn't forget the look of hurt on her sister's face earlier, the pain at their mother's words. She needed time alone with Rebecca, the chance to talk to her in private. Finally, after what seemed like hours, their mother stood up.

"Right, I should be getting home," she said, gathering up her bags. "Libby, I imagine I'll be seeing a lot more of you soon, once you've moved back in with Simon."

Libby opened her mouth, but Pauline hadn't finished.

"Make sure you tell him today, because I'm bound to bump into his mother in Waitrose this week, and I want to be able to celebrate the good news with her. All right?" She gave Libby's shoulder a too-hard squeeze and then breezed out.

Libby waited until she heard the front door slam, then turned to her sister.

"Bex, I'm so sorry you had to find out like that. I wanted to tell you privately but it's all been so—"

"I've got work to do."

Rebecca stood up and swayed, knocking over her empty champagne glass. Libby jumped up to steady her, but her sister shook her hand away as if it were contaminated, then rushed out of the room.

Libby sank back down at the table. She knew how desperate Rebecca and Tom were for a second child, and how devastating her sister was finding their struggles to conceive again. Libby's accidental pregnancy must have been a punch in the guts for her, and their mother had made it all one hundred times worse.

With a sigh, Libby picked up her phone. At this very moment, her mum would be calling her dad, telling him the news. Pretty soon she'd start telling her friends, and in no time at all the news would get back to Simon's family. Libby couldn't put the call off any longer. She went upstairs, tiptoed past her sister's closed bedroom door on the way to her room, then sat down on the bed and dialed Simon's number.

He answered on the second ring. "Libby? Everything okay?"

"Why are you whispering?"

"I'm afraid this isn't a great time. I'm in the middle of something."

"Okay, I'll be quick. But there's something important I need to tell you."

"Hold on, then."

Libby heard the sound of a door opening, followed by a strange, muffled noise. When Simon spoke again, he sounded as if he was in a padded cell. "Okay, what is it?"

"Where are you?"

"In the downstairs toilet."

Libby pictured the space, a tiny, windowless room that doubled as a cupboard so that when you sat on the loo, you invariably had someone's coat hanging in your face. For some reason, the idea of Simon hiding in there gave Libby confidence, and she took a deep breath.

"There's something you need to know . . ." Come on, rip the plaster off. "I'm pregnant."

There was no sound from the other end of the line.

"Simon?"

Still nothing.

"Si—"

"Is it mine?"

"What? Yes!"

"Are you sure?"

"Of course I'm sure. I'm fifteen weeks; the baby was conceived back in March."

More silence, then . . .

"Fuck."

Libby could hear the panic in his voice, and she imagined him sitting in that tiny toilet, his head in his hands.

"This has come as a shock to me too," Libby said. "I had no idea until last week."

"And you want to . . ."

"Yes, I want to keep it. You know I've always wanted a baby, even if this isn't quite how I'd planned it."

"Okay . . . Christ, this is a lot to take in."

"I know it is. But look, I want you to know that you're not under any pressure here. I'm not expecting us to get back together. I'm sure we can find a way to make it work amicably; loads of separated couples do."

"I can't believe this is happening today of all days."

"What do you mean?" There was quiet on the other end of the line, so long that Libby began to wonder if he'd hung up. "Simon?"

"Look, this wasn't how I wanted you to find out, but you may as well know. Olivia and I . . . Well, she's moving in. Moved in, in fact. Yesterday."

It took Libby a second to process what she'd heard.

"What do you mean, she's moved in, Simon? All my stuff is still in the house."

"Well, actually, it's not. I put it all in the garage."

"What?"

"It's all right; it's all in black bin bags, so it's safe."

Libby felt rage burn the back of her throat. "You put all my worldly belongings in rubbish bags and moved someone else into our home, and you didn't even bother to tell me?"

"It's *my* home, actually," Simon said in a whiny voice that made her toes curl. "It's my name on the mortgage."

"That might make it your house, Simon, but until very recently it was *our* home."

"Well, how was I supposed to know you'd get yourself pregnant?" he said, his voice getting higher. "Olivia and I are serious, Libby. Do you have any idea how much she's going to freak out when she finds out you're having my baby?"

"Oh, I'm so sorry for the inconvenience." Libby's voice was thick with sarcasm, but Simon didn't seem to hear her.

"I don't know what to do with this information, Libs. I'm not sure I can deal with this right now."

"Well, you're going to have to deal with it, Simon, because it's happening, whether you like it or not. Your only choice is whether you want to be involved or not."

There was another long pause, and Libby felt sick. She knew what Simon was going to say, had known it from his very first reaction when she'd said the words "I'm pregnant," but still she found she was holding her breath.

"I'm sorry, Libs." His voice was barely a whisper. "I just can't do it. I can't be involved with this baby."

And the line went dead.

Libby wasn't sure if she wanted to scream, laugh, or sob. So much for her mum's confidence that Simon would drop everything and come running back to her the second he found out. The man was a coward. Libby should have known he'd react like this. And how dared he throw all her belongings into bin bags, as if they were being cast off to a charity shop? Libby felt the heat of anger again. But behind it, there was something else. However much she hated Simon right now, she couldn't ignore the sting of rejection once again. Simon had moved on with his life, and he wanted nothing to do with her or their child.

Libby's phone buzzed, making her jump. She snatched it up again and pressed answer.

"What do you want now?" she snapped.

There was no response from Simon.

"I don't have time for this. Either tell me or leave me alone."

"It's me . . . Dylan."

Every nerve in Libby's body fired at the unexpected sound of his voice. "Dylan, hi. I'm—"

"It's fine," he said, and his tone was cold and businesslike. "I wanted to let you know that there's been an e-mail to the girl on the 88 bus account."

"Oh, okay."

"It's from a woman who thinks she might have a lead."

Libby's breath caught. "Really? Who?"

"You should read it," Dylan said, and his tone was still emotionless.

"I will. Dylan, I—"

"I've got to go. Bye."

For the second time in less than five minutes, Libby's phone line cut off. She stared at the phone for a moment, stung by Dylan's abrupt tone. He must really hate her right now, and Libby could hardly blame him. She blinked back tears and then opened the "girl on the 88" e-mail account, scanning through the spam until she found the message Dylan had been referring to.

Hi,

A few days ago I saw your poster in Pimlico, and I think I may be able to help. There's an old lady who lives near me in Clapham, and she's mentioned to me before that she studied art at college in the sixties. I've spoken to her and she says she had red hair back then and she remembers meeting a man on the bus who never called her. She can't remember his name, but she says he was very handsome! She's 80 and her husband is in a home, but she says she's happy to meet your friend again and reminisce about the old days. Her name is Mrs. Stokes. Let's make this happen!

Nasima

26

PEGGY

Sorry, I might be a bit late on Tuesday, love. You know how I told you about that man I'm going to meet? Well, it's been booked for Tuesday afternoon. I'll come straight after and tell you how it went. Wish me luck!

27

Libby and Nasima exchanged a number of e-mails over the next few days, and a plan was put in place for a meeting between Frank and Mrs. Stokes the following Tuesday at Oxford Circus.

Frank asked Libby to accompany him, which she was delighted about. She'd spent so much of the last six weeks thinking about this incredible-sounding woman, she was almost as excited as Frank about potentially getting to meet her. Libby didn't dare ask if Dylan was coming too, but on Sunday, Frank had texted to say that Dylan wasn't going to join them. Libby didn't know whether to be relieved or disappointed.

Seeing as today was the first time Libby was going to see Frank since their failed trip to the National Gallery, she spent ages trying to work out what to wear. She knew she couldn't hide her pregnancy from him forever, but today didn't feel like the right time. Frank had enough on his mind without her suddenly announcing she was four months pregnant. In the end she chose a loose-fitting sundress that hid her small bump, and she put on a denim jacket over the top for good measure.

As she approached the bus stop near Frank's house, Libby spotted him straightaway. His usual faded velvet jacket had been replaced by a sky blue linen suit, which must have once fitted perfectly, but now hung off his stooped frame. He'd clearly tried to style his chaotic white hair specially for the occasion, although his attempt at a quiff was rather flat and a bit skew-whiff. On his feet was a pair of shoes that Libby realized, as she got closer, were blue suede. The whole ensemble was quite remarkable. Libby was about to call out hello when she saw someone step out from inside the bus shelter, and her stomach flipped.

Dylan glanced up and for a moment their eyes met, but his face remained expressionless and she quickly looked away.

"Libby!" Frank threw his arms wide and pulled her into an embrace, and she tried not to choke at the overpowering smell of aftershave. "Isn't this exciting! I'm so glad you're here to witness my reunion."

"I'm very happy to be here, Frank."

"Dylan was much more reluctant. I had to drag him along, kicking and screaming."

"I don't want to overwhelm this woman," Dylan mumbled, but Libby could tell that wasn't the truth. He hadn't wanted to come because Libby had ignored him and then been so rude on the phone. For a brief second, Libby remembered the last time she'd seen Dylan, the electricity she'd felt and his offer to take her to the art class, but she quickly pushed the memory away. Everything had changed since then.

"This whole thing today is thanks to your and Libby's hard work, so it's only right you're here," Frank was saying to Dylan. "Although for the actual meeting itself, I may ask for a little privacy." He gave Libby a wink.

"Your suit is amazing, Frank."

"Thank you. I thought it might have gone to the charity

shop years ago, but Dylan managed to dig it out for me. You don't think I look silly?"

"Are you kidding me? You look very handsome."

"Well, I looked a lot better the last time she saw me. But I wanted to make an effort for her after all this time."

An 88 drew up to the bus stop, and Frank stepped on board and began his usual animated chat with the bus driver. As Libby waited behind him, she was conscious of Dylan standing nearby, so she pulled her jacket round herself in the hope that might cover any signs of the bump. When Frank finished his chat, the three of them made their way upstairs, Dylan supporting Frank, who was looking a little unsteady on his feet today. As it was the first stop on the line, the bus was empty and Frank took his seat on the left side of the front row. Libby sat next to him, and Dylan sat across the aisle.

"So, have you thought what you're going to say to her?" Libby asked as the bus pulled off.

"I've thought of little else since you called me about the e-mail," Frank said. "I've spent sixty years waiting for this day, but now it's here, my mind is blank."

"Are you sure you still want to meet her on here? It would be easier in a café; that way you can have a cup of tea and it might feel more relaxed."

Frank shook his head. "Cafés are too noisy. Besides, the last time we saw each other, she was getting off the bus at Oxford Circus. It seems only fitting that today we should be reunited in the same spot."

The bus wound its way south through Kentish Town and Camden, and the whole while Frank chatted nonstop. Libby could tell how anxious he was, and she asked questions and tried to be as reassuring as possible. Dylan sat across the aisle from them, staring the other way like a moody teenager.

"What has got into you today, Dylan?" Frank asked as they reached Euston Road. "Have you had another fight with your dad?"

"Nah, I'm fine," Dylan said. "Look, boss, I know this is all very exciting. But can you prepare yourself for—"

"I know what you're going to say and I don't want to hear it," Frank interrupted.

"But—"

"No, Dylan. I understand it's your job to care for my physical needs, but my emotional needs are different. So for once can you please stop fussing and let me enjoy my moment?"

Dylan looked as though he was about to say something but stopped himself.

They rode on in silence, each of them looking out of the bus window. This was the first time Libby had ridden the 88 into town since that fateful day when she and Frank had gone to Trafalgar Square. Now she saw that all the yellow posters were gone, having been either taken down or washed away by the recent rainstorms, all evidence of her and Dylan's endeavors removed. Libby glanced across at Dylan, but he was staring forward and wouldn't meet her eye. Blinking away her disappointment, she turned back to look out the window. As she did, she noticed a sole yellow poster attached to a lamppost. They must have taped that one really well for it to have survived this long. And as the bus pulled forward, Libby saw another one, and then a third, all of them in pristine condition. She sat up in her seat, confused. And then—

"Sunny!" Libby shouted so loudly that Frank jerked next to

her. She leaned across him and banged on the window, trying to get the attention of a man standing at the bus stop, his back to them as he secured a poster to the shelter.

"Is that him?" Frank said. "Sunny!" And he too banged on the glass.

Sunny turned around and looked up then, his face splitting into a grin when he saw Libby and Frank. He disappeared from view, and a moment later Libby heard the sound of footsteps running up the stairs.

"Libby! Frank! Oh, and Dylan too!" Sunny said as he reached them. "How fortunate to see you again."

"Sunny, what on earth are you doing?" Libby said, laughing as the young man slid into a seat behind them.

"Well, to tell you the truth, I have been putting up some more of these posters on my lunch breaks. I know you did not ask me to, Libby, but I photocopied some more at work. Are you angry?"

"Of course we're not angry," Frank said, reaching out and patting Sunny's arm. "It's so good to see you again, my dear boy. And you look so much jollier than when I last saw you."

"Oh, yes, life is much better now, thank you," Sunny said. "I am so happy to see you too, Frank. When Libby and Dylan told me about your search, I was overjoyed. I have never forgotten your story about the woman on the bus."

"Well, you'll never guess who we're off to meet now," Frank said.

"What?" Sunny's eyes went wide. "No!"

"Yes, we found her!" Frank laughed at the expression on Sunny's face. "Her friend saw a poster and told her. Perhaps it was one of the posters you put up, Sunny?"

"Oh, I am so pleased for you, Frank," Sunny said, and Libby

could see the genuine delight in his face. "You deserve this happy ending; you really do. Where are you meeting her?"

"At the Oxford Circus bus stop," Frank said.

"Speaking of which," Libby said as the bus curved around the edge of All Saints Church toward Regent Street. She pulled out her phone. "I need to text Mrs. Stokes and let her know we're arriving."

Next to her, she heard Frank inhale sharply.

"This is really about to happen, isn't it?"

"How are you feeling, Frank?" Sunny said.

"Excited . . . and terrified. I've spent so long waiting for this moment, I can't believe it's really here."

The bus had stopped at traffic lights. Up ahead, they could see the bus stop on the left-hand side. Libby's eyes scanned the passengers waiting to board. There was one older lady, who was short with silvery white hair, leaning on a walking stick for support. Her eyes were fixed on the bus as it approached.

"Do you think that is her?" Sunny said.

"It must be." Libby turned to Frank, who was suddenly looking very pale. "Are you okay?"

"Yes. I . . ." His voice cracked and he faltered. "What if I get confused, Libby? What if I say the wrong thing or have one of my funny turns?"

"I'm sure you won't. And if anything does happen, Dylan and I are here."

"But what if she's angry with me? I did stand her up all those years ago, after all."

Libby couldn't help smiling. "If it is her, do you really think she's come all this way today to tell you off?"

"No, I suppose not."

"She's probably feeling nervous too."

"I'm not sure about that. The girl I met sixty years ago wasn't scared of anything."

The traffic lights turned green and the bus pushed forward.

"Do you think I should go downstairs to greet her?" Frank said.

"No, you stay up here," Dylan said, the first time he'd spoken in ages. "I can go downstairs and then help her up if she needs it."

"Thank you," Frank said, and Libby could tell he was relieved not to have to tackle the stairs again.

"I have to go. I have to get back to work," Sunny said. "Good luck, Frank. I will be holding my breath for you."

"Thank you, Sunny."

"I'll go down too, so you can meet her on your own," Libby said. She gave his hand a squeeze. "Good luck, Frank. We're downstairs if you need us."

Frank nodded but he seemed to have lost his words. Libby gave him an encouraging smile, then turned toward the aisle to stand up. As she did, Dylan was also standing up in his seat, and for a moment their faces were inches from each other.

"Eh . . . you first," Dylan said, looking away.

They reached the lower deck and said good-bye to Sunny as the bus pulled up at the stop and the doors opened. Libby waited by the bottom of the steps, watching as passengers boarded. The woman was the last to get on, looking around at the other passengers before beginning to make her way down the aisle toward the stairs.

"Mrs. Stokes?" Libby said.

She looked up, and Libby could immediately tell how nervous she was too. She was wearing too much makeup, the lipstick slightly smudged in the creases around her mouth.

"You Libby?"

"Yes, hi. It's lovely to meet you."

"Is Frank here?"

"He's upstairs."

"Would you like me to help you up?" Dylan said.

Libby saw the woman take in Dylan, but she didn't bat an eyelid. "No, thanks, dear. I'll be fine."

"Okay. We'll be down here if you need anything," Libby said.

The woman nodded and turned toward the stairs, taking a deep breath before she started to climb. Libby watched her until she reached the top and disappeared out of view. Then she took a deep breath herself and turned to face Dylan.

28

They stood awkwardly for a moment, neither looking at the other. Then the bus pulled away from the stop sharply, and Libby was caught off-balance. She wobbled forward, almost falling on top of Dylan, who reached out to steady her. Libby quickly righted herself and stepped away.

"Wanna sit down?" Dylan said, and she nodded, embarrassed.

There was an empty seat opposite the stairs, and Libby slid into it. Dylan sat down next to her, their bodies not quite touching. Neither of them spoke as the bus made its way down Regent Street, and Libby stared out the window at the shoppers and tourists milling past so she didn't have to look at him. She and Dylan had done this journey together many times, yet now she felt as if she were sitting next to a stranger.

"How have you been?" Libby said when she couldn't bear the strained atmosphere any longer.

"All right. You?"

"Fine, thanks. How's Esme?"

"Good. She was gutted she couldn't make today; I think she's more excited about this reunion than the rest of us put together."

"Please give her my love."

They stared forward as the bus approached Piccadilly Circus.

"How's Hector?" Dylan said.

"He's okay. Still driving my sister mad with his loud music. The woman next door has been banging on the wall so much, I think she might break through it one day."

Dylan sniffed. "Sorry. I think I might be to blame for that one. Is he—"

"There's something I want to say," Libby blurted out, interrupting him.

He looked at her and she halted. What the hell was it she wanted to say?

"I wanted to . . . er . . . apologize. You . . . you know, for not meeting you to put up the last posters and for ignoring your messages and being so rude on the phone."

"It's fine," Dylan said, and he turned to look forward again.

"No, it's not fine, Dylan. I've had a weird few weeks and I didn't know what to—"

"You don't have to explain anything."

"But I do. You see . . ." Libby paused, suddenly unsure she should carry on. But what harm could it do? This might be the last time she ever saw Dylan, so she might as well tell him the truth. "I'm pregnant."

The words still felt strange to say out loud, here on the bus. Libby heard Dylan inhale.

"Wow! Well . . . congratulations."

"Thank you," she said formally, not sure what else to say. "It was totally unexpected, so it's taken me a bit of time to get used to the idea."

"I'm sure. How do you feel about it now?"

"I'm happy about it," Libby said, and as she looked across at Dylan, she saw his face soften.

"Then I'm happy for you too, Libby. It's great news."

"Yes, I think it is. I mean, it's certainly not how I'd planned to have a baby, but I feel lucky."

"How many weeks are you?"

"Sixteen."

"Oh." She could see the confusion in Dylan's face. "Then . . ."

"Simon is the father, yeah."

"Wow," Dylan said, and that word seemed loaded with understanding. He was the one person, Libby realized, whom she'd been completely honest with about her feelings about Simon. "And how has he taken the news?"

"Oh, brilliantly. It turns out he's moved his new girlfriend into our house, and a baby doesn't exactly fit into their life plans, so he wants nothing to do with it."

Libby said it as lightly as possible, but she saw Dylan frown. "I'm sorry; that's really shit."

"It's okay. I mean, given the way he's behaved over the past few months, he probably wasn't going to be winning any 'father of the month' awards anyway."

"He sounds like a massive knob."

"Yeah, to be fair, I think he might be."

"You want me to go round and beat him up?"

"What?" Libby looked at Dylan in horror. "No! I mean, thanks for the offer bu—"

She stopped when she saw him smile. "I was kidding, Libby."

"Oh, right."

"I'm afraid I can't even hurt a spider in the bath, let alone another person."

"I'm sorry. I didn't mean to assume you were the beating-up type."

"That's okay. Looking like this, people always think I'm up for a fight. My tactic is usually to run in the opposite direction as fast as I can, as you saw with those coppers."

"I can't imagine anyone trying to pick a fight with you."

"Oh, they do all the time, but I'm a massive coward. In fact, I'll let you into a little secret . . ." Dylan leaned toward her, and Libby's breath caught at his sudden proximity. "I'm scared of blood. Even the tiniest bit and I freak out like a little kid."

She laughed. "I thought you said you wanted to be a nurse."

"I do, which makes it even more embarrassing."

They carried on chatting as the bus made its way south, and Libby felt her body slowly unwinding. She hadn't realized until now how much she'd missed hanging out with Dylan, their conversation so free-flowing and fun. When Libby was with him, it felt like there was no one else around, even when they were on a crowded bus with a crying baby and a child shouting about snacks behind them. At one point Libby caught Dylan's eye and felt a lightness in her chest, but she quickly pushed the feeling away. Maybe he could be a friend after all, but nothing more than that. Not now.

"I wonder how they're getting on up there," Libby said as the bus passed the Cenotaph war memorial, Big Ben rising up ahead of them.

"I dunno. But it's got to be a good sign neither of them has come down shouting yet."

"I didn't expect Frank to be so nervous. He looked as white as a sheet when we left him."

"The guy has spent six decades waiting for this moment. He's built this woman up in his mind to be some sort of goddess. It's no wonder he's panicking."

"I really hope it goes well."

"Me too."

Neither of them spoke for a moment, and Libby listened out for any sounds of Frank upstairs, but she couldn't hear anything above the noise of the children.

"So, is Hector excited about having a cousin?" Dylan said.

"I haven't told him yet."

"Oh?"

"It's a bit sensitive, as my sister and brother-in-law are try-ing for a baby themselves."

"I see."

"Anyway, by the time the baby arrives, I won't be living there. Their nanny is returning next month, and then I'll be moving out."

"Have you found anywhere to live yet?"

"No. I've been looking online this week but everything in London is so expensive."

"I can ask around if you like, see if anyone has a spare room to rent?"

"Thanks, but I'm not sure how many people want a flatmate with a baby in tow."

"The council might be able to help you if you don't have anywhere to live. Especially given you're pregnant, they might be able to—"

Dylan was interrupted by the appearance of Mrs. Stokes on the stairs. He and Libby both jumped up.

"Oh, I remember that place; it was fancy," Mrs. Stokes was saying with a laugh as she reached the bottom of the steps.

"Ah, there you both are," Frank said when he appeared be-hind her. "We've had such fun reminiscing about the good old days."

"That's great," Libby said, feeling relief rush through her

body. She glanced at Dylan and saw the same hopeful expression reflected back at her.

"I could chat to Frank all day," the woman said, her eyes glowing. "But sadly I've got to go and visit my husband; he's in a care home and I go to see him most days."

The bus pulled up and they all disembarked, calling thanks to the driver. Once the bus had pulled off, Libby and Dylan held back while Frank and Mrs. Stokes said their good-byes.

"Well, it was lovely to chat to you, Frank," she said.

"The pleasure was all mine." He reached out and took her hand. "Thanks once again for agreeing to meet me."

"Not at all. You've got my number now, so let's do this again soon."

They smiled at each other, and then Frank released her hand. "Good-bye."

The elderly lady turned and made her way down the road. Libby, Frank, and Dylan watched her go. Only once she was well out of earshot did Libby turn to Frank.

"Well?"

"Ah, dear Libby, thank you so much for all your help."

"So it *was* her, then?" Libby grasped his arm. "That's amazing, Frank. I can't believe we actually found her!"

He gave a small, sad smile. "No. No, I'm afraid it wasn't her."

29

PEGGY

Well, yesterday turned out to be an eventful day, and not in the way I was expecting.

I told you that I was going to meet that solicitor man David had set up about my power of attorney? Well, that turned out to be dull as ditchwater. I went to his office in town, which wasn't anywhere near as fancy as I'd hoped. They gave me a cup of tea but it tasted like rat's piss, and there weren't any biscuits, not even digestives, which I thought was pretty poor. He explained how it all works, which I knew, of course, from when we did it for you. So frankly, I'm not sure why David wanted me to see him, but anything to make my boy happy.

Anyway, the real excitement came on the bus home.

I caught the 88 at New Cavendish Street, and it was quite busy but I managed to get my favorite seat, back behind the wheelchair area. So I'm sitting there, minding my own business, when we get to the top of Haymarket and this posh-looking lady gets on with a pram. It's one of those big, fancy contraptions that fit two kids in, a baby at the bottom and a toddler on top, and she's got to park this tank in the wheelchair spot. Well, let me tell you, she made a complete hash out of it. She was huffing and puffing, trying to push it in the wrong way, but it was never going to fit. I watched her for a minute or two, but it was too painful, so eventually I had to pipe up and tell her she was doing it wrong.

Well, you should have seen the look on her face.

She turns to me, her eyes all screwed up like I'm something the cat dragged in, and in the most hoity-toity voice, she says, "I know how to do it, thank you very much."

Can you believe the cheek of it?

I nearly let loose and gave her a piece of my mind, but you'd have been proud of me, Percy. I bit my tongue. Instead I sat back in my seat, arms crossed, and watched the show.

Her face was getting redder and redder as she tried to force the back wheel to make it fit round the pole, and of course it wouldn't go but she kept on trying. It was like you always say: you can buy yourself a fancy education, but you can't buy common sense. And then the woman started swearing under her breath and suddenly she kicks the wheel of the pram. Well, of course the thing doesn't budge, but the jolt wakes up her baby, who lets out a howl of rage. I'm not going to lie. I did have a little smile to myself at that. What was it Maisie used to say that always made us laugh? *Karma's a bitch, baby.*

So now the baby's crying and the pram is still sticking out into the aisle, blocking everyone's way, and then from the top seat, the toddler pipes up.

"Mummy, I'm hungry."

This kid must have been at least three years old and far too big to still be in a pushchair, in my opinion. And he's got one of those really annoying whingy voices.

"In a minute, darling," the woman says, sounding like the Duchess of bleedin' Cambridge.

"But I need a snack *noooow*," the kid shouts, and he starts swinging his legs backward and forward so he's kicking the end of the baby's bassinet, which makes the little one scream louder.

Well, what that child needed was a smack, not a snack. But of course she doesn't tell him off; instead she bends down and lifts the baby out of the pram.

I have to tell you, love, when I saw the little one, my heart stopped.

She was absolutely tiny; looked like she couldn't have been more than a few days old. And the woman is balancing the baby in one arm while she's bending down to rummage under the pram to find something, and the boy is still chanting, "Snack! Snack! Snack!" and the baby is howling her head off and the woman's scrabbling around, looking like she's about to explode.

So do you know what I did?

I leant forward and I held out my arms, and I said to her, "Give the baby to me."

Well, she turns and looks at me then, and I could see her doing the mental calculation of whether I looked like a serial killer or not. And then she handed this baby over to me.

Honestly, love, the thing was so small, I could barely feel her in my arms. And do you know what it made me think of? Jack.

After all these years, it made me think of Jack.

I remembered holding him in the hospital when he was so tiny, he could almost fit in the palm of my hand.

Do you remember the hat I'd knitted for him, which was so big it covered his whole upper body?

This baby was larger than Jack, of course; otherwise they'd never have let her out of hospital. But still, holding her I felt like I was back there with you and him in the hospital that day he was born.

Finally, the woman finds a packet of crisps and she hands them to the boy, who stops shouting and starts shoveling them into his mouth, the greedy little brat. And this woman collapses down onto the seat next to me, and I think she's going to ask for her baby back, but she doesn't. She lets out this long sigh and closes her eyes and just sits there, not moving.

And as I'm watching her, do you know what I see?

Tears.

And I remembered you, on the bus back from the hospital, sitting next to me crying. It was such a shock to see, love. I was always the crier, but there you were, not making a sound, your shoulders shaking with the sobs. And I didn't know what to do; I was in so much pain myself that I didn't know whether to comfort you or pretend I hadn't seen. So I just sat there, staring out the bus window at gray London, and by the time I turned back, you'd stopped.

I'm not sure I ever saw you cry again, after that. It was like there were no tears left.

The following Tuesday, Libby sat outside the Parliament Hill café, waiting for Frank to arrive. It had been a week since their trip on the bus to meet Ingrid Stokes, and Libby had been worrying about him nonstop. Dylan had been texting her updates and said that Frank was okay but subdued and avoiding talking about what happened on the bus. What was more, he'd apparently stopped going out on the 88, giving tenuous excuses each time as to why he couldn't go. Frank himself had ignored all of Libby's messages suggesting they meet up, until yesterday, when he'd finally replied and agreed to join her for a walk.

Libby saw him heading slowly up the path toward her, dressed in his usual velvet jacket, and she hurried over to meet him.

"Hi, Frank."

"Hello, Libby." He smiled at her, but Libby couldn't help noticing he'd lost some of the sparkle in his eyes.

"It's so lovely to see you again," Libby said. "Shall we head up Parliament Hill as usual? I've brought my sketchbook with me."

"Can we walk along to the ponds instead? I'm not sure I'm up to the climb today."

"Of course."

This was the first time Libby had ever heard Frank admit defeat, and she felt a knot of anxiety. Dylan had warned her this might happen, that the disappointment if they didn't find Frank's woman might be too much for him. But Libby had insisted on pushing on with her search anyway, determined that she knew better. What had she done?

They turned and began to make their way along the path toward the ponds.

"How have you been?" Libby said as they passed the infants' playground, the sound of children's laughter floating over to them. "Dylan tells me you've not been on the 88 this week."

"No, I've not really felt like it."

"Are you okay?"

"I've been a little under the weather. I think I may have a head cold. I've been enjoying catching up on some nature documentaries."

"Is that so?"

"Yes. I really do enjoy TV; I should watch it more."

"And how have you been feeling about what happened last week?"

"Last week?"

"Yes, your meeting with Mrs. Stokes."

Frank hesitated for a fraction of a second, and when he spoke again, it was in a too-jovial voice. "She was a nice lady, wasn't she? Very friendly."

"She did seem lovely," Libby said carefully. "What did the two of you chat about?"

"Oh, this and that: the weather, her grandchildren, how expensive London is these days. The usual conversation of two lonely pensioners on the bus."

Libby was unused to hearing Frank talk like this, and she

stopped in the middle of the path. "I'm so sorry it wasn't her, Frank. I feel terrible."

"Why? It's not *your* fault that it wasn't her."

"I know, but I was the one who suggested the whole search, who got your hopes up. If it wasn't for me, you would never have been disappointed like this."

Frank shook his head. "It had to happen sooner or later. I've been living in a dreamland and it's time I woke up to the truth."

"What truth?"

"That I'm never going to find her."

"Oh, Frank, that's not—"

He held his hand up to stop her. "I know that sounds very dramatic of me, Libby, but it's quite all right; you don't need to try and make me feel better. I know that she probably left London decades ago or that she's passed away."

"That's not true. Just because this woman wasn't her doesn't mean she isn't out there somewhere."

Frank turned and walked over to a bench on the side of the path, then sat down heavily.

"Even if she is still alive, the chances of me finding her are minuscule, aren't they?" he said as Libby sat down next to him. "I've been holding on to this fantasy of some grand reunion on the bus, but it's silly, really. I can see that now."

"I believed we could find her too; otherwise I'd never have offered to help."

"You were being kind."

"No, I wanted to find her. Her story . . ."

Libby paused. Why had she been so keen to find this woman, investing so much of her time and energy in the search? Yes, she'd wanted to find her for Frank, but it wasn't only that.

"Your girl on the bus did the thing I've always regretted not doing. She defied her parents and went to art school, while I let my parents talk me out of it. So I think I wanted to know if she made the right decision. Were her sacrifices worth it? Was she happy?"

Frank was watching Libby as she spoke. "Please don't think I'm not grateful for your help, Libby, but it's time we stopped. You and I have both been hiding behind this search, and we need to face up to our own lives."

"What do you mean?"

He raised his chin. "I spoke to Clara on Friday. I'm going to have the care assessment and move into a home."

"What?" Libby tried to hide the horror in her voice. "But why?"

"It's what Clara wants. And after all the worry I've caused her over the years, it feels like the least I can do now."

"But, Frank, you said yourself, if you move into a care home, you won't be able to go out on the bus anymore."

"Haven't you been listening, Libby? My days on the 88 are over."

"But what about your walks up Parliament Hill? Do you really want to give up that freedom before you have to?"

He shook his head. "I have dementia, dear. Sooner or later, I won't be able to do any of those things anyway. So I might as well give up now, with my dignity intact."

"Oh, Frank—" Libby started, but he put his hand up to stop her.

"Please don't feel sorry for me. I've made peace with my decision. I have the care assessment in three weeks' time, and I'll tell the social worker that I can't cope in the house anymore and I want to move to a home. It's all for the best."

"And Dylan?"

Frank shrugged. "We'll still be friends, I'm sure."

Libby slumped back on the bench. She couldn't believe this was really it, the end of the search.

"You need to get on with living your life as well," Frank said gently. "I know this has given you a much-needed project these past few months, but it's time you moved on too. You're young, single, and carefree; you shouldn't be spending your days riding the bus for an old fogy like me."

"Frank, I'm not young and carefree. I'm turning thirty in a few weeks, I'm pregnant, and my ex-boyfriend wants nothing to do with me or the baby."

Frank's eyes went wide. "You're pregnant?"

"Yep." She pulled her loose dress against her body to show him the bump, which seemed to be getting bigger by the day.

"My goodness, why didn't you tell me?"

"I only found out a few weeks ago at the hospital, and I was in shock to begin with. And then Nasima got in touch, and I didn't want to tell you right before you met Mrs. Stokes."

"But this is wonderful news, Libby. You'll make a fantastic mother."

"Thank you."

"And your birthday so soon as well? What are you doing to celebrate?"

"I hadn't really planned anything. My sister's family are going on holiday and my parents are staying with them that week, so I'll probably have a quiet night in front of the TV."

"Why don't you go away with them?"

"They did invite me, but honestly, the thought of being in close quarters with my sister and mum is more than I can handle," Libby said, wincing. "I'm not the flavor of the month with either of them right now."

"Well, you can't spend your thirtieth birthday on your own. You have to celebrate it with friends."

"Thank you, but I'm not really in the mood for a party."

"Neither am I, but it will do us both good. We can combine your birthday with a last hurrah for me before my assessment."

Libby frowned. "Are you sure?"

"Yes. We'll invite Dylan, of course, and Esme too. Are we okay to hold it at yours? My place is far too cluttered but I'll bring champagne and we could . . ."

Libby watched Frank as he began listing suggestions. She'd never loved birthdays, and in recent years she and Simon had barely celebrated them. But Frank was right: they all needed something positive and fun in their lives right now, especially Frank. She reached into her bag, pulled out her sketchbook, and started to write a list.

CHAPTER

31

By eight p.m. on her birthday evening, Libby was dressed and busy in the kitchen. She'd bought a leg of lamb, at great expense, which was now roasting in the oven along with vegetables for a salad, and she was putting the final touches to a salsa verde. It was a pleasure to be making a proper meal again; Libby had always loved cooking, but Simon had tended to do all the "special" meals, leaving her with the dull weeknight suppers. Now she reveled in using every utensil and pan in the kitchen. Rebecca would have had a fit if she were here.

The doorbell rang, and Libby glanced in the hallway mirror as she went to answer it. She'd overcome her nerves and this morning had been to a local hairdresser, who had given her a stylish trim and blow-dry, so her usually chaotic curls now hung in sleek ringlets. Libby dabbed on a quick slick of lipstick, then opened the front door.

"Happy birthday!" Frank, Esme, and Dylan were standing on the top step, all grinning at her.

Frank, who was wearing his powder blue suit for the occasion, stepped forward first and gave Libby a bottle of champagne, a box of chocolates, and a kiss on the cheek. Behind him, Esme was wearing a floral jumpsuit, and she gave Libby a huge hug. Dylan was the last to come in. He was wearing his leather jacket but with a black collared shirt underneath, and he gave a small cough as he greeted Libby.

"Happy birthday," he said. "You look lovely."

Libby felt herself flush as she mumbled thanks and led them through to the garden.

"Isn't this wonderful?" Frank said as they stepped outside. "Did you do all of this?"

Libby nodded. It was only a tiny garden but she'd spent most of the morning getting it ready. She'd cleared Hector's toys off the patio and cleaned the table, decorating it with small vases of cut flowers. She'd dug Rebecca's Christmas fairy lights out of the attic and suspended them along the back wall, and she'd also found two dozen tea lights, which she'd put in jam jars and glasses dotted round the garden. Now that the sun was starting to set, the whole space looked magical.

Dylan opened the bottle of champagne Frank had brought and soon the conversation was flowing. After one glass, Frank started regaling them with funny stories from his acting days, causing them all to cry with laughter. Libby served her roast lamb and warm vegetable salad, which everyone declared was a triumph, and while they ate, Esme excitedly shared with them the plans for her wedding in November. Libby listened, adding suggestions and ideas, but the whole time all she could think about was Dylan sitting across the table from her. A couple of times she glanced up and caught him watching her, but he always looked away. Still, Libby felt as if she had a swarm of butterflies circling inside her stomach, and she was pretty sure it wasn't the baby wriggling.

When they'd finished eating, Frank cleared his throat.

"There's something I want to tell you all," he said, and waited for them to quieten. "First off, I wanted to apologize to Dylan. I know that I've been a bit down in the dumps lately, and I'm sorry if I've been grumpy with you."

"You can say that again," Dylan said, raising an eyebrow.

"That whole thing with that Ingrid woman completely threw me. I was so sure she was going to be my woman on the bus, and when she wasn't . . . well, I felt humiliated, like a silly old fool." Frank turned to Libby. "When we met for our walk, I'd just come off the phone from Clara. She'd been nagging at me about the care assessment, and I didn't have the energy to fight her anymore. I wanted to quit."

He picked up his glass, his hand shaking, and they all waited while he took a sip.

"But I've been doing a lot of thinking about this, and I've realized I was wrong. So I called Clara yesterday and told her I won't go into the care home. I know that time will come eventually, but I'm not ready to give up on my independence just yet."

"And what did she say?" Libby asked.

"She wasn't delighted, as you can imagine. And she says I still have to have my care assessment on Tuesday, as it's booked and she can't cancel it. But Dylan's going to be there for the assessment, and together we'll show the social worker that I'm still perfectly capable of living at home and looking after myself. If I can prove that, then no one can make me move into a care home if I don't want to."

"And what about your hunt for the lady?" Esme said.

Frank smiled. "I took a trip out on the 88 today."

"You and that bloody bus," Dylan said, but he was smiling too.

"I know what you think, Dylan. But I promise you, I'm being more realistic now. I know that I'll probably never find her, and that's okay. I want to keep on looking while I still can."

"Well, I think it's wonderful." Libby raised her glass. "To Frank and his independence!"

They all raised their glasses and chinked.

"Is there birthday cake now?" Esme said.

"Of course!" Libby started clearing the plates.

"Let me help." Dylan stood up and picked up some dishes, following Libby into the kitchen. "That meal was amazing."

"Thanks. It's been a while since I cooked for pleasure and I'd forgotten how much I enjoyed it. Frank seems well?"

"Yeah, this has done him a world of good. Turns out he just needed an audience again."

Libby laughed as she started to load plates into the dishwasher. Dylan came to stand next to her.

"Bloody hell, did you make this too?" he said, pointing at the chocolate cake on the counter. Libby had baked it yesterday, decorating the surface with shards of dark, milk, and white chocolate. "It looks incredible."

"I hope it tastes all right. Can you pass that?"

She indicated the bowl next to Dylan, and he picked it up and handed it to her. As he did, his hand brushed against hers, and Libby felt a familiar jolt of electricity through her arm. Beside her, she heard Dylan draw breath. Libby put the bowl in the dishwasher, her skin still tingling.

"So, I got you a little something . . ." Dylan went over to his bag on the counter and pulled out a small object, wrapped in tissue paper. He handed it to Libby. "Don't get excited; it's nothing fancy."

"You didn't have to get me anything."

"Sorry if you think it's stupid."

Libby started unwrapping the gift, aware Dylan was watching her. Inside was a piece of white fabric, and as she unfolded it, she saw it was a baby's onesie, on the front of which was a drawing of a red London bus.

"Oh, Dylan."

"It's the 88," he said, pointing at the number on the front of the bus. "I've got a mate who runs a stall in Camden Market and she made it specially."

"It's gorgeous. Thank you." Libby felt tears pricking her eyes, and she put the onesie down and picked up another plate to put in the dishwasher so he wouldn't see her face. She wasn't sure anyone had ever given her such a thoughtful present before.

"I'm sorry it's small. But I also wanted to say something . . ."

Dylan trailed off, and when Libby glanced up at him, he was staring at the onesie, chewing his lip. He cleared his throat before he spoke.

"I know we haven't known each other very long. And I know that we haven't even really hung out properly, unless you count riding the 88 bus, which I'm pretty sure doesn't actually count as a date. And I know that you've had a crazy few months with your ex being such a prick and moving to London and finding out you're pregnant and . . . Sorry. I'm waffling."

Libby could see Dylan's cheeks were almost as red as the bus on the baby onesie.

"What I'm trying to say is: I think you're amazing," Dylan continued. "The way you organized this whole poster campaign to try and help Frank. The way you've taken the pregnancy news in your stride. And I know you're nervous about doing it on your own, but you're going to be a brilliant mum; this kid is bloody lucky to have you. And I want you to know that I don't think you need anyone else to do this with. You are going to absolutely smash it all on your own."

He paused again to draw breath, his eyes still focused on the gift.

"But I also wanted to say that you don't have to do it all on your own, if you don't want to. I mean, I don't know the first thing about babies, so I'm not sure I'd actually be much help, but I want to be there for you, if you'd like. As a friend, or . . ."

"Or?" The word was out of Libby's mouth before she realized it.

Dylan looked up from the onesie now, into Libby's eyes. The nervous expression had gone and was replaced with something else, something that made her chest contract.

"Or as more than friends," he said, not taking his eyes off hers.

Libby didn't speak, and for a moment neither of them moved. Then Dylan stepped forward, very slowly, until he was so close that she had to tilt her head up to see his face. His dark eyes were fixed on her mouth, and Libby felt such a rush of emotion that she closed her eyes. A second later she felt his lips brush against hers, so softly they were barely there. She let out a small gasp as his hand found her cheek, gently pushing her hair back from her face. She opened her eyes, and stared into his face as it hovered above hers. And then Dylan kissed her again, this time with an urgency that took Libby by surprise. She reached up and put her hands on the back of his head, feeling the curve of his skull under the soft shaved scalp. Dylan let out a small moan, and Libby felt it reverberate through her whole body.

"AH, we were wondering where the two of you had got to." Frank was watching Libby as she walked back out into the garden, and she was grateful it was dark and he couldn't see how flushed her face was.

"Sorry. I . . . I couldn't find the cake forks," Libby said, not looking him in the eye. She lifted up the knife to cut a slice and noticed that her hand was still trembling.

"No! We need to sing first," Esme said.

"Oh, there's no need," Libby started to say, but Esme was already launching into "Happy Birthday," followed by the other two.

Libby laughed and caught Dylan's eye. Even in the low candlelight, she could see his face was flushed too, and she had a sudden urge to drag him back into the kitchen and pick up from where they'd left off a moment ago. When the singing had finished, there was a round of riotous applause.

"I'd like to propose a toast, if I may," Frank said, once the clapping had died down. He lifted up his wineglass and turned to face her. "Libby, I want to thank you for your kindness over the past few months. I know we might not have had the outcome we hoped for—"

"Yet," Esme interrupted, and Frank smiled.

"Quite right, Esme. But whatever happens, I'm so grateful for everything you've done, Libby. I feel blessed to be able to call you my friend, and I know that Dylan and Esme feel the same." Libby could still feel Dylan's eyes on her, and she smiled. "I also wanted to say that all three of us will be here for you over the coming months, as you enter this exciting new phase as a mother. I know that right now it must all feel very daunting, but please know that we're here to support you every step of the way. So here's to the very happiest of thirtieth birthdays, dearest Libby!"

An echo of "Cheers!" went round the table as they all clinked glasses.

Libby felt tears threatening again. "Thank you," she said,

blinking them away. "The last few months have been . . . well, they've been life changing, and that's mainly because of meeting the three of you. I feel very lucky to have you in my life."

"You are very lucky," Esme said with a grin. "Now let's have cake."

"Yes, boss!" Libby started to cut large slices. As she did, she heard the sound of the doorbell from inside the house.

"Do you want me to get that?" Dylan said.

"It's fine. I'll go."

She jumped up from the table and made her way into the house, licking cake off her fingers as she did. Behind her, Libby could hear Esme say something and Dylan laugh. The sound of his voice sent a thrill of excitement through her body, and Libby smiled to herself as she reached the front door. She pulled it open, and her stomach dropped.

"Surprise!"

32

Simon was holding a bunch of flowers so huge, he could barely see over the top of them. Libby didn't say anything, too horrified at the sight of her ex-boyfriend standing on the doorstep minutes after she'd kissed another man.

Simon stepped forward, peering at her through the petals. "Happy birthday!" He tried to hand Libby the flowers, but as he did, he staggered and had to lean against the wall to steady himself. "Sorry. I started the celebrations a bit early."

A strong smell of lager hit Libby, and she found her voice. "What the hell are you doing here, Simon?"

"It's your birthday!"

"And?"

"And I saw on Rebecca's Instagram that they're away, and I hated the thought of you all sad and alone on your big day."

"Well, thanks for your concern but I'm fine, so you can go now."

"I wanted to talk to you as well, Libs. I've been doing a lot of thinking about the baby and everything and I—"

"Libby, can I get more wine from the fridge?" Dylan's voice came through from the kitchen.

"Help yourself," she called back.

Simon was looking at Libby, bewildered. "You're having a party?"

"I've got some friends round for dinner."

"Who?" He moved his head to one side, trying to see past her into the house.

"No one you know. Look, I don't know why you're here but—"

"Can I come in and meet them?"

"No! Go home, Simon."

She watched his face fall. "I thought you'd be pleased to see me."

"You can't turn up here unannounced. Not after everything that's happened."

"But I wanted to see you and . . ." He trailed off, staring at her with his brow creased as if trying to work out a difficult sum. "I guess I'll go, then."

He thrust the flowers toward her, and this time Libby took them—anything to get rid of him.

"Good-bye, Libby."

Simon turned around too quickly and staggered at the top of the stairs. As he began to make his way down the steps, Libby could sense him focusing all his attention on placing one foot in front of the other. When he reached the bottom, she heaved a sigh of relief. She was turning back into the house when she heard a heavy thump and looked round to see Simon sprawled face-first on the paving stones.

"Oh, crap!" Libby dropped the flowers and ran down to him. "Are you okay?"

Simon didn't respond, and Libby bent down next to him.

He wasn't moving, and she was about to shout for help when he turned his head toward her and grinned. Libby opened her mouth to yell at him, then spotted the blood.

"Jesus, you've cut your head."

He put his hand to his forehead, wincing as he touched it. "Oops. That's embarrassing."

"You'd better come inside and clean it up."

"No, I'll be fine." Simon started to pull himself up tentatively, like a toddler learning to stand. Libby took his arm and helped him.

"You can't go home like this; you've got blood running down your face. Come on, there are plasters in the kitchen."

Libby helped him back up the steps: not an easy task, as he was swaying left and right. She finally got him and the ridiculous bouquet of flowers through the front door and down the hall to the kitchen.

"There's a first aid kit in here somewhere," she said in a low voice, hoping the others in the garden wouldn't hear her. But Simon ignored her as he walked through the kitchen toward the back door.

"No—" Libby started to say, but it was too late.

"Woo-hoo, *par-tay!*" Simon shouted, staggering out into the garden.

From Libby's position in the kitchen, she could see past him to the scene outside. Frank, Esme, and Dylan all stopped talking and were staring at Simon. Frank and Esme both looked confused at the sudden arrival of another guest, but Dylan's expression was different. He was sitting up tall in his seat, his eyes narrow as he glared at Simon with undisguised contempt. Libby stepped out into the garden.

"This is Simon," she said to them all, but her eyes were fixed on Dylan. "He's just here for one minute to—"

"I'm the father of Libby's baby," Simon interrupted, and Libby saw Dylan's eyes narrow, as if this was confirmation of what he'd suspected.

"Oh, good evening," Frank said, reaching his hand out toward Simon. But Simon ignored it, and when Libby glanced at him, she saw he was staring back at Dylan. For a moment nobody spoke, and she felt the energy shift.

"You have blood on your head," Esme said.

"I'm just getting Simon a plaster before he leaves," Libby said, but she didn't move. Simon and Dylan were still eyeing each other across the table.

Frank must have sensed the tension too, because he gave a loud cough. "Would you like a drink, Simon? A glass of water, perhaps?"

"Got any beer?" Simon said, and he finally turned from Dylan and half sat, half slumped into a seat.

Libby hurried back into the kitchen. Rebecca kept a first aid box in one of the cupboards, but Libby couldn't remember which one, and she started pulling doors open as fast as she could. In the background she could hear Simon's slurring voice from the garden, and as she frantically searched, she imagined all the totally inappropriate things he could be saying to her guests. To Dylan.

At last she found the green box and rushed back outside. Simon was midflow.

"And then one year I took her to the Ivy for her birthday and afterward we—"

"Here, I've found it," Libby interrupted.

Simon turned to her. "Thanks, Piglet."

She winced at his use of her old nickname; why had she ever put up with him calling her that? She opened the first aid box, her hands shaking, and pulled out a bottle of TCP, some cotton wool, and a plaster.

"You should clean it before you put the plaster on," she said, thrusting the bottle at Simon.

"Would you mind doing it for me? I'm feeling a bit dizzy."

Libby gritted her teeth, but she knew the sooner she got it done, the sooner he'd leave. She put some TCP on a piece of cotton wool, conscious of everyone watching her. When she stepped toward Simon, he closed his eyes as if waiting for a kiss. Libby took a deep breath and began to dab his cut, acutely aware of how close she was to his face and how Dylan was watching her every move.

"You've always been an excellent nurse," Simon said, opening his eyes and smiling up at her. "Thank you, Libs."

"How's Olivia?" Libby said as she ripped open the plaster, and the smile disappeared from his face.

"She's fine."

"Who's Olivia?" Esme said.

"She's Simon's new girlfriend," Libby said, pressing the plaster on his cut with a little more force than was perhaps necessary. "It turns out that when he said he wasn't ready for commitment, he just meant he wasn't ready for it with *me*."

"Libs, it wasn't like that," Simon said. "I know I hurt you with our breakup, but it wasn't all my fault."

"Oh, I'm sorry. Whose fault was it, then?" There was a sharp tone to Libby's voice, and Simon looked at her, surprised.

"You have to take some responsibility for what happened to us," he said. "I mean, maybe if you'd taken a bit more—"

"Don't you fucking dare!"

They were the first words Dylan had uttered since Simon arrived, and his voice was low.

"What did you say?" Simon said.

"I said, don't you dare try and blame Libby."

"Excuse me, but I'm not sure this is any of your business. Who the hell are you anyway?"

Dylan ignored the question. "I know guys like you. Pricks who treat women like dirt and then try and blame it on them."

Simon let out a sharp laugh. "You have no idea what you're talking about."

"I know enough to know you're bad news."

"Are these the friends you're keeping now?" Simon said, turning back to Libby. "Because I'm not sure they're the kind of people I want my child growing up around."

"Simon, stop it," Libby said, but he ignored her.

"I mean, I know you've always liked a charity case, but this is a bit much, even for you."

"Fuck off and leave her alone," Dylan snarled.

"I'm not going anywhere. You're the one who needs to leave, you freak."

There was the sudden sound of scraping chairs, and before Libby realized what was happening, both Simon and Dylan had sprung to their feet. Only Simon was so drunk that he wobbled and fell against the table, knocking a glass of red wine everywhere.

"Sit down, both of you," Frank said sharply, but neither of them listened, their bodies straining toward each other across the table.

"Do you want to sleep with her? Is that it?" Simon spat at Dylan. "Because let me tell you, you're barking up the wrong tree there, mate. Libby prefers her men a bit more manly, less jewelry and stupid hair."

"You little—"

Esme let out a scream and Libby sprang forward, putting her body between them.

"Stop it!" she shouted. "Both of you, stop it now!"

No one moved, the air electric. Libby looked between Dylan and Simon, their faces both twisted in anger. She needed one of them out of the house before they killed each other. She took a deep breath. "Simon, you need to l—"

"Oh, I don't feel well," Simon groaned, and he sank back down into a chair and put his face in his hands.

"What's the matter?"

"I feel dizzy."

"How did he cut his head?" Frank asked.

"He fell off the bottom step outside," Libby said.

"Maybe he has a concussion."

"He doesn't have a concussion," Dylan spat. "He's faking it."

But Libby had to admit that Simon was looking pale. "Should we call one-one-one?"

"No, I'm okay," Simon said. "I just need to rest for a minute; then I'll leave."

"I don't think you should be going anywhere if you've hit your head," Frank said, and when Libby looked at him, he shrugged in apology. "I'm sorry, Libby, but he's not safe out there on public transport, not like this."

"Jesus, can't you see he's putting it on?" Dylan said.

"Piss off," Simon said, glaring up at Dylan. "I really do feel—"

"Will you two give it a rest?" Libby said. She looked at

Dylan. "I'm sorry but Frank's right. I can't let Simon travel back to Surrey in this state."

"You don't need to look after him, Libby." The aggression had disappeared from Dylan's voice, and he was looking at her imploringly. "You don't owe him anything."

"I know I don't. But I can't let him roam the streets when he's this drunk; he might get hit by a bus or something."

Dylan opened his mouth to reply, but then he stopped and his whole body seemed to deflate. "Fine."

All the laughter and joy from earlier had gone, and when Libby looked at her friends, their faces were serious.

"We should probably be heading off," Frank said, pulling himself up. "Libby, would you like one of us to stay and help you with Simon?"

"No, I'll be fine, thank you."

Frank and Esme started toward the kitchen. Dylan stayed where he was a moment longer, glowering at Simon; then he turned and followed the other two inside.

In the hallway, they all found their coats and Libby opened the front door to let them out.

"Thank you for a lovely party," Esme said, giving her a tight hug.

"Are you free for a walk on Monday?" Frank asked, and when Libby nodded, he gave her a kiss on the cheek and stepped outside with Esme.

Dylan was the last one to leave. She felt him squeeze against the wall as he moved past, so as not to accidentally brush against her. All the intimacy of earlier had disappeared, and he wouldn't even look at her as he stepped outside.

"Good night, Dylan."

He faltered on the doorstep and then turned back, their eyes meeting. "You know you don't have to do this, don't you?" he said in a quiet voice. "You don't have to do anything for him anymore."

"I know."

Dylan stood still, staring into her eyes, and for a second Libby wondered if he was going to kiss her again. Then he turned and made his way down the front steps, not looking back.

33

Libby was woken the following morning by clattering sounds from the kitchen. She'd gone to bed shortly after her guests had left the night before, leaving Simon in Hector's room with a glass of water and one of Tom's old T-shirts to sleep in. She'd been hoping that he'd have left before she woke up, but from the sounds coming from downstairs, it didn't seem like Simon was going anywhere in a hurry. Libby showered and dressed slowly, putting off the moment she had to face him.

When she did eventually head down to the kitchen, she walked in and did a double take. All the mess from last night's meal had been cleared away, the dishes washed and the surfaces spotless. Simon was over by the mixer, weighing flour into a bowl. He was wearing Rebecca's silk dressing gown, which barely reached his thighs. When he saw Libby, he did a little shimmy.

"What do you think of my outfit? Sexy, huh?"

"What are you doing?"

"I'm making pancakes. Although I couldn't find any normal flour in this place, so I'm afraid they're gluten free, god help us." He broke eggs into the flour and reached for a measuring jug filled with milk.

Libby crossed her arms. "You need to leave."

Simon didn't look up at her. "Look, I'm sorry about behaving like an idiot last night. You know what I'm like when I've had a few drinks. I didn't mean any harm."

"You were a complete arse."

"Well, if it makes you feel any better, I've got a storming hangover this morning and my head feels like it might explode at any minute. I need food."

"Why did you come last night?"

He hesitated and then turned toward her. "When I woke up yesterday and realized it was your birthday, I started thinking about all the amazing times we'd had together. Do you remember that time I surprised you with a trip to Paris on the Eurostar? And when we did the *Star Wars* marathon in bed and didn't leave the house all weekend?"

"So what?"

"Well, the memories just made me realize how much I've messed everything up with you, especially how I reacted to the pregnancy news. And then I went to the pub for a drink, and somehow I ended up having five pints and then getting on a train to see you." He added a pinch of salt to the batter with a flick of his wrist.

"Why are you here, Simon?"

"I told you. I got drunk and sad, and I wanted to see you on your—"

"No, I mean, why are you still here now, making pancakes? You're living with another woman."

"I know, but it's all so complicated. I mean, look at you . . ." He pointed at Libby. "You're pregnant, with *my* child."

Libby let out a bark of a laugh. "Well, I'm so sorry this is complicated for *you*, Simon. What a nightmare it must be for *you*." She opened the fridge, took out some orange juice, and then slammed the door shut, wishing it would make a more satisfying bang.

Simon shook his head ruefully. "I know I've handled this all so badly, Piglet."

"Don't call me that," she snapped.

Simon frowned but carried on. "When you called me the other week, I panicked. Olivia had literally just moved her stuff into my house and there were boxes everywhere. But that's why I'm here now, because I want to apologize. And I want to try and make it up to you."

He reached out to touch Libby's arm and she recoiled. "No! You can't do this, Simon. You can't turn up drunk, cook me a pancake, and then expect me to forgive you."

"I know that. But if you'd let me explain—"

"What is there to explain? You dumped me, made me virtually homeless. Then when I discovered I was pregnant, you told me you wanted nothing to do with me or the baby. That's all pretty self-explanatory, no?"

"But that's what I'm trying to say. I was wrong when I said that, Libs. I was freaking out but I didn't mean it."

Libby could feel a headache coming on, and she pinched the bridge of her nose. "So what *are* you saying?"

"I don't exactly know," he said. "But I do know that I want to be involved in my child's life. At this point I have no idea how that might work, but I would love the chance to talk to you and see if we can come up with some kind of a plan."

"Does Olivia know you're here?"

She watched Simon cringe. "Olivia's . . . We broke up. She's moved out."

Libby wanted to laugh out loud. So that was why Simon had turned up at her front door drunk. He'd been dumped.

"But look, this isn't about Olivia; this is about us and our baby. Please, can we sit down and talk over breakfast?"

"Simon, I asked you to leave."

"Please, Libby. Please, hear me out, and then you never have to see me again if you don't want to."

Libby inhaled. She desperately wanted Simon out of the house, but she knew from experience how stubborn he was. "Fine, let's get this over and done with, then. But for god's sake, put some clothes on first."

LIBBY sat in silence at the kitchen table while Simon cooked the pancakes. While he did so, she checked her phone. Frank had texted her first thing this morning, a brief message saying he hoped she was okay and he was looking forward to seeing her tomorrow at Parliament Hill. And Esme had sent a message this morning too, all in caps, pronouncing, I DON'T LIKE YOUR EX. DYLAN IS MUCH NICER.

Yet the message Libby really wanted to receive hadn't arrived. She thought back to last night and their moment in the kitchen—the bus onesie . . . Dylan's words . . . that extraordinary kiss—and she picked up her phone to compose a text. But as she started to type, Libby remembered the look in Dylan's eyes when Simon had walked into the garden, the way he'd strained across the table as if he wanted to kill him. Libby had seen Dylan angry before, but that had been nothing compared to his fury last night. No wonder he hadn't texted her; he probably never wanted to see her again. She put the phone down as the baby gave an unsettled squirm.

"Here you go." Simon placed a plate of pancakes in front of

Libby. "I even found some syrup at the back of the cupboard; I'm amazed your sister allows this stuff in the house."

"Okay, so, what is it you wanted to say?" Libby said. There was no way she was going to let him sit and make small talk as if they were two friends having a social breakfast together.

Simon ate a mouthful before he answered. "Well, for one, I wanted to apologize about the way I reacted when you told me."

"You've done that already. What else?"

Libby saw anger flick across Simon's face. He'd never seen this version of her before, the one who spoke up to him, and he clearly didn't like it. But when he opened his mouth again, his tone was light.

"I've done a lot of thinking over the past few weeks, and I realize that I was wrong when I said I didn't want anything to do with the baby. You know how much I've always wanted to be a dad, and I can't just walk away from my own child."

Libby took a deep breath. This had been what she'd hoped for originally, for Simon to say he wanted to be involved. But now she was hearing these words, they filled her with dread. "So what are you proposing?"

"For one thing, I can help you financially. I know you've not worked in three months, so you must be running out of savings. I'm happy to pay my share of costs, and there's always your old job at my company if you want it."

"Okay. What else?"

"Well, I'd like to be part of the baby's life. I'd like to see him or her regularly, have them for weekends and holidays when they're a bit older. I've got a spare room, as you know, so I can turn that into a bedroom for the little one. I don't want to be some distant dad the kid never sees. I want to be there on the football sidelines cheering them on, you know?"

Libby put a small piece of pancake in her mouth but her throat was dry and she couldn't swallow it. She sipped some water so she didn't gag.

"Have you thought about where you're going to live?" Simon said, helping himself to more syrup.

"I'm not sure yet. I've been looking online for places to rent round here."

He sucked in through his teeth. "You won't find anything you can afford in this part of town."

"I'm looking farther out as well."

"Have you thought about coming back to Surrey?"

"No, Simon. Surrey is pretty much the last place I want to live right now."

"Ouch!" Simon said, and he grabbed his chest dramatically as if he'd been stabbed.

Libby smiled before she could stop herself. She quickly straightened her face, but Simon was smirking in triumph.

"Surrey's not that bad, is it?" he continued. "There're great schools, lots of outdoor space; you have family and friends there . . . Plus, I'd be nearby, an extra pair of hands in those difficult early months. I'd love to be able to help you."

"That's not what you said before."

"I told you, I made a mistake."

"And what if you change your mind again?"

"That's not going to happen." Simon looked across the table, his blue eyes fixed on her face, and Libby had to look away. "I really do mean it, Libs. If you're nearby, then I can be there to support you and the baby, as much or as little as you want."

Libby pushed her plate of food away. "So, what are you suggesting, that I move in next door? That would be nice and cozy. The kid and I could pop round for Sunday lunch with you and whichever girl you're dating at the time."

She saw Simon wince.

"Come on, I'm being serious," he said. "Rent is so much cheaper round us. Plus, my parents are there, and yours too."

"If you're trying to encourage me, that's not helping."

Simon laughed. "Okay, we wouldn't have to tell your mum, then. But look, having a baby is bloody hard. And you've always been a bit nervous around kids, haven't you? Do you really wanna bring one up on your own?"

"I'm not on my own," Libby said as Dylan's face flickered into her mind. What had he said last night? *I want to be there for you.* But that had been before Simon turned up, before she'd pretty much thrown Dylan out of the house.

"I know you've made some friends here, and that's great," Simon said. "But seriously, do you think some old dude and a guy wearing fancy dress are really going to give you the same support as your family?"

"Don't you dare be rude about them," Libby said sharply. "I can't imagine they're that impressed with you either after last night's performance."

"Sorry," Simon said, raising his hands. "I just want you to think about it, all right? I know it might feel a bit weird at first, but people make things like this work all the time. And it has to be better for the baby to have its father nearby, right?"

"Have you finished?" Libby nodded toward his empty plate.

"Sure." There it was again, that twitch of anger, although Simon hid it quicker this time. He stood up, gathering up his phone and keys. Libby stayed sitting.

"Right, well, I'll see myself out, then." He turned to leave and then stopped. "Promise me you'll think about what I'm suggesting. I know things have been difficult between us these past few months, but we have to move beyond that, for the sake of the baby. Yeah?"

He stared at Libby, his eyes so piercing, she felt he could see right into her mind. For a moment neither of them moved; then Libby gave a small nod of her head.

Simon smiled, but it didn't reach his eyes. "Good. I'm the father, after all. I have rights too."

34

Libby had arranged to meet Frank at the top of Parliament Hill on Monday morning, and as she approached the summit, she saw him sitting on his usual bench and staring out at the view. He turned to look at her as she sat down.

"Libby, how are you? You look tired."

"I'm fine, thanks. I just didn't sleep very well last night."

"Tell me about it. I can't remember the last time I had a proper night's sleep."

"How are you feeling about the assessment tomorrow?"

Frank shook his head. "I have to admit, I'm pretty nervous. What if the social worker asks me to do something difficult?"

"I'm sure they won't. Besides, you'll have Dylan with you for moral support."

"Thank god. Clara's coming down too." Frank grimaced as he said his daughter's name.

"Try not to worry too much, Frank. It's not an exam."

"It feels like one, though." He exhaled. "Anyway, enough about me. How did everything go with Simon after we left?"

"About that. I wanted to apologize about his behavior."

"Don't you apologize; you did nothing wrong."

"Simon's not usually like that, I swear. He'd had too much to drink and—"

"Libby, it's fine. You don't have to make excuses for him."

"But I feel terrible that he ruined the evening. Poor Esme looked petrified."

"Oh, I wouldn't worry about her; she's a tough cookie. Was Simon okay after a night's sleep?"

"He was fine." Libby stared out at the view in front of them. There was a heavy gray haze hanging over London this morning, and the Shard was barely visible through the fog.

"Did you have a chance to talk about the pregnancy?" Frank asked.

"Simon says he's changed his mind and wants to be part of the baby's life. He's suggested I move back to Surrey, so he can be near me to help."

Frank let out a long, low whistle. "Goodness. And how does that make you feel?"

"I don't know. I've got used to the idea of having this child on my own, here in London, so this has completely thrown me. And what if he changes his mind again?"

"Do you think he might?"

Libby thought before she answered. "No, I don't think so. He seemed genuine when he talked about it yesterday."

"And what about you? What do you want?"

"Honestly, I don't know. I saw how hard my sister found having a baby, and that was with a husband and a nanny, not to mention a massive house and plenty of money. I'm not sure if I can do it on my own."

"Of course you can. I'm not saying it will be easy, but you're stronger than you think, Libby."

"But Simon does have a right to be involved if he wants to. He's the biological father."

Frank nodded. "Sure, but that doesn't mean you have to move back to Surrey. You could stay in London and still let Simon be involved."

"But maybe it would be easier to move back to Surrey, though? I could afford a bigger place there, and my parents are nearby as well as Simon. I'd have more of a support network there."

"And what about Dylan?"

Libby looked across at Frank, surprised to hear him say that name. "Did he tell you what happened on Saturday night?"

"No, but I could tell from your flushed faces when you came out with the cake that *something* had happened." Frank smiled at her, and Libby felt herself blush.

"It wasn't just that. Dylan said some things . . . some amazing things. He offered to be part of my and the baby's life."

Frank was staring out at the view, but Libby could tell he was hiding a smile. "Dylan is a good man" was all he said.

"I know he is. Which is why this is all so confusing."

"Yes, it must be. What's that saying about buses? You wait ages for one, and then two come along at once."

"Except in this case, I fear that one of the buses may no longer be willing to have me on board."

"Why do you say that?" Frank said.

"You saw Dylan when Simon turned up. He was furious at him, and with me when I let Simon stay."

"He wasn't furious with you, Libby. But he was angry at Simon; there's no doubt about that."

"I've never seen him like that."

"Dylan won't tolerate bullies. Especially not when the person being bullied is someone he cares about."

"Simon's not really a bully, though. I mean, he behaved appallingly the other night, but he's not a bad person."

"Did Dylan ever tell you about his parents?" Frank said.

"No, why?"

"I'm afraid it's not my story to tell. But I will just say that Dylan's reaction to Simon makes a lot more sense when you know what he's been through with his family."

Libby leaned back on the bench. "What am I going to do, Frank?"

"Have you spoken to Dylan since Saturday?"

"No, he's not been in touch."

"I imagine he's giving you some space. Dylan's not the kind of person who'd want you to feel pressured."

"I thought he might be avoiding me after what happened. Maybe he regrets what he said?"

"I'm almost certain that's not true. I think it's much more likely he's being respectful and giving you time."

"Oh god, what a mess," Libby said, putting her head in her hands. "I have to move out of Rebecca's place soon, so I need to make a decision. What should I do, Frank?"

"Only you can make that decision, my dear. But before you do, I strongly recommend you speak to Dylan. Why don't you text him now and see if he's around this afternoon?"

"Now?"

"No time like the present, as they say."

"Okay." Libby pulled her phone out of her pocket and typed out a message, then pressed SEND before she could change her mind.

CHAPTER

35

L ibby received a reply from Dylan within half an hour, telling her he'd be over soon. There was no "x" at the end of
the message, but as Libby walked home from seeing Frank,
she still found herself feeling lighter than she had done since
her birthday. Frank was right: she had to talk to Dylan before she made any decisions. Because what if he hadn't changed
his mind? What if he still meant what he'd said about wanting
a relationship with her? If he did, then perhaps there was a
way Libby could be with Dylan and still let Simon be involved in the baby's life. Yes, it would be complicated, especially given the two of them had got off on such terrible
footing. But surely they could all make it work, for the sake of
the baby?

As she approached the house, Libby spotted someone sitting on the front steps, reading a newspaper. She felt a rush of
excitement and was about to call out Dylan's name when the
figure lowered the newspaper.

"Libs!" Simon's face lit up when he saw her.

"What are you doing here?"

"Sorry. I know I should have called you first, but there's
something important I need to talk to you about."

"This isn't a good time," Libby said. What if Dylan were to turn up while Simon was here? That would *not* be helpful.

"I'll be quick, I promise. But please, I've come all the way up here. Can I have five minutes?"

"Okay, but only five minutes."

Libby climbed the stairs and unlocked the front door, then hung up her bag and led Simon down to the kitchen. She poured herself a glass of water and turned to face him across the island.

"All right, then, what do you want to say?"

"Okay. So . . ." He was bouncing on the balls of his feet like an excited puppy. "After I left you yesterday, I couldn't stop thinking about your living situation. I even went online to look for flats near me and your parents, but everything's so expensive, it's insane. Honestly, I'm tempted to give up the gardening business and go into property development because—"

"Simon."

"Sorry. So, I was lying in bed last night, thinking about it, when I had this absolute brain wave." He paused for dramatic effect. "What if you didn't have to rent somewhere? What if you could live somewhere for free?"

Libby scrunched up her nose. "What are you talking about?"

"I'm talking about my place, of course! I've got a spare room that's currently sitting completely empty. You and the baby could use that!"

It was so absurd that Libby let out a snort of laughter. "Oh my god, Simon, are you kidding me?"

"What? Why is that such a crazy idea?"

"Because you broke my heart, packed my life belongings

into bin bags, and then moved your new girlfriend into the house."

"Well, yeah, but—"

"What happens when you meet someone new? Are you going to move them in with me and the baby too? That would be cozy. Or will you throw me out again?"

"Of course I won't!" Simon said, his voice full of indignation. "I told you, the Olivia thing was a stupid mistake. I was bored and restless and it was just a fling. I swear, I never felt about her the way I felt about you. Besides, everything changed the moment you told me I was going to be a father."

"But you don't seriously think we could live together?"

"Of course we can. This way you don't have to worry about rent or living in some scummy, damp bedsit, and I can be there for you and the baby. And we've got the garden, plus, there are lots of parks and there's that great nursery up the road."

Libby took a swig of water. It was true: the house was perfect for a family—that was one of the reasons she'd never pushed for them to move, even though she'd have preferred them to own a property jointly. But moving back in with him, after everything that had happened—surely that was crazy?

"It's not a good idea, Si. I mean, it might work for the first six months while the baby's tiny and can sleep in with me. But what happens when it's a bit older and needs its own room?"

"That's ages away, Libs. Who knows where we'll be at by then? I mean, maybe by that point . . ." He trailed off, and it took Libby a second to work out what he was suggesting.

"No, Simon, we are *not* getting back together. Seriously, after everything you put me through, you think—"

"All right, all right," Simon interrupted. "Fine, so once the baby is older, you can move out and find somewhere new. But at least for the first year or so you'll want to be sharing a room with the baby, so why not do it for free at my place? Just think, Libs, I could change nappies, cook for you, do the night feeds so you can get some rest. There's so much I could do to help."

"But wouldn't it be weird, us living under one roof again, in the same house we lived in together as a couple?"

"Maybe it would be a bit odd to begin with, but we'd adjust to it. And pretty soon we'll be so busy with the baby that we won't even remember what it was like before."

Libby's head was spinning with it all, and she slumped down on a stool by the counter.

"So, what do you think?" Simon said.

"I need time to consider it, Simon. It's a lot to take in."

"Of course, of course, I'll leave you to it. But promise me you'll consider it properly. I know it might feel weird at first, but the more I've thought about it, the more I'm convinced it's the perfect solution."

"I've said I'll think about it and I will."

Libby heard a buzzing sound, and when she looked down, her phone was vibrating on the counter. What if it was Dylan? She quickly snatched it up before Simon could see the screen.

"You need to leave." Libby stood up, led him down the hallway, and opened the front door. "Good-bye, Simon."

"Bye, Libs. Oh, this is so exciting." He leaned forward as if to give her a kiss. Libby quickly moved out of the way, and Simon grinned. "Sorry, old habits!" He gave her a wink and then trotted down the front steps.

Libby closed the door and then fell against it, exhaling

slowly. She was still holding her phone, and she looked down at the message on her screen. It was from Dylan.

> Really sorry, something's come up and I can't meet today. Are you free tomorrow instead? Usual time, usual place? D

36

PEGGY

've some news, love. Not good news, I'm afraid, although it rarely is when you get to our age.

Eileen from number eighteen passed away.

The first I knew about it was when I saw an ambulance turn up and paramedics go into her flat on Saturday. Then an hour later I saw them coming out with a stretcher, and her son, Jeremy, was there, looking all pale faced. I wanted to go up and talk to him, check he was all right, but bloody Betty Fincher swooped in there first.

Later, she told me that apparently Eileen had a heart attack sometime on Friday, and Jeremy found her when he went round to see her on Saturday morning. But I don't know if that's true; Betty's never been the most reliable source.

Still, I'm not gonna lie, Percy: it sent chills through me when she said that. As you well know, it's always been my biggest fear, something like that happening and no one being there to find me. And it's not as if David comes round regularly to check on me, like Eileen's son does. I could be there for . . . Well, it doesn't bear thinking about, does it?

I saw Eileen last week, in Asda. She stopped me in the freezer aisle to show me the swimsuit she'd bought for her trip to Dubai with Jeremy. I pretended to admire it, but really, I was looking over her shoulder to see which was cheaper, the frozen cod or the haddock. She'll never get to use that swimsuit now. Shame, it looked expensive.

I called David on Saturday night, just to check in and see how he is. He said he couldn't chat for long, as he and Emma were going out for dinner. I told him what had happened with Eileen but I'm not sure he heard me. He said he'd call back on Sunday for a proper chat, so I stayed in all day waiting, but he must have been busy, 'cos he never got round to it. Perhaps he'll call today.

Sorry. I know I'm sounding a bit maudlin. I don't know what's wrong with me but I've felt knackered all week, a proper bone-aching tired. I nearly didn't come up here 'cos I felt so exhausted. And I know what you'll say, love, that I should have stayed at home and rested rather than trek all the way here. But honestly, if I don't come here, then I don't have anyone else to talk to, apart from the odd stranger on the bus.

Jesus, that makes me sound like a pathetic old bugger, doesn't it?

Maybe I should book a trip to Dubai. I've never been abroad, after all. Or New York. You've always said I'd love it there. Imagine what David and Emma would say if I told them I was going to New York on my own. They'd never believe it!

Maybe you could come with me too, love? I mean, it's not a totally absurd idea. You've been before, after all, so you could show me the sights. Percy and Peggy in New York together, painting the city red. That would be a lot of fun, wouldn't it?

37

Libby arrived at the bus stop outside Kentish Town Station at nine fifteen on the dot. She'd spent the past eighteen hours replaying Simon's suggestion in her head. The whole thing was completely ridiculous, so why the hell hadn't she said no yesterday and got it over and done with? *Because you're scared of having this baby on your own,* a voice in Libby's head kept saying. *Wouldn't it be easier to live with Simon and have his help, rather than trying to carve out a new life in London on your own?*

And then there was eccentric, surprising, dark-eyed Dylan. Libby thought about the way he'd looked at her on Saturday night, the feel of his lips on her neck, the offer he'd made to help her. She glanced up Highgate Road, waiting to see his tall profile strolling toward the bus stop. Frank had told her yesterday that his care assessment was at twelve o'clock, so Dylan should have a couple of hours between his regular morning visit to Frank and needing to get back there for the assessment. Perhaps they could go to one of the cafés on Kentish Town Road, or walk up to the heath? Wherever they went, Libby had promised herself she'd tell Dylan everything: she didn't want to hide things from him anymore; he deserved to know the whole messy truth. She glanced back up the road. Still no sign of Dylan. Libby checked her phone and saw it was nine twenty-five. He usually messaged if he was running late, but when she looked at WhatsApp, she saw that he hadn't been online since seven o'clock the previous evening.

At nine thirty-five, Libby pulled out her phone again and dialed Dylan's number. She held her breath as she waited for him to answer, imagining the sound of his deep voice. But the phone rang and rang and eventually clicked into an automated voice mail. She hung up before the tone and then called Frank's number.

Frank answered on the fifth ring, his voice bellowing down the line. "HELLO?"

"Frank, it's Libby."

"This isn't a good time, Libby. I'm sorry."

"I was wondering if Dylan has left yours yet."

"No, he hasn't turned up this morning."

"What?"

"He's never done this before. And today . . . I need him today." Frank's voice wobbled.

"Did he call and say why?"

"It's my care assessment; my daughter will be here soon. Dylan promised he'd be here to help me."

"I'm sure he'll turn up for the assessment, Frank; please try not to worry. Maybe he overslept?" Libby knew she didn't sound very convincing.

"I need him here today."

"Do you want me to come up there now? I could stay for the—"

"No!" Frank shouted, startling Libby. "It's Dylan I need. He knows everything, my medication and routine. He has to be here so the social worker will know I'm fine."

Libby could hear the panic rising in his voice. "It's okay, calm down. I'm sure there's a good explanation. Do you have an address for Dylan, and I can try going to his house?"

"I do . . . somewhere. What's that smell?"

"What smell?"

"Oh, where's Dylan? Everything's going wrong today."

"Are you sure you don't want me to come up there now, Frank?"

"No. I'd better go."

"Okay, good luck with your—" But she didn't get to finish the sentence because the line went dead.

Libby checked the time again: it was nine forty-five, so Dylan was now half an hour late. Where the hell was he? He of all people knew how important today was for Frank. What if something bad had happened to him? Or perhaps there was a perfectly good explanation for this? Whatever it was, she needed to track Dylan down so he didn't miss Frank's assessment.

A thought occurred to Libby, and she dialed the number Esme had given her. When the young woman answered, Libby explained what was going on.

"Dylan never misses work," Esme said.

"When did you last see him?"

"Yesterday. We went to get him a suit for my wedding."

"And how did he seem?"

"Sad. He was worrying about you."

Libby's stomach contracted. "Did he say that?"

"No, he didn't have to, Libby. I'm very good at reading people."

"This is so weird," Libby said. "Do you have his address?"

"Yes. I'll text it to you now."

When the address arrived, Libby put the postcode into Google Maps, which showed her a spot near Regent's Park. It was right on the 88 bus route, Libby realized. How strange that Dylan had never pointed out where he lived, given they'd ridden the bus past there so many times. But then, he'd never told her anything about his home life; Libby didn't even know if he lived alone or with flatmates. She wavered for a moment. Was this mad, turning up uninvited at his flat? Then she remembered Frank's tone on the phone, the rising panic in his voice at the thought of having to do the assessment without Dylan. An 88 bus was approaching, and Libby stuck out her arm and signaled for it to stop.

Twenty minutes later, she got off the bus on Albany Street, at the exact stop where she and Dylan had first started putting up posters. The address for his flat was in a large housing estate that stretched back from the main road. Libby followed the directions on her phone down Robert Street, past long, squat buildings with external walkways running along each of the upper floors. Finding the entrance marked "200–350," she opened it and headed up to the second floor. As she walked past the row of identical front doors, the occasional sound of voices or music drifted out from inside. Libby stopped when she reached number 278. Net curtains were drawn across the window, and there was no immediate sign of life inside. Taking a deep breath, she rang the bell.

Within seconds there was an explosion of barking so loud that Libby jolted. Dylan had never mentioned he had a dog. There was a banging sound and the door rattled as the animal threw itself against it from the inside, and Libby stepped away in case it burst through. Then she heard a man's voice on the other side of the door shouting at the dog. This was clearly not

Dylan's flat; Esme must have given her the wrong address. Libby was about to turn and walk away when she heard a scraping sound, and then the door opened to reveal a man dressed in tracksuit bottoms and a saggy sweatshirt, gray stubble lining his face. There was scrabbling and a whining sound behind him, suggesting the dog was still nearby and trying to get out.

"What do you want?" the man snapped.

"I'm so sorry to disturb you. I must have the wrong flat." Libby started to walk away.

"Who you looking for?" the man called after her.

"Eh, Dylan. Dylan . . ." She realized with a start that she didn't know his surname.

"He lives here," the man said with a sniff. "Why you looking for him?"

"Well, he was supposed to meet me this morning and he didn't turn up for his work either, so—"

The man let out a bark of a laugh. "Let me guess. He got you in this state, did he?" He nodded at Libby's baby bump.

"What? No, this isn't—"

"At least this explains why he's done a runner."

"What?"

"He's gone, love, taken off. Packed a bag yesterday afternoon and I ain't seen him since."

Libby blinked at the man. "Are you sure?"

"Shut it, Vincent!" he shouted at the dog behind him, who'd started to bark again. The animal immediately fell silent and the man turned back to Libby. "I heard him chatting on the phone and then he packed a bag and left. I wasn't sure why, but now I've seen you, it all makes sense."

Libby's head was spinning. There was no way Dylan would have left, not the night before Frank's assessment.

"It turns out he's just like his mother, after all." The man gave a leering smile, revealing yellow smoke-stained teeth. "That bitch did a runner too when he was a little 'un; did he tell you that? Couldn't cope with being a mum, so she pissed off in the middle of the night and left me to deal with him."

My god, poor Dylan. Libby couldn't imagine what that must have been like, to be abandoned by his own mother and left with this . . . this brute.

"Have you registered him as missing with the police?" she asked.

The man let out a sharp laugh, which quickly dissolved into a fit of violent coughs. Libby watched as he hacked and choked for a solid minute. When he stopped he was wheezing heavily. "Of course I haven't registered him missing, because he ain't. He's probably gone off with that other bird."

"What other bird?"

"Oh, I don't know her bloody name, but they've been on and off for years. She's some waster punk like him." The man gave another harsh cough. "I thought they were off again but it was her who called him yesterday. He's probably moved in with her, so you can't chase him down for money. He's always been a tight bastard."

Libby opened her mouth to defend Dylan, but no words came out. Dylan's father was watching her with that horrible smile.

"I've got to go," she said, suddenly desperate to get away. "If you see Dylan, please will you tell him to call Libby?"

"I won't waste my breath," the man said, and Libby turned and hurried away, his cruel laughter chasing her down the walkway.

ibby spent the bus ride home in a daze. Had Dylan gone? She couldn't imagine him deserting Frank with no warning; it seemed so unlike him. But what if Dylan had turned up at the house yesterday, seen Simon there, and assumed the worst? And then there was this whole girlfriend thing. Surely Dylan would never have kissed Libby and said what he'd said if he had a girlfriend? He'd always struck Libby as honest and trustworthy. But then again, she'd always thought Simon was honest and trustworthy too, and look what had happened there. Libby shuddered and the baby gave a restless kick.

Libby got off the bus on Kentish Town Road and walked back toward Rebecca's house. As usual, the baby settled once she was on the move, and as Libby walked, she composed a message to Esme telling her what Dylan's father had said. She left out the bit about the girlfriend, the words too unreal to type. Libby was pressing SEND as she turned through Rebecca's front gate, and then she stopped dead. The front door to the house was hanging wide open.

Libby felt the blood draining from her face. Had she shut the front door when she left this morning? She was always so careful, but she'd been distracted about meeting Dylan and might have forgotten. Her legs were shaking as she crept up the front steps. Were the burglars still in the house, or had they gone already, taking all of Rebecca and Tom's valuables with them? Libby still had her phone in her hand, and as she reached the front door, she dialed 999. She was about to press CALL when she saw a flash of movement at the end of the hallway and then heard a familiar voice.

"There you are, Elizabeth."

"Mum?"

"Well, don't stand there like a lemon. Come on in."

"I thought you guys weren't back until Friday?"

"Change of plan—we flew home early." She came forward and gave Libby a dry peck on the cheek. "Happy birthday, darling."

"Is everyone okay?"

Her mum looked up and down the corridor to check no one was in earshot, then lowered her voice. "Rebecca took a pregnancy test in France and . . ." She tapped the side of her nose.

"Oh, wow, that's amazing!"

"Shh, you did not hear it from me!" Pauline hissed. "Of course, the second Rebecca found out, she wanted to rush back to London. I mean, the Dordogne is lovely but you can't trust the French not to sneak blue cheese or raw meat into your food."

"Where is she now?"

"Upstairs having a lie-down. Your father and Tom have taken Hector across to the park. Now, come on, I'm gasping for an Earl Grey. Tea is another thing the French manage to completely mess up." Her mother led her through to the kitchen, where every surface was covered with bags and holiday detritus.

"So, how was your birthday?" she said as she turned on the kettle. "I can't imagine you got up to much in your condition."

"Actually, it was lovely. I had friends round for dinner."

"Really? And what else have you been up to?"

"Oh, not much." It was possibly the biggest lie she'd ever told, what with the bus search and Simon's invitation, so Libby kept her back turned so her mum couldn't see her face.

"No other news, then? Nothing to report?"

Libby paused, mug in hand. Her mum's tone was casual, *too* casual. "When did he tell you?"

"When did who tell me what?"

"You know what I'm talking about, Mum. When did Simon tell you he asked me to move back in?"

A grin spread across Pauline's face. "He called me yesterday evening. Oh, darling, I am *so* relieved for you."

"Really?"

"Yes, really. I mean, a marriage proposal would have been even better, but one step at a time, hey? Have you started packing yet? I'd say we'd give you a lift back today, but we've got all our luggage to fit in the car."

"No, I haven't started packing."

"Have you thought about nursery furniture? John Lewis does some fabulous sets; we could pop to Bluewater next week and take a look if you like?"

"Mum—"

"Simon's mother will be delighted. Of course, she'll want to hold the baby shower at her place but as your mother I get—"

"Mum, stop."

"What?"

"I haven't said yes to Simon."

There was a beat of silence.

"Elizabeth Anne Nicholls, what do you mean, you haven't said yes?"

Libby pulled her shoulders back. "I'm not sure I want to move in with Simon again."

"Why on earth not? He's the father of your child."

"I know, but that doesn't mean I have to live with him."

"This is ridiculous," Pauline said. "I know you're still cross with Simon, but as he explained to me on the phone yesterday, he really regrets the way he handled the pregnancy news. The poor guy was taken by surprise, that's all."

"Don't you think I was taken by surprise too? What would have happened if I'd reacted in the way he did? And why do you *always* have to side with Simon?"

"I do not."

"Yes, you do. It's always 'poor Simon this' and 'poor Simon that.' I wish, just for once, you'd say, 'Poor Libby, how rubbish that your boyfriend of eight years dumped you, kicked you out, and wanted nothing to do with your baby.'"

"What has got into you, Elizabeth?" her mum said. "I've never heard you talk like this before."

Libby sighed. Part of her wanted to give up and acquiesce, like she always did with her family. But what had Dylan said? *You need to stop caring so much what your family think.*

"Mum, I'm thirty years old and about to become a mother," Libby said, trying to keep her voice steady. "You need to stop treating me like a disappointing child who messes everything up."

"Oh, for goodness' sake, don't be so ridiculous," Pauline said, rolling her eyes.

"See, this is exactly what I mean," Libby said. "You never listen to what I have to say or what I want. You think I'm incapable of making decisions on my own and treat me like an idiot. And I'm sick and tired of it."

"I do not think you're incapable of making decisions. I just worry about you. You threw away a promising medical career on a foolish whim, and I don't want to see you make the same mistake with Simon."

"It wasn't a promising medical career. I hated every second of that degree! I only stuck it out so long because I knew how much it meant to you and Dad. And I'm not going to make the same mistake and move back in with Simon because it's what you want."

"Quite right."

Libby spun round at the sound of another voice. Rebecca was standing in the kitchen doorway, watching them.

"Ah, Rebecca, maybe you can talk some sense into your sister," Pauline said. "She's saying she's not going to move back in with Simon, which is utter madness."

"It's not madness, Mum," Libby said. "If these last three months in London have taught me anything, it's that I'm tougher than I realized. I know you'll find this hard to believe, but maybe I'm strong enough to have this baby on my own."

"See what I mean?" Pauline said to Rebecca, her eyebrows shooting up in dismay. "She hasn't got a clue. Tell her, Rebecca. Tell her she doesn't stand a hope in hell of raising a child on her own."

The room was quiet as they waited for Rebecca to speak. She was looking at Pauline, her brow furrowed. "Actually, Mum, I think Libby's right."

"What?" Libby and Pauline said in unison.

"I think Libby's right. Simon has treated her like shit, and I think she's probably better off doing this alone."

Pauline's face had gone a strange shade of purple. "Are you serious?"

"Yes, Mum. And you need to let Libby make up her own mind and support her in whatever she decides."

Libby was so shocked, she didn't know what to say. She had never known her sister to stick up for her like this, even when they were kids.

"I see," Pauline said stiffly. "This is how it's going to be, is it? My own children ganging up on me."

"We're not ganging up on you," Rebecca said. "But we're both adults now. You need to let go of the reins a bit, let us live our own lives."

"Of course, I let you live your own lives," Pauline hissed.

"Mum, you just insisted I cut my precious family holiday short because I found out I'm pregnant and you didn't think France was safe for me," Rebecca said. "And I agreed because that's what I always do. But Libby was right a moment ago: we're capable of making our own decisions now."

Pauline looked between her two daughters, her mouth open, apparently too stunned to speak. In the distance, Libby could hear sounds at the front door, the click of it opening and the thud of Hector's footsteps as he ran in. The noise seemed to startle Pauline back to reality as she turned and reached for her handbag.

"Right. Well, I know when I'm not wanted."

"Oh, Mum, don't be like that," Libby said, but Pauline was already striding out of the kitchen.

"Roger, get our bags. We're leaving!" she shouted from the hallway.

Libby looked at Rebecca. "Thank you for your support there."

Rebecca shrugged. "I should have said it a lot sooner."

"And congratulations on the pregnancy news too. That's amazing."

"It's still very early days, so we're not celebrating yet," Rebecca said brusquely. Then she gave Libby a small smile. "But thanks."

39

By the time Pauline finally left the house, still refusing to be calmed down by either her daughters or her baffled husband, it was gone two and Libby was ravenous. Rebecca and Tom still had all their luggage to unpack, so Libby decided to give them some space and headed out to her favorite café. As she was eating a sandwich, she checked her phone. Still no word from Dylan, and it didn't look as if he'd checked his messages since last night either. Where the hell could he be? Had he made it to Frank's assessment? At the thought of her friend, Libby flicked to his number and pressed CALL, but there was no answer. Perhaps he was still doing the assessment, although it should have been finished by now. How would Frank have got on without Dylan there? Libby wondered with a lurch. She ate the last two mouthfuls of her sandwich, ordered some cakes to go, and then set off toward Frank's.

When she reached his house, Libby rang the doorbell and stood back to wait for him to answer. She knew he was usually slow to get to the door, but within seconds she heard the sound of footsteps, long, fast strides that couldn't possibly have belonged to Frank. Was it Dylan? Libby felt a flush of relief as the door opened.

The person on the other side wasn't Dylan, but a middle-aged woman with an exhausted expression. Libby tried to conceal her disappointment.

"Can I help you?" the woman said in a clipped tone with a faint Scottish accent. This must be Clara, Frank's daughter.

"Hi, is Frank in? I brought him éclairs." Libby thrust the cake box toward Clara, but the woman ignored it, running a hand through her graying hair.

"Sorry. Who are you?"

"I'm Libby, a friend of Frank's."

"Well, I'm afraid now's not a good time. My dad's had a long day and he's tired."

"Could I quickly pop in and say hi? I won't be long, but I promised him I'd come round and see how today went."

The woman scrunched up her nose. "Okay, but keep it quick."

"Of course." Libby followed her inside.

As they approached the living room, Clara turned to her again. "Please don't upset him."

"Of course not," Libby whispered back. What an odd request.

"Dad, you've got a visitor," Clara said in a loud voice as she stepped into the living room. Libby followed her through, then stopped in her tracks.

Frank was sitting in his usual armchair, staring at the muted TV screen. He was wearing a dressing gown that reached down to his knees, revealing knobbly, varicose-vein-lined legs underneath. His shoulders were hunched forward and his hair was even more unkempt than usual. He was resting his right arm in his lap in a strange way, and when Libby looked closer, she saw his hand was wrapped in a white bandage.

"Frank, what happened?" she said, hurrying toward him, but if Frank heard her, he didn't respond. He was watching some nature documentary on TV, but his eyes were glassy, as if he was looking at but not seeing the images on the screen.

"Dad burned himself this morning," Clara said, walking to stand behind him and rest her hands on his shoulders.

"Oh, no!" The bandage was thick, with only the tips of his fingers poking out. "How did it happen?"

"He was making himself breakfast and the toast caught on fire," Clara said. "And rather than leave it, Dad decided to grab the toast with his bare hand and gave himself second-degree burns."

Libby drew breath. "Is it going to be okay?"

"The doctor said it should heal all right, but his hand is going to be out of action for a while."

Frank was still staring at the TV, apparently oblivious to their conversation.

"He says something distracted him halfway through making breakfast, which is why he forgot about the toast, but he can't remember what it was," Clara continued. "Between you and me, I think he had one of his funny spells, when he zones out. It's a common symptom of his type of dementia."

At the word "dementia," Frank's head snapped round. "There was smoke," he said. "Smoke and a strange smell."

"Yes, Dad, that was because the toast was burning," Clara said, enunciating the words.

"Oh, shit!" Libby said as a thought dawned on her. "I'm so sorry, but I think it was me."

"What was you?" Clara said.

"I think I was the one who distracted Frank. I phoned him this morning and he said there was a funny smell, but it didn't occur to me he was burning something. My phone call must have been the thing that distracted him."

"I see," Clara said slowly. "Well, that clears that up, at least."

Libby bent down next to Frank's chair so her face was level with his. "I'm so sorry, Frank. You said something about a funny smell before you hung up, but I didn't think anything of it. I should have come straight up here."

Frank didn't respond. His eyes had gone back to the silent TV screen, on which a lion was stalking a pack of gazelles.

"The doctor gave him some strong painkillers earlier and they've knocked him out a bit," Clara said.

"I feel terrible," Libby said. "I should have come up and checked on him when he said Dylan wasn't here."

"It's not your fault. I blame that bloody carer. It's gross negligence, what he did; if he's ill, he's supposed to call the agency so they can send a replacement."

"I think something has happened to Dylan," Libby said, but Clara ignored her.

"I should have trusted my instinct. The first time I saw him, I knew he'd be trouble."

"That's not fair. I'm sure Dylan will have a good explanation for this."

Frank must have heard Dylan's name, because his head jerked again. "Where's Dylan? Is he here?"

"No, Dad, Dylan didn't come," Clara shouted, and Libby saw him wince. "The agency are sending a new carer for you tomorrow morning."

"But I need Dylan." Frank's voice was weak, and he reminded Libby of a small child.

"What happened with the care assessment?" Libby asked.

"I had to cancel it because we spent the whole morning in

A and E getting his hand seen to," Clara said. "We only got home half an hour ago."

"What does that mean? Will they reschedule?"

Clara shook her head. "There's no point. I don't need a care assessment to tell me that Dad's not safe to live here alone, especially now he can't use one hand. I'm going to start looking for a care home for him ASAP."

"Really?" Libby said in alarm, and Clara looked at her sharply. "I mean, your dad obviously had a bad morning today, but when Dylan's here, he's usually fine."

Clara let out an impatient sigh. "I'm sorry, but who are you, again?"

"I'm a friend of your dad's."

"And how long have you known him?"

"A couple of months."

"Right. And I'm his daughter, who's known him for almost fifty-five years, so I think I can look after my father's interests a little better than you can."

"Of course you can. I'm sorry; I didn't mean to suggest otherwise. I just know how much he was hoping to retain his independence, at least for a little while longer."

"Look, I'm aware Dad's not exactly delighted at the idea of moving into a care home. But this house is too big for him and full of hazards: it's not just the kitchen; he could easily trip and fall down the stairs or hurt himself getting out of the shower. And with the dementia, he's going to need more and more specialist care."

Libby looked down at Frank, huddled in his chair, cradling his bandaged arm. For the first time ever, he looked old and frail.

"He'll get used to it soon enough," Clara said, her voice

softening. "And it will be good for him. He's been far too lonely, shut up in this house and riding the bus on his own. At a care home he'll be able to socialize with people his own age."

Libby remembered what Frank had said to her, not long after they first met. *If they put me in a care home, they might as well put me in a box and bury me.*

"Would you mind sitting with Dad for five minutes while I make him some tea?" Clara said.

"Of course."

Clara nodded at her and then walked out of the room. Libby turned to Frank and rested her hand on his arm.

"Frank, what a day you've had."

He didn't say anything, but she saw a flicker on his face. Libby pulled up a chair so she could sit next to him.

"I went looking for Dylan this morning. He wasn't at home but his dad said he's been missing since last night."

"Where is Dylan?" Frank was still staring at the TV, but she could see him trying to battle through the painkiller fug.

"I don't know, but I'm going to try and find him." Libby swallowed. "Did Dylan ever mention a girlfriend to you?"

Frank blinked slowly.

"His dad said he might have gone to stay with her."

Frank lifted his right hand up to rub his face, and then looked confused when he felt the bandage. He stared at his hand.

"You hurt your hand this morning," Libby said. "Apparently you were making breakfast and you burned it on the grill. I'm so sorry. I feel responsible."

"It's your fault?"

"You told me on the phone that you could smell something. I should have realized what was going on and come up here."

Frank's brow furrowed. "It's your fault."

"I really am sorry, Frank. But Clara said your hand will heal."

He turned his head and looked at Libby as if noticing her for the first time. "It's your fault about Dylan."

"What do you mean?"

"He should have been here today . . . for my assessment. But because of you he missed it and I burned myself."

"I'm not sure that's strictly true. I mean, wherever Dylan is, I don't think—"

"You broke his heart," Frank interrupted. "He was so sad and now he's gone."

"He's not gone, Frank. I don't know where he is, but I'm sure he'll be back."

"He won't." There was a tremble in Frank's voice. "You scared him off. And because of you, I missed my assessment and they're going to lock me up in prison."

"Oh, Frank, it's a care home, not prison. And I really don't think Dylan missed today because of me."

"He did!" Frank slammed his hand on the arm of the chair and then gasped in pain. "It's your fault."

"What on earth's going on in here?" Clara came in through the door. "Dad, what's wrong?"

"Get her out!"

Clara glared at Libby. "I told you not to upset him."

"I'm sorry. He started blaming me for what happened today."

"Dad, it's not Libby's fault you burned your hand," Clara said. "You know you shouldn't have been using the grill in the first place. I've told you that dozens of times."

"Just get her out," Frank growled. "Now!"

Clara looked at Libby. "I think you need to go."

"Okay." Libby's voice wobbled and she stood up and started

moving toward the door. "I'm so sorry, Frank. I'll see you soon."

"No!"

She stared at him for a moment, his face contorted with anger. Then she felt Clara tugging her arm.

"I'm so sorry," Libby said as they went to the front door. "I really didn't mean to upset him."

"He's had a long day."

"Can I come back and visit him tomorrow?"

Clara pulled the front door open and waited while Libby stepped outside. "I think it's probably best you don't. Dad's going to have a lot to adjust to over the next few weeks, and I don't want him upset more than is necessary." She gave Libby a curt nod and then closed the door in her face.

40

Libby went to bed early that night, exhausted after the events of the day. But every time she closed her eyes, she saw Frank's face twisted with anger and heard Dylan's dad's mocking laughter. How had everything gone so horribly wrong in the space of one day? Dylan had disappeared, possibly with another woman, and Frank wanted nothing to do with her ever again. All of a sudden the London life she'd felt so optimistic about had crumbled into nothing.

Libby sat up and reached for her phone in the dark. The illuminated screen told her it was 2:06 a.m. She opened WhatsApp and instinctively clicked on Dylan's name, but all she could see were her own unread messages, taunting her. She typed out another short one saying she hoped he was okay. Her finger hovered over the x button, and then she pressed it twice.

No sooner had she pressed SEND than her phone began to ring, making Libby jump. She scrambled to answer it, praying she was about to hear Dylan's deep voice.

"Hello?"

"Can't sleep either, huh?"

Libby exhaled. "What is it, Simon?"

"I saw you were online and wanted to say hi."

"It's two in the morning!"

"Can't you sleep?"

Libby slumped back on her pillow. "It's been a long day."

"You need to find time to unwind, Libs. You're pregnant; you should be taking things easy."

"You don't need to worry about me. I'm capable of looking after myself."

"I know you are, but I can't help worrying about you. You and my baby."

His voice was gentle in her ear, and out of nowhere Libby felt a sob building in her throat. She tried to stifle it, but it emerged as a strangled gasp.

"Libby?"

"I'm sorry," she said, feeling the now-familiar warmth of tears.

"Wanna talk about it?"

"No." Libby pressed her hand against her eyes to stop the tears. "I had a fight with a friend."

"I'm so sorry to hear that."

"He was really angry at me and . . . I messed things up."

"I'm sure you didn't."

"I did. This morning I should have gone to help him but I was too absorbed with my own problems. And then he burned himself."

"Is this the old guy I met at your birthday?" Simon said. "If so, you can't blame yourself. He's not your responsibility."

"But he blames me for all of it."

"All of what?"

Libby didn't answer because any explanation would involve mentioning Dylan's name.

"I'm sure he'll calm down tomorrow," Simon said when Libby hadn't replied. "No one can stay mad at you, Libs."

"He said he never wanted to see me again." Her voice wobbled, and she took a deep breath.

"Oh, I'm so sorry. You don't deserve this."

His tone was so gentle, and before Libby realized what was happening, her tears had started to flow. This time she didn't fight them, and for several minutes, she allowed herself to sob in the dark. She cried for Frank, who would now have to move into a care home, and for Dylan, who could be out there in the city right now hurt or worse. And she cried for herself: alone, pregnant, and scared.

The whole time she cried, Simon whispered softly into her ear. "It's going to be okay . . . Everything's going to be all right."

"I'm sorry," Libby hiccupped when the tears had finally stopped. She felt utterly exhausted, and she allowed her eyes to drift closed.

"Don't apologize. I'm so glad I could be here for you tonight."

"Thank you."

"I want to be here for you when the baby arrives too, Libs."

"Not now, Simon, please. I really need some sleep."

"Let me help look after you, Libby. You need someone to support you."

"Good night, Simon."

Libby moved the phone away from her ear to end the call. As she did, the last words she heard were "You don't have to do this on your own."

41

ibby was woken by the sound of her phone ringing. She was about to roll over and ignore it when she remembered Dylan and sat up with a start, scrambling blindly for her phone on the bedside table.

"Dylan?"

"It's Esme."

"Any news on him?"

"I've found him," Esme said.

"Oh, thank god! Where is he?"

"He's in UCH hospital."

Libby felt the blood draining from her face. "Is he okay?"

"I knew he wouldn't disappear, Libby. So I made Mum help me ring all the hospitals."

"What's happened to him?"

"I don't know; they wouldn't say."

"Can we visit him?"

"Yes. I have an appointment this morning, but you can go now."

Libby wasn't sure she'd ever got dressed and left the house so fast. Rebecca was down in the kitchen with Hector, and Libby ignored her sister's questions as she sprinted out the front door. The 134 bus took her directly to the hospital, and she spent the whole journey chewing her fingernails and willing the bus to hurry in the early-morning traffic. When it finally reached the hospital, she dashed into the large glass-fronted atrium and was given directions to Dylan's ward by a man on reception.

It took Libby a while to find the ward, and when she reached it, a nurse pointed her in the direction of Dylan's bay. There were eight beds, four on each side, and Libby walked cautiously along to Dylan's at the end, steeling herself for what she was about to see.

At first she thought there'd been a mistake. The man lying there had no distinctive hairstyle or ear piercings, only a white bandage that was wrapped tightly around his skull. He had a huge bruise around his right eye so dark it looked like some horrible Halloween makeup, and the side of his face was red and puffy. As Libby stepped closer, she saw a tube running out of his nose and a drip connected to his right hand. It was only the tattoos snaking up his arm that let her know it really was Dylan.

For a moment, Libby had a strong urge to throw her arms around his poor broken body, but instead she sank down into the plastic chair next to the bed.

"Oh, Dylan," she muttered.

"Looks pretty rough, doesn't he?" a croaky voice said, and Libby spun round to see an elderly man in the adjacent bed. He was sitting up against his pillow, eating from a large bunch of grapes. "He's been like that since they moved him up here yesterday morning. I think they must have him sedated or something."

"Do you know what happened to him?" Libby asked.

"From what I can gather, he was in a fight. Sounds like it was pretty nasty and he had to have some kind of operation, hence all the bandages."

Libby turned back to look at Dylan. His left arm was resting on top of the sheet, and she reached out and took his hand between her own. "Is he going to be okay?"

"Dunno. They won't tell me anything. I only knows this much because I eavesdropped."

Libby stroked the back of Dylan's hand. His skin was warm and surprisingly smooth, and she remembered the feel of it on her face. How had that been less than four days ago?

"If you ask one of the nurses, they might tell you more," the man said. "Are you family?"

"No, I'm just a friend."

"You should ask his girlfriend, then; she'll be able to tell you more."

Libby swung round. The man was studying the bunch of grapes on his lap.

"Has she been here?"

"Yeah, yesterday." He found a suitable grape and popped it in his mouth with satisfaction. "That's when I heard her telling the nurses what happened. It sounds like she was there at the fight, poor love."

Libby released Dylan's hand and sank back in her seat.

"I tried to chat with her too, but she wasn't interested. She was a funny-looking thing, black makeup and hair all over the place. I never understand why some young people do that to themselves."

So Dylan's dad had been right. Libby felt a strange lurching feeling, like vertigo, and she closed her eyes.

"She's the one who gave him those flowers," the man was

saying, but Libby turned away. She didn't want to hear any more.

"He's not botherin' you, is he, darlin'?" came a thick Scottish accent, and when Libby opened her eyes, a middle-aged nurse was approaching Dylan's bed, her Crocs squeaking on the linoleum floor. "I hope you're not disturbing this young lady, Sam?"

"Of course not, sister. We've been having a lovely chat."

"Even so, let's give her some privacy. I need to change your dressing anyway." The nurse winked at Libby and began to pull a curtain around Dylan's bed.

"Can he hear me?" Libby asked her.

"Probably not, but yous can chat to him anyway; there's no harm."

The nurse moved away and Libby could hear her busying herself with the old man in the next bed. She looked at Dylan lying in front of her, the bandaged head and the tube running out of his nose. Without his Mohawk and piercings, he looked so different, younger and more vulnerable.

"Dylan, what happened?" she said in a whisper. "You told me you always run away from fights."

He was so still she couldn't even see his chest moving. The only signal that he was alive was the steady beep of the monitor next to the bed.

"I've been so worried about you. And Frank . . ." She stopped; Frank's troubles were the last thing Dylan needed to hear about right now. "Frank misses you too" was all she said.

Libby faltered, feeling self-conscious talking to someone who couldn't hear her. On the other side of the curtain, she could make out the soft chatter of the nurse as she changed the old man's dressing, but her words were indecipherable.

"Esme sends her love; she'll come to visit you later. She was the one who found you here. I went looking for you, at your flat . . ."

Libby took a deep breath.

"Why didn't you tell me you had a girlfriend, Dylan? Your dad told me and I didn't want to believe him, but then I heard she was here . . ."

Libby trailed off and it was a while before she spoke again.

"Simon's asked me to move back in with him."

She studied Dylan's face, looking for any twitch or movement, but he remained motionless. She looked down at his hand resting on the edge of the bed.

"I know if you were awake you'd probably tell me to run a mile. But I'm scared, Dylan, scared to do this all alone. I thought I was strong enough after everything that's happened, but now I'm not so sure."

Out of the corner of her eye, Libby saw something move and she snapped her head up. But it was only the curtain blowing in a breeze as the nurse walked away.

"I think I'm going to say yes to Simon. It's what's best for the baby, so it can grow up with its biological father. And I think it might be what's best for me too."

Libby stopped, half hoping that Dylan might suddenly sit up and tell her she was making a terrible mistake, but he didn't move. She reached out and touched the bandage on his head, running her hand along where his Mohawk once sat.

"I wish it hadn't ended up like this, Dylan. I wish things could have turned out differently."

From inside her bag, Libby heard a buzzing sound, and she reached down and pulled out her phone. Simon's name was flashing on the screen. She stared at it for a moment, then slipped it back into her bag.

"I have to go. I need to speak to Simon."

Libby stood up but didn't walk away immediately. She looked down at Dylan, at his peaceful, handsome face. Then she leaned forward and placed a gentle kiss on his lips.

"Good-bye, Dylan. I love you."

The words slipped out of Libby's mouth before she realized what she was saying. Tears stinging her eyes, she turned and hurried out of the ward.

42

Three Months Later

Libby let herself out of the house and walked up the road toward the bus stop. There was a chill this morning, her breath visible in the autumn air, and she pulled her coat around her body as best she could. She'd not bothered to buy a proper maternity coat, thinking it was a waste of money, but at thirty-four weeks pregnant, she was beginning to regret not having anything that would cover her ever-expanding bump.

It was only a ten-minute bus ride to the library, where she and Simon were attending an NCT course today. It had been his suggestion that they go, as a way for Libby to make "mum friends," as Simon had put it. And it was true that she hadn't done much socializing since she'd moved back to Surrey; with everything she needed to do to get ready for the baby's arrival, she'd not had much spare time.

As Libby approached the library, she heard her phone ringing.

"Si, I'm just arriving," she said as she answered.

"Libs, I'm so sorry but I'm not there yet. I'm still at the

rugby club. The bloody car has broken down in the car park and I've got to wait for the RAC to come."

"What's wrong with it?"

"I don't know; the engine won't start. I'm so sorry; will you be okay going on your own?"

Libby stifled a sigh. "Sure, I'll be fine."

She hung up and headed into the library, where a librarian pointed her toward a meeting room at the back. When she got to the door, Libby glanced in. There were five couples, all sitting in chairs arranged in a semicircle, facing a middle-aged woman wearing a cheesecloth top and floral boots. The woman was holding a plastic model baby and what looked like a knitted breast. There were two empty chairs in the semicircle.

"Ah, you must be Libby," the cheesecloth woman said when she spotted her. "Come on in. We've left spaces for you and Simon."

Libby faltered at the door.

"Don't be shy; we won't bite."

The five couples were all staring at her, and Libby could see some of them looking behind her for her partner. Did she really want to go through this today, discussing placentas and cracked nipples with a bunch of strangers all pitying her for being there alone? Surely, there were better things she could be doing with her time.

"I'm sorry; something's come up," Libby said, and she turned and fled.

As she walked away from the library, Libby congratulated herself on her decision. Now she could go to Sainsbury's to do some food shopping, and then she could spend the afternoon washing, labeling, and putting away the baby clothes that her sister had given her. Rebecca had recently discovered she was having a girl and had immediately announced that all the clothes she'd used for Hector were no longer suitable. Libby had happily agreed to take Hector's old baby clothes and had been surprised when her sister had volunteered to drive down and drop them off last weekend. They still weren't exactly close, but Rebecca had been uncharacteristically supportive over the past few months. Libby had also reached a tentative peace with her parents, who were delighted she was back in Surrey and were clearly making an effort to support her rather than control her. Although, true to form, her mum hadn't been able to stop herself from making the odd critical remark about Libby's choice of pram, cot, and even nappy brand.

As Libby was walking past the train station, she heard an announcement drift over the wall.

"The next train is the ten thirteen service to London Waterloo."

Libby paused. If she hurried, she might have time to buy a ticket and catch the train to London, her last chance for a day in the city before the baby was born. Or she could stick to the plan, go to Sainsbury's, and prepare for the baby's arrival.

An hour later, Libby emerged into the bustle of Vauxhall Bus Station. It was almost six months to the day since she'd last been here, carrying two hastily packed rucksacks, her life in tatters. Libby could remember getting lost trying to find the right stop for the 88, and then being tutted at by passengers as she struggled to pay for her bus journey. Now she strode toward stop E, boarded the waiting bus, and paid with a touch of her card.

Libby moved instinctively toward the stairs to the upper deck, then stopped. That was where she and Frank had always sat together, but she hadn't heard from him since the horrible day of their fight, back in July. She'd initially given him space like he'd wanted and because she'd been so busy with everything going on in her own life. When she'd finally plucked up the courage to call him, about a month later, his phone had rung and rung and eventually cut off. Libby had tried calling several times since, but the same thing always happened, and she'd come to the reluctant conclusion that Frank didn't want to hear from her. With a small sigh, Libby moved away from the stairs. The lower deck was busy, and despite her heavily pregnant state, no one offered her a seat as she moved down the aisle.

The bus pulled off and Libby looked out the window, taking in the view as they drove up toward Vauxhall Bridge. She remembered how strange and overwhelming this had felt when she first arrived in London, an unfamiliar city with its traffic and tourists and constant buzz of movement. Now she realized how much she'd grown used to it over her short stay in the city and how much she'd missed it since moving back to Surrey.

"Oi, are you blind?"

A loud voice to Libby's left caused her to look round. An elderly lady wearing a transparent plastic rain hood was glaring at the teenage boy in the seat next to her.

"Can't you see that girl's pregnant? Or were you pretending you hadn't noticed so you wouldn't have to give up your seat?"

The teenager looked between the old woman and Libby in confusion.

"It's fine. I'm quite happy standing," Libby said.

"That's not the point," the woman barked. "In my day,

young men were taught to give up their seats for women, especially those in your condition. Come on, lad, move it."

She gave the boy a sharp jab in the ribs with her elbow. For a moment Libby thought he was going to shout at the old woman, but she was giving him such a steely look that he obviously thought better of it, and with a grunt he stood up and slouched away.

"Well, come on, then, sit down."

Libby really had been happy to stand, but there was no way she could disobey this formidable woman, so she lowered herself into the vacant seat next to her.

"That's quite a bump you got there. You expecting triplets?" the woman said, nodding at Libby's tummy.

"Just the one."

"Blimey. When you due?"

"Tenth December."

"Good luck with that. It's going to be a whopper by then."

Libby was used to this by now, complete strangers approaching her to talk about her pregnancy. A few weeks ago, she'd been in Boots when a stranger had walked up to her, put both hands on her stomach without asking permission, and pronounced it was going to be a boy.

"This your first?" the woman on the bus asked, and when Libby nodded, she sucked her teeth. "I remember when my son was born. The labor took three days and the doctors said it nearly killed me."

"Wow, I'm sorry to hear that."

"I was fine, love. I'm as tough as old boots. And you should be all right too, with those big hips of yours."

Libby wasn't sure if that was a compliment or an insult, so she nodded and then turned the other way to look out of the opposite window. The bus was on John Islip Street, making its way up toward Chelsea College of Art and Design. She remembered putting up posters around here with Dylan; it had been a wet day and they'd gone to a café for a cup of coffee while they waited for the rain to pass. She'd not heard from Dylan since that day she'd visited him in the hospital, and the memory of him made her chest ache. Libby suddenly wished she'd taken the underground today, rather than the bus with all its painful memories.

She felt a sharp tap on her arm and turned back to the woman sitting next to her.

"The thing I always say to people is: realize you're not in control."

"I beg your pardon?"

"You youngsters these days are so used to planning and controlling everything, and you approach giving birth in the same way, with your books and birth plans and all that malarkey. It's nonsense."

"I do like to plan things," Libby said with a small smile.

"Well, you can forget all that right now. A baby's gonna come the way a baby wants to come, and there's not much you can do besides lie back and let Mother Nature do her work."

Libby looked at the woman. "Do you know what? I was meant to be at an NCT course today, but I think you've summed up in one minute everything I need to know about having a baby."

Her companion chuckled. "Well, I'm no NCT expert, whatever the hell that is. But anything you want to know about birth and babies, you just ask."

"All right, then." Libby thought for a moment. "Is the pain really as bad as people say?"

"Worse. That's why you've got to take all the drugs they offer you. Next?"

"How did you cope with all the sleepless nights? I'm really bad when I'm tired. I can't function properly."

"You got to sleep when the baby sleeps. But having a baby also gives you all these strange hormones, which means you can survive on hardly any sleep. Next?"

"How do you know when labor's starting? I keep getting these little twinges every now and then, Braxton-Hicks contractions, they call them, but how do you know when it's the real thing?"

The woman gave a wry laugh. "Oh, you'll know all right, love. A woman has a sense when the baby's about to arrive; it's instinctive. When your time comes, you'll know it's for real."

"Thank you. That's been genuinely helpful."

"You're welcome."

They rode on, and Libby watched the familiar sights of the 88 bus route fly past the window. The Home Office, where Dylan had gone off on a rant about the British government and Libby had got the giggles. Parliament Square, where they'd been accosted by tourists wanting to take Dylan's photo. Horse Guards, where Libby had stopped for ages to watch the soldiers on their beautiful horses. It was hard to believe that had been only a few months ago; it felt like another lifetime.

As the bus approached Trafalgar Square, Libby leaned down to try to pick her bag up from the floor, but she couldn't reach past her bump.

"Here, let me," the woman next to her said.

"Thank you."

"You getting off here?"

"Yes, I'm going to the National Gallery."

"Oh, you like that place, do you?"

"I've only been once. I thought I might visit today, though, my last chance for a while."

"I've not been for years," the woman said. "I used to go all the time before I had my son. I could spend days wandering round."

"You sound like a friend of mine," Libby said as she reached forward to ring the bell.

"There was this painting I used to love. I can't remember its name now. That's a sure sign I'm getting old, isn't it?"

"Trafalgar Square," the bus announcement declared, and passengers began to move toward the doors.

"Well, thanks for all the baby advice," Libby said, standing up.

"Good luck with it all, love. And remember, you can't control your birth, so don't even try."

"I won't! Bye."

Libby joined the passengers waiting to disembark. There was a woman with bags of shopping up ahead struggling to carry them all off the bus, and a queue was building up around her.

Bacchus and Ariadne," Libby heard muttered behind her. "How could I forget that?"

The shopper finally managed to get off, and Libby was caught up in the flow of passengers toward the bus door. As she disembarked, she was hit by a blast of cold wind from Trafalgar Square, and she pulled her collar up. The lights on the pedestrian crossing had turned green, and Libby stepped out into the road. It was almost twelve thirty now, so she had plenty of time to wander round the gallery, maybe even treat herself to lunch in the café. What should she go and see first?

Frank had said the Renaissance rooms were his favorite, so maybe she should start there.

Libby reached the other side of the crossing and stepped up on the pavement, then stopped as something in her brain clicked. *Bacchus and Ariadne.* Why was that name ringing a bell? She'd heard it before; someone had told her about the painting.

Frank had told her about the painting.

Libby spun back round. The pedestrian lights had turned red and the traffic had started to move again. At the other side of the road, she could see the 88 bus driving past, and Libby caught a flash of the old woman. She lifted her arm and waved at the bus.

"Wait!" she shouted, but her voice got lost in the hubbub of Trafalgar Square.

Libby watched the bus crawl on toward Pall Mall. The traffic was heavy and the bus was moving slowly, but Libby could hardly rush through the vehicles and bang on the window. She knew from her excursions with Dylan that the 88 would turn right onto Waterloo Place and then stop by Charles II Street. If she ran, could she get there in time? Libby looked down at her stomach, so swollen she couldn't see her own feet. Then she looked back up at the departing bus, took a deep breath, and started to run.

43

It was almost two by the time Libby arrived at Frank's house, out of breath after her hurried walk from the bus stop. She rang the bell, praying he would answer. As she waited, she felt a sharp kick from the baby. It usually fell asleep when she was walking, but clearly Libby's excitement was contagious, and the little one was as nervous as she was. Perhaps Frank was out on the 88? Or maybe he'd moved already? Libby stepped forward and rang again. She waited for a minute, her foot tapping on the path, before her heart started to sink. Even with his slow shuffle, Frank would have answered the door by now if he was at home. Damn.

Libby reached into her bag for a piece of paper to scribble down a note asking Frank to call her back if he got it. As she went to post it through the letter box, she caught a glimpse inside through a pane of glass in the door.

The hall was empty. No coats on the rack, no furniture or rug as there had been last time she was here. Libby stepped off the path into the front garden and crossed to the window. There was an old net curtain pulled across it, but she could see through it well enough to make out the living room on the other side. Everything was gone: the stuffed bear, the suit of armor, the throne.

Frank had moved, and Libby had no idea where he'd gone. What was more, she had no way of contacting him, given his mobile phone always rang out. Her shoulders heavy, she turned and began to walk down the pavement, away from the house. But Libby had not made it more than ten steps when she heard a noise behind her and spun around.

"Frank!"

He looked older than Libby remembered, his face gaunt and his shoulders stooped. She hurried back to him.

"Frank, it's me, Libby."

"Libby?" His forehead wrinkled, and he lifted a hand to rub his chin. "I don't know a Libby."

"We met on the 88."

"The what?"

Libby opened her mouth to answer, but then Frank looked at her, a twinkle in his eye. "Hello, trouble!"

"Frank! Jeez, you had me there." Libby stepped forward and gave him a tight hug.

"The look on your face," he said, laughing as he hugged her back. "I'm not completely doolally. At least not yet."

"I thought you'd gone already. Your house . . ." Her voice trailed off.

"You've caught me just in time. I'm moving today."

"Where?"

"Willow Court, the place is called; Clara chose it for me. Apparently they have bingo every Monday and movie night on a Friday. Lucky me." His voice was thick with sarcasm.

"I'm so sorry, Frank."

"Oh, well, it had to happen eventually. I've been lucky it

was full, so I got an extra few months here. But some poor sod must have popped their clogs, because a room became free."

"Are you going now?"

"In a bit. Clara's there at the moment, moving my stuff in. I asked for some time on my own in the house to say good-bye."

Libby checked the time on her phone. "Frank, I know this might sound strange, but how would you feel about a quick walk up Parliament Hill?"

"What, now?"

"Yes. There's someone I'd like you to meet."

"I don't know . . ." He stared at her for a moment. "Oh, go on, then. There's no point in me moping round this empty place any longer. Let me leave a note for Clara and we'll go."

THEY'D been walking for twenty minutes when Libby realized the mistake she'd made. She'd underestimated how far it was from Frank's to the top of the hill and how slow their progress would be. Frank's footsteps were small and shuffling, and every couple of hundred meters, he had to stop for a rest.

"Frank, maybe we should head home now? Clara must be coming to get you soon," Libby said as she saw the final, steepest part of the ascent ahead of them.

"It's fine; she can wait."

"We could come back another time, with a wheelchair?"

Frank scoffed. "I've been climbing this hill for fifty-odd years. Anyway, didn't you say you wanted me to meet someone?"

"Yes, but we can rearrange for another day."

"Nonsense. We're almost there now."

He pushed on forward, but Libby could tell how much the climb was taking out of him. Several times his feet stumbled,

and Libby had to grab his arm to steady him. Sweat was forming on his brow, but his mouth was pursed in determination.

"Frank—"

"I can do it," he said through gritted teeth. "I don't know if
I'll ever get to walk up here again, Libby. Please, let me do it
this one last time."

CHAPTER

44

PEGGY

From my spot at the top of the hill, I can see the pair of them coming. The man, who must be Frank, has wild hair all over the place and he's leaning on Libby's arm, his face bright red. Jesus, it would be just my luck if he croaked it on the way to meet me, wouldn't it?

It takes him bloody ages, and by the time he gets to me, he collapses on the bench, huffing and puffing. Libby sits down on the other side of him, and I can tell she's worried he's about to cark it too. But eventually he catches his breath, and then he turns to look at me.

I see him taking me in: the silver hair, the old-lady clothes, my shopper, and I can tell he's disappointed. Well, what the hell did he expect, Doris bloody Day? He's hardly an oil painting himself. And then he holds out his hand to me, and I can see it's shaking and I recognize it straightaway. Well, I would, wouldn't I, love, after everything we've been through?

"Hello," he says to me. "I'm Frank Weiss."

So I say hello back, and tell him my name.

"Peggy," he says, rolling the word round his mouth like he's testing to see what it tastes like.

And then he doesn't say anything, just sits staring into the distance, like he's drifted off somewhere else entirely. So I don't say anything either. I just look out too, take in this view I know so well. My beautiful London.

You know, I still have one of the first sketches I did up here, back in the days when I was still drawing. It's of this very view, although you'd hardly recognize it now. That was back when St. Paul's Cathedral was still one of the tallest buildings in the city, can you believe? Now the poor thing's dwarfed by the Shard and the Gherkin and all those other fancy skyscrapers they've built. Not that I mind. You know me, love. I've never been one to care about things changing. And this city of ours is the best kind of shape-shifter.

There's a cough to my left, and I turn back to see Frank looking at me. His face is a normal color now, thank god.

"Do you come here often?" he asks, and I almost laugh 'cos it's like a cheesy line from one of those American films you and I used to watch together.

So I tell him yes, yes, I do. I come here every week.

"And how do you know Libby?" he says, and that's when I realize that she hasn't told him yet. And I look at her and she nods, like she's saying she wants me to be the one to tell him.

"We just met, on the 88," I say. "Libby told me about your search."

And I see his eyes go wide then, like the penny's dropped, and he looks at me but he doesn't say anything, and I start to panic again that he's gonna have a heart attack right here on our bench.

"Are you . . ." he says, and his voice is all quavery, like his hands. "Are you my girl on the bus?"

Let me tell you, when Libby told me about him earlier, this old man and his sixty-year search . . . well, I didn't quite believe it, to be truthful. What kind of person spends sixty years looking for someone they met once? I thought he must be off his rocker. But now I look at him and I can see it in his eyes, see the answer to that very question.

Hope.

That's what's been driving him, why he hasn't been able to give up. His search has given him hope, and now he's terrified I'm going to crush it. So I take a deep breath before I answer.

"No."

I see him blink.

"I'm not your girl on the bus."

His eyes flicker then, like a candle that's been caught in a draft.

"But I think I know who she was," I say before the candle goes out altogether.

"Are you sure?" he says.

I can't help chuckling at this. When Libby described her to me earlier, an art student with bright red hair and a beret who liked to draw people on London buses . . . well, there can't have been that many of them around in the early sixties, can there? Especially not ones who had a thing for that *Bacchus and Ariadne* painting. So I nod at him and tell him I'm sure.

Frank's staring at his hands, clasped in his lap like he's trying to stop them shaking.

"What's her name?" he says, his voice so quiet I can hardly hear him.

"Persephone Fitzgerald." It feels funny, saying that name out loud after all these years.

"Persephone." He gives a little smile, a small shake of his head, and then he looks at me. "Will you tell me about her?"

And I smile too, because you know me: there's nothing I love more than a good story. So I sit back on the bench, and I tell him all about you.

I tell him how we met, back on our first day at art school. I tell him how everyone else spoke all la-di-da and walked around like they owned the bloody place, and then there was you standing in the corner looking like a beautiful Victorian waif and swearing like a trooper. I remember we caught each other's eyes, and it was like looking in a mirror: we both recognized, without saying a word, how hard we'd had to fight to be there, the sacrifices we'd both made that those other kids would never understand. And then you grinned at me and strolled across the room, your eyes never leaving mine.

"I'm Percy," you said, and you must have seen me screw up my nose, 'cos you said, "My real name's Persephone but that's a bore."

I tell him how we got a room together, down in Clapham, in a house full of girls trying to make their way in the city. How we were inseparable: Percy and Peggy, Peggy and Percy. How you opened my eyes to London, took me to dodgy little drinking dens in Soho where we were the only girls in the place, taught me to smoke and play poker. And the art galleries, of course. I'd never been to the National Gallery, and you took me that first Saturday and made me sit for an hour in front of one painting. I thought you were barking, but by god, you taught me more about art than any of those stuffy old men at college.

And then, I have to confess, I detour a little bit to tell him what happened to me. Well, you can't blame me, can you?

I explain how I met Arthur—handsome, charming, dangerous Arthur—and how naive I was when he told me we were safe; he was taking care of things. And then how, a few months later, you held me as I sobbed in the loo with the realization of what had happened. How you were with me when I told my parents, who were so furious they made me and Arthur get married, even though we didn't love each other. How I had to drop out of art school in our final year and move into that little flat in Clapham Junction and how Arthur had started cheating on me even before David was born.

I can see the girl, Libby, is watching me the whole time I tell them this, biting her lip as she strokes her big pregnant bump. So I stop then, because it's not my story they're interested in, after all. It's yours.

I tell them how you graduated top of our class but stayed in London to help me when David was born, sleeping on the floor next to my bed when Arthur was out drinking all night, barricading the bedroom door when he got home. How you wanted me to leave him and us to get a flat together, you working to support me and the baby. I still wonder sometimes what would have happened if I'd said yes, how differently things might have turned out for both of us. But I didn't, did I? Too scared of that bloody man and his fists. Besides, I didn't want to hold you back, love. You were never meant to be tied down.

Then I tell them about the postcards you sent: first from Rome, when you studied there, then from Paris, and finally from New York. I still have them all at home in a box, the weekly cards with your spidery scrawl on the back. I remember standing at the sink in my tiny kitchen, reading in wonder these unfamiliar words: Andy Warhol and the Factory and someone called Edie Sedgwick. And Frank nods at this, his face bright, and I can see that these names mean more to him than they ever did to me.

"So she really did become an artist, like she said she would?" he asks, and I tell him too bloody right; you set the New York scene alight. And he grins, his eyes shining, and I almost want to stop the story here, leave him at the part where everything is so promising and bright. But then he asks me to go on, and I know I have to finish your story. For years I've been waiting to tell it, Percy. I can't stop now.

So I tell him how the postcards started to slow down sometime in the mid-seventies. At first they'd be a few days late, then a week or so, and eventually I was only getting them sporadically. I still wrote to you every week, like a worried mother hen, but I wasn't even sure I had the right address anymore. *I'm fine, I've just been busy,* you'd write, when a card finally came. *I've had the flu but I'm on the mend.* I didn't believe you for one second, love; you've always been a terrible liar. But still, nothing prepared me for that day you rang my doorbell.

Do you remember how I opened the door and couldn't speak, I was so shocked? I'd never seen a person look so near to death: even with you wrapped up in all those coats, I could see how skinny you were, and you had those dark circles round your eyes. And your hair! My god, that beautiful red hair had almost all gone.

And then came the dark days of your withdrawal. The days when you moaned and cried for hours on end, unable to sleep or eat but refusing to see a doctor. The days when you scratched your skin till it bled, and I had to lie there and hold your hands to make you stop. David would peer in through the door and watch, fascinated, like you were some kind of wild animal. And then, just when we'd got through the worst of it, when you could eat a bowl of soup without being sick, you told me.

I'm pregnant, Pegs.

"What?" Libby says, and the surprise in her voice reminds me of exactly how I felt back then. I mean, you'd been at death's door a moment ago; how could you possibly be pregnant? But you were so sure. And when you finally let me take you to see a doctor, he confirmed it was true. Somehow, through it all, you'd carried a baby.

Do you remember those months that followed, how excited we were? You got that little flat round the corner, and together we painted a mural on the nursery walls. Well, I say "together," but you did all the artistic bits. I just stood there and watched. You had color back in your cheeks and you were full of energy, although you were still far too skinny. You used to sing all the time, Bob Dylan and Nina Simone, and you were always dancing. You were so happy, my love. So happy.

I stop then, for the first time not sure whether I should go on. Libby's watching me, a blissful look on her face 'cos she knows that feeling, that excited bubble when you're about to meet your baby for the first time. But it's not just her that's bothering me. For some reason, I'm suddenly worrying whether you'd want me to tell this part of the story. These are two complete strangers, after all. Would you want them to know?

And then I look up, out over Parliament Hill, and do you know what I see?

A kite. A red-and-white kite dancing in the air above us.

And I know then. I know you want me to tell the story. To say his name.

Jack.

I tell them how perfect he was, tiny but utterly perfect. How the midwives wouldn't look at you properly, but you never noticed because you only had eyes for your son. I tell them about the six days and nights you sat with him in hospital, even when the doctor told you there was nothing you could do and you should go home. How you dressed him in the hat and clothes I'd knitted for him, all far too big, and sang him Bob Dylan and Nina Simone. And as I'm talking, I can see tears in Libby's eyes, and Frank reaches across and squeezes her hand. But she looks at me and nods, and I know she wants me to go on.

So I do. I tell them how we brought his ashes up here, you clutching the tiny box to your chest. How you said you wanted Jack to play here forever, with the kites, London at his feet. And how, when you opened the box, there was a gust of wind and you howled, a sound I've never heard a human make, before or since.

And then I tell them how we returned to the flat in Clapham Junction, how the days turned to weeks and then months, and somehow life went on. How, with your support, I finally mustered the courage to kick that piece-of-shit husband of mine out, and you moved into the flat and took his place, hanging your paintings alongside mine on the walls. How you got a job as an art teacher at a local school, a job you loved and did for the next thirty years. How you became a second mother to David, the support you gave me when he went through his difficult years, how we celebrated the birth of my granddaughter, Maisie, together. And how you would come up here every week, without fail, to sit on this bench and talk to Jack.

And Frank, who's barely said a word since the start of the story, turns to me then, his mouth open.

"She came here every week?" he says, and I tell him yes, sometimes more than once a week.

And he shakes his head as if he can't believe me. "I come here as well, have done for decades. This is the bench I always sit on."

His eyes are wet now, and I think he might start crying. But then he starts giggling.

"Isn't that something?" he says. "All this time I've spent looking for her on the bus, and all along she was sitting up here, right under my nose."

And Libby starts to laugh then too, and I join in, and before I know it, we're all cackling, tears running down our cheeks. What a sight we must look! And I don't even know why we're laughing, to be honest, but it feels good. After everything that's happened, by god, it feels good.

When we finally stop, I tell them the end of the story. How we noticed you getting forgetful first, an item missed off the shopping list or a misplaced mobile phone. How you refused to see a doctor for ages until I frog-marched you to the GP. How you never let the Alzheimer's diagnosis define you. I tell them that you eventually had to give up teaching at the school, which broke your heart, but how you volunteered to run art classes at the local old people's home. How you swore you'd make it to Maisie's wedding, and you did, wearing a bright purple dress and dancing with all the young men under the giant glitter ball.

How you died a few days later, twelve years ago this month, with me holding your hand.

How I brought your ashes up here and released you into the sky, to fly with Jack and the kites.

And then I've reached the end of your story . . . our story . . . and I stop talking.

CHAPTER

45

The three of them sat in silence, staring out over the view. It had been busy up here when they'd arrived, walkers and dogs and a young child flying a kite, but now the sun had set and it had quietened down.

Libby's mind was spinning with Percy's story. What an extraordinary life the woman had lived, so uncompromising and brave. And how tragic too. Libby had found the part of the story about Jack unbearably sad, and Frank must have sensed it, because he'd held her hand throughout. Yet Libby hadn't wanted to stop Peggy because the woman was so caught up in the story, reliving it moment by moment. Libby glanced at her now and saw she'd closed her eyes, a small smile on her face.

Between them, Frank was motionless too, his eyes fixed on the view in front of them. Libby could see how tired he was, and she put her hand on his arm.

"We should probably be getting you back, Frank."

"Of course."

She watched him take a deep breath before he turned to Peggy.

"Thank you so much for sharing Percy's story," he said. "She led quite a life."

Peggy opened her eyes. "She did indeed."

"Can I ask you one more question before I go?"

"'Course."

"Did she ever . . ." Frank paused, and Libby could see him searching for the right words. "I've thought so much about her over the years. And I can't help wondering if she ever remembered me once she'd got off the bus that day."

He was looking at Peggy with such intensity that Libby found she was holding her breath. Please, Peggy, tell him she did. Even if it's a lie.

Peggy leaned back against the bench. "I'm not gonna lie to you, Frank. She didn't spend the past sixty years searching for you on the 88, if that's what you mean."

"No, of course. But did she ever mention me, back at the time?"

"She never told me about meeting you on the bus, no."

Frank let out a small sigh, his shoulders sagging.

"But let me tell you one more story before you go," Peggy said. "I can remember this quite clearly, because of what happened to me.

"It must have been spring of 1962, 'cos we were in the summer term of our second year at art college. This was after I'd started seeing Arthur, and it must have been a Sunday, 'cos he'd taken me to the flicks. I can't remember what we went to see, I'm afraid. But I do remember that I was wearing a new blue dress I'd made myself, using this lovely fabric I'd got from Petticoat Lane Market, and I'd had to let the waistline out 'cos I'd put on a bit of weight since I started making it."

Libby bit her tongue. Peggy was a wonderful storyteller, but as they'd discovered over the past two hours, she did have something of a tendency to disappear off on a tangent. Earlier, she'd spent a good fifteen minutes telling them all about her son, David, which, while interesting, had had nothing whatsoever to do with Percy's story. Now it seemed as though Peggy might be about to go off on another one.

"The reason I remember this day so clearly is because halfway through the film, I was violently sick all over the back row of the Clapham Grand. Arthur was furious, 'cos I got some on his new shoes, and we ended up having a big fight and him disappearing off and leaving me to get home on my own."

She tutted and shook her head as if annoyed at young Peggy for putting up with such behavior.

"I remember getting back to the house, all upset about the fight, and waiting for Percy to come back. I knew she'd been meeting some lad that morning, but by three o'clock, she still wasn't home. I was sick another two or three times in our shared bathroom, all the other girls moaning at me to get out, when finally, around five o'clock, Percy gets back.

"Well, she takes one look at me, and she just knows. I mean, I told you we were thick as thieves, and she looks at me and goes, 'Oh, no, Peg, you're pregnant, aren't you?' At which point I burst into tears, 'cos I'd been fearing as much myself, what with the weight gain and the sickness. And Percy gets down on the floor next to me and wraps me in her arms, and she holds me while I sob, whispering that it's going to be all right, she'll look after me."

Peggy was quiet for a moment, her eyes damp. Libby remembered her own pregnancy discovery, the day she and Frank had gone to the National Gallery. How she'd gone home alone, scared and overwhelmed, without a friend like Percy to hug her and reassure her. The memory made goose bumps prickle on Libby's arm.

"I'm sorry," Peggy said. "It's strange to do all this remembering. It brings up . . . well, it brings up lots of feelings, doesn't it?"

"I understand," Frank said, nodding.

Peggy wiped the back of her hand across her eyes before she continued.

"The reason I'm telling you all this is that later, once Percy had tucked me up in bed with a hot Bovril, I said to her it must have been a good date she'd had, seeing as she'd been gone all day. And I remember this so clearly, Frank. She gave a little smile and shook her head and said it was a funny thing, but the lad she was meeting had never turned up. She said they were meant to go to the National Gallery, and she'd been so sure he'd come that she'd sat there all day in front of that bloody *Bacchus and Ariadne* painting, but he never came."

"Oh, no," Frank said, his face turning pale.

"But here's the strange thing. Percy, as you've probably gathered by now, was not the kind of girl who'd sit there waiting for a boy all day. She was fierce and independent and bloody-minded, and boys chased her round seven days a week, but she never usually gave them the time of day. So her saying she'd sat there from ten in the morning till gone four in the afternoon, waiting for some lad to come meet her—well, I'd never heard anything like it. And I said as much, asked her why she'd waited so long. And she said something like 'I don't know, Pegs. I just had a good feeling about this one.' And then she shrugged, picked up her book, and never talked about him again."

Libby watched Frank, waiting for his reaction. His eyes were glazed, and for a horrible moment, Libby wondered if he'd gone into one of his confused states. Eventually he spoke.

"She waited all day." His voice was faint. "She waited for me at the gallery all day, while I waited for her at the bus stop."

Peggy nodded. "I always wondered who the boy was who could make Percy Fitzgerald sit there all day. And now I know."

"I lost her number," Frank said, his voice still quiet. "I was so sure I'd catch her at the bus stop."

"Well, I can't say for sure she'd have even caught the bus that day," Peggy said. "She liked to walk, always did, right up till the end. She may well have set off early and gone up there on foot."

Frank shook his head. "It never occurred to me to go to the gallery. I didn't think."

"No, well, that's the problem with you men, isn't it?" Peggy looked at Libby and raised an eyebrow. "Still, you must have made quite an impression on her, Frank. I've never known Percy to wait for a man, before or since."

Frank didn't say anything. It was almost dark now, and London was lit up in front of them with thousands of twinkling lights. Libby didn't want to tear Frank away, but she knew Clara must have been going crazy with worry.

"Thank you so much for telling us all of this, Peggy," she said.

"Not at all, love. I spend so much time up here on my own, chatting to Percy in my head, it's been lovely to talk about her out loud."

"It's a beautiful spot," Frank said, looking around them. "I've done some of my best thinking up here over the years."

"She loved this place. I like to think she's up here when I come, flying kites with Jack and listening to me blabber on."

Frank looked at Peggy. "Do you think . . . May I?"

"'Course you can, love."

He cleared his throat.

"Hello, Percy."

Frank's voice was loud and clear as he looked out into the darkness.

"I'm Frank Weiss, the boy on the 88 bus. I lost your number, and then I stupidly never thought to come to the gallery. I hope you weren't too cross."

Libby watched him take a deep breath.

"I've been looking for you these past sixty years because I wanted to say thank you. Our conversation that day changed the course of my life. Thanks to you, I had the confidence to stand up to my parents and tell them I wanted to be an actor. I got a place at drama school and went on to have a long and moderately successful career. I don't think any of that would have ever happened if I'd not met you."

Somewhere in the distance, an owl hooted.

"I've often wondered what would have happened if we'd met each other for that date or if I'd found you again on the bus. This may sound silly, but I've always thought that we might have been good together, you and me, that we might have been happy." He paused, running a hand through his hair. "But hearing your story today, Percy, I realize that you didn't need me in your life. You've had someone who has made you far happier than I ever could."

He turned to Peggy. "I'm very glad she had you."

Peggy smiled. "Me too, Frank. We were a good pair, me and her."

A gust of wind blew, and Frank started to pull himself up from the bench. Libby stood up to help him.

"Are you coming too, Peggy?"

"Nah, I'm going to stay here a bit longer, love. I want to say good-bye to Percy before I leave."

"Well, thank you again," Frank said to her. "After all these years, it's good to finally know what happened to my girl on the 88 bus."

"She'll love this, you know," Peggy said. "She'll be out there right now, chuckling away to herself about the daft old bugger who spent sixty years looking for her. She was a romantic at heart, even though she'd never admit it."

"Well, I'm glad I got the chance to make her laugh again," Frank said. "Her and Jack."

He nodded good-bye to Peggy and then turned, leaning heavily on Libby's arm.

"You know, I've always loved the name Jack," he said as they moved away from the bench.

"He was named after Percy's favorite writer," Peggy called from behind them. "I can never remember the man's name. Jack Ker-oo-ic or something like that."

Frank looked at Libby, a smile spreading across his face. "Jack Kerouac. Of course."

46

Two weeks later, Libby caught the train back up to London. She hadn't intended to come up again before the baby was born, but the decision had been made for her by Esme, who'd sent Libby a text message the previous week.

> I visited Frank who told me he saw you.
> My wedding is this Saturday. Johnny is
> excited to meet you. There will be karaoke
> and dancing! E xx

Libby had considered replying saying she was busy and couldn't make it, but she hadn't the heart to let Esme down. Besides, the wedding gave her the perfect excuse to skip the second part of the NCT course, much to Simon's annoyance.

Rather than get off the train at Vauxhall today, Libby disembarked at Clapham Junction instead. From there, she walked ten minutes to a row of flats with neat front gardens and rang on the bell of number twelve.

Peggy answered the door, beaming at her. "It's good to see you again, love. Here, give me your bag and come on in. Frank's already here."

She showed Libby into a small sitting room and then disappeared to make tea. It was a cozy room, with an old floral settee in front of a TV, a sewing bag resting on a table with its contents spilling out. But what was most striking were the framed pictures that hung on every wall. Most of them were paintings, bright slashes of abstract color, like fireworks against the white walls. Frank was standing looking at one of them, dressed in his blue suit, his back to Libby. She walked over to join him, and for a moment he didn't seem to notice her presence.

"They're extraordinary, aren't they?" he said eventually.

"I've never seen anything like them," Libby said, and she meant it.

The painting Frank was studying looked, at first glimpse, like a large splash of green paint. But when she looked closer, Libby saw that there were actually dozens of different shades of green in there, hundreds of small, delicate strokes making up the larger block. The only other color was a small blob of red at the top right of the canvas.

"You're having a gallery tour, I see," Peggy said when she came back in.

"Are they yours?" Frank asked.

Peggy let out a laugh. "No, love. These are Percy's."

Next to her, Libby heard Frank take a sharp breath.

"Quite something, aren't they?" Peggy came over to join them.

"They're absolutely stunning," Frank said. He still hadn't taken his eyes off the painting in front of them.

"This one's called *On Parliament Hill*," Peggy said.

"Is that a kite?" Libby pointed to the small splatter of red.

Peggy nodded. "It's one of my favorites. It's also one of the last Percy ever painted. Her Alzheimer's was pretty bad by this point and some days she could barely get out of bed. But that morning, she picked up a brush and started painting for the first time in months. For those few hours, it was like the old Percy was back."

Libby glanced at Peggy and saw she was looking at the painting, her eyes misty. Then Peggy gave a small cough.

"Come on, let's have a cup of tea before it goes cold, shall we?"

It turned out a cup of tea at Peggy's also involved an elaborate spread of food, including triangular-cut sandwiches, homemade Victoria sponge cake, and a sherry trifle large enough to feed a dozen. While they ate, Frank told them about his new home, Willow Court.

"It smells of boiled cabbages and they make you eat at the most ridiculous times," he grumbled. "And I've already had a stand-up row with the matron because she told me off for changing the TV channel the other night. I said to her, 'Everyone else here is asleep in their chairs. Why can't I watch David Attenborough instead of the stupid soaps?'"

"Oh, I love the soaps," Peggy said. "This place sounds right up my street; maybe I should come live there too."

"Well, it's not all bad, I suppose," Frank said grudgingly. "They do serve rather delicious puddings. And I have to admit, I don't miss all the stairs. Plus, I have been sleeping better since I moved there."

"Maybe they have a better bed?" Libby said.

"It could be that. Or maybe it's something else." Frank looked up at them both. "Maybe it's because I finally know what happened to my girl on the bus?"

Libby couldn't help but exhale in relief. She'd spent the past fortnight worrying that she'd done the wrong thing by taking

Frank to meet Peggy; that the news that his girl on the bus was gone, alongside his move to a new home, might have been too much for him. But as he helped himself to seconds of trifle, she could see that it had had quite the opposite effect.

"Right, we should be heading off," Frank said once he'd finished his third helping. "Thank you for having us, Peggy."

"It was lovely to see you both," Peggy said. "I don't get many visitors these days. My David is very busy, you see."

"I promise I'll be back soon," Frank said. "Next time I'd love to see those postcards of Percy's that you mentioned. And I wouldn't say no to another trifle too!"

"And you must bring the little 'un up when it's born," Peggy said to Libby as she showed them to the front door. "And remember what I said . . ."

"You can't control the birth, so don't even try!" Libby said, and they both laughed.

Libby and Frank walked across Clapham Common and caught the 88 bus from outside the station. Libby had been a little concerned that riding the bus might upset Frank, but she was delighted to see how happy he was to be back on it, greeting the driver and saying hello to other passengers as they made their way north toward the river. Once they'd crossed over the Thames into Pimlico, they got off the bus near Tate Britain and walked up to the church where the wedding was being held.

By the time they arrived, it was almost five o'clock. The sun was starting to set, throwing its autumnal evening light through the huge stained glass window behind the altar. Dozens of candles in glass storm lanterns had been lit along the nave, and the air was filled with the heady scent of jasmine from the floral arrangements. A string quartet were performing music at the back, and a low chatter of voices hung over the church as Libby and Frank found their seats. At the front, a young man in black tie, who Libby assumed must be the groom, Johnny, was waving at guests and high-fiving people as they walked past. Libby looked around the church, seeing if there was anyone she recognized.

"I'm sure he'll be here somewhere," Frank said in her ear.

"Who?"

"Dylan."

"Oh . . . I wasn't looking for him," Libby mumbled.

The string quartet launched into a new piece of music, and a ripple of laughter went round the congregation as they recognized it as "Dancing Queen" by ABBA. The vicar signaled for them all to stand. At the back of the church, the heavy doors creaked open, and everyone turned around to get their first glimpse of the bride.

As soon as Libby saw Esme, tears sprang to her eyes. She was wearing a white fifties-style tea dress, covered in hundreds of tiny crystals so that her whole body sparkled in the light of the candles that clustered around the entrance. She had a lace veil over her face, and through it Libby could see a huge, radiant grin. Esme stopped in the doorway, giggling as she looked behind her, waiting for someone. Libby smiled at Frank next to her; his eyes were damp too. Then she looked back as a tall figure stepped into the church.

It took a second for Libby to realize who she was looking at. Dylan had swapped his usual leather jacket and jeans for a dark suit, although Esme had obviously been in charge of his styling, because the lapels of his suit were also decorated with small crystals, like the ones on her dress. Dylan's hair still hadn't grown back fully since his operation, but he'd managed to style a small Mohawk, the tips of which were dyed orange to match Esme's flowers. His whole face was bursting with pride as he began to walk her down the aisle. Libby watched him as they passed, but Dylan had eyes only for the bride and didn't glance up once.

The service began, and Libby sat back to enjoy it. The vicar was wonderful, making jokes and doing everything she could to put Esme and Johnny at ease. Esme's mum read a passage from *Winnie-the-Pooh*, and some of their friends performed an a cappella version of "Stand by Me," which had the whole congregation in tears. When it came to the first hymn, "Give Me Joy in My Heart," the church was filled with loud, boisterous singing.

Later, as Johnny and Esme were saying their vows, Libby heard a sniff to her left and looked over to see Frank's cheeks glistening.

"Are you all right?" she whispered, and he smiled through the tears.

"I was thinking how beautiful their love is. I wish I'd been so lucky."

"Me too, Frank."

At the front, Esme and Johnny stepped forward to kiss each other, and the whole congregation erupted into cheers of approval. Behind the wedding couple, Libby could see Dylan wolf-whistling with glee. He must have felt Libby watching him, because he glanced over for the first time, catching her eye. For a moment they stared at each other across the church; then Libby looked away.

. . .

AFTER the service, everyone poured out of the church and down the road to a nearby hotel for the reception. When they reached the venue, Libby lost Frank in the excited crush of guests flowing into the room where drinks were being served. Someone handed her a soft drink, and Libby found herself standing with one of Esme's friends, who introduced herself as Laura and squealed with excitement when she saw Libby's heavily pregnant state.

"When's the baby coming?" Laura asked.

"In a month."

"Is it a boy or a girl?"

"I haven't found out; it's going to be a surprise."

"It's a girl," the young woman said confidently. "Have you chosen a name yet?"

"Not yet, no. I'm struggling a bit with that."

"Where's the dad?"

"He's not h—"

"Is that him?"

Libby turned to see where Laura was pointing. Dylan was standing with a group of people across the room, and glanced away when he saw Libby look at him.

"No," she said quickly. "He's not here today."

"Well, that man's been staring at you."

"He has?"

"He's very handsome. Are you married?"

"So, how do you know Esme?" Libby said, keen to change the subject.

"Me and my boyfriend are in a theater group with her. *Ohh*, he's coming over here now."

"Your boyfriend?"

"No, the handsome man!"

"Shit," Libby said. A moment later, she felt Dylan move in beside her.

"Hello!" Laura thrust her hand at him. "I'm Laura."

"Hi, Laura, lovely to meet you," Dylan said, shaking her hand.

"We were just talking about you."

Libby widened her eyes at Laura, who grinned back at her.

"Oh, right," Dylan said, looking awkward. "And how do you know Esme?"

"Laura!" A young man came bounding over and threw his arms round her shoulders. Laura turned to him, leaving Libby and Dylan on their own.

"I thought I should come and say hello," Dylan said, staring at his shoes.

"How are you?"

"All right, thanks. You?"

"Yeah, fine."

Up close, Libby could see a scar running along the edge of Dylan's skull, above his right ear. He must have sensed her staring at it, because he put his hand up to his head and touched it.

"I almost didn't recognize you in the church," she said. "You look so different."

"Yeah, this outfit was Esme's idea. To be honest, I feel like a right knobhead in it."

They must have both remembered Libby's drawing at the same moment, because they looked at each other and smiled. Then Dylan looked away.

"I'm so sorry you ended up in hospital," Libby said. "It must have been awful."

"I don't remember much about it, to be honest. One minute I was walking to the bus stop, and then the next thing I knew, I woke up in hospital three days later."

"Bloody hell," Libby said. "Was it a fight?"

"A fight? No, I was beaten up. Apparently one guy hit the back of my head and knocked me to the ground, and then him and his mate started kicking me. They ran off when they realized I was unconscious."

"Bloody hell. Did the police catch them?"

"Nah. There were witnesses who gave descriptions to the police, but they never found them. Probably some pissed-up kids."

"I'm so sorry, Dylan. Are you okay now?"

"Apart from this scar and my hurt pride, I'm fine. Can I get a top-up, please?" Dylan held his glass out to a waiter who was walking past, and waited for it to be refilled. "So, how's everything with the pregnancy?" he said once the waiter had moved on.

"All good. Not long to go now."

"And you're back in Surrey?"

"I am."

"That's good." He took a sip of champagne. "Simon all right?"

Libby glanced up; Simon was the last person she'd expected Dylan to ask about. "Yeah, he's fine."

"Dinner is about to be served," the master of ceremonies called through the crowd. "Could everybody move into the dining room, please?"

There was a bustle as the guests started to head toward the door.

"I'd better get in," Dylan said. "I'm sitting at a table with Esme and Johnny, so I can't be late."

"Okay. Maybe catch up with you after the meal?"

"Sure." Dylan started to walk inside the dining room and then stopped. "If I don't see you then, good luck with all the baby stuff, yeah?"

For a moment Libby caught something in Dylan's eyes, a look that she remembered from her birthday night. "Thank you."

"You deserve to be happy, Libby. I hope Simon realizes how lucky he is."

"Pardon?"

"Everybody take your seats, please!" the MC shouted, and Dylan started to walk away.

"Hang on, Dylan. What do you mean?"

He looked back at her. "I meant Simon's lucky to have been given a second chance. I hope he's a good boyfriend to you, that's all."

Libby felt her stomach lurch. "Oh my god."

"Come on, Dylan." Esme's mum was walking past and grabbed his arm. "We need to get in. Esme and Johnny are about to make their entrance."

"I'm coming."

He turned and followed her into the room. Libby watched him go, her head reeling.

"Wait!" she shouted so loudly that he turned around to look, along with several other people nearby.

"What?"

"Dylan, I'm not with Simon. I never moved back in with him."

She watched his brow crease as he processed what she'd said; then his eyes went wide. Behind him, loud music kicked in, announcing the imminent arrival of the bride and groom. Dylan stared at Libby for a second longer, then turned and hurried into the room.

47

The meal passed at a snail's pace. There were speeches first and then three courses of food. Libby was seated at one of the round tables with Frank, Laura and her boyfriend, and several of Esme's other friends. They were all lovely, chatting with her and asking questions about the pregnancy, but Libby could barely concentrate on anything anyone said. She kept glancing over at Dylan, who was sitting a few tables away with his back to her. She couldn't see his face, but she could tell by the twitching of his head that he was distracted too.

As dessert was served, Esme's friends were sharing funny anecdotes from her hen do, and Libby allowed her mind to wander back to that afternoon at the hospital. She could re-member it so clearly: Dylan's injured face, the old man in the adjacent bed telling her about Dylan's girlfriend coming to visit, the feeling of despair, Simon's name flashing up on her mobile phone screen. The moment she'd kissed Dylan on the lips, and those three words had tumbled out of her mouth.

I love you.

After that, Libby had run straight to the hospital toilet, where she'd cried so much that the Scottish nurse had come in to check she was okay. Through her snotty tears, Libby had tried to explain that the father of her baby wanted her to move back in with him, but she'd realized she was in love with another man, who probably had a girlfriend. The nurse had handed Libby some toilet roll to blow her nose and then told her in no uncertain terms that this all sounded far too complicated, and it was probably not a good idea to live with her ex if she was in love with someone else. And just like that, Libby had felt as if a great weight had been lifted from her shoulders.

"Are you all right?" Frank was watching her.

"I might step outside for a minute. I'm really hot in here."

"Would you like me to come with you?"

"No, I'll be fine, thanks."

She stood up and made her way toward the exit. As she did, she passed by Dylan's table, but he was deep in conversation with Johnny and didn't look up.

Libby stepped outside onto the hotel terrace, inhaling the cool evening air. There was a dull ache in her pelvis from all the standing up today, so she crossed to the far side of the terrace and sat down on a bench. After the noise and excitement of the wedding, it was quiet and still out here, and she took several deep breaths as she looked out over the garden, bright in the moonlight.

Libby heard a cough behind her, and when she turned around, she saw Dylan standing in the doorway, silhouetted against the light from inside. At the sight of him, she felt another throb in her stomach.

"Frank said you were out here," he said as he walked across to join her. "You all right?"

"Yes, just needed some fresh air. This little one is pummeling me today."

"Aren't you cold?"

"Not really." As she said it, Libby realized she was starting to shiver.

"Here, have this." Dylan took off his jacket, and before she could say anything, he wrapped it round her shoulders.

He sat down next to her, and for a moment neither of them spoke.

"About the—"

"I wanted to—"

"Sorry, you first," Libby said.

Dylan was staring at his feet. "I really thought you'd got back together with Simon."

"What on earth made you think that?"

"You told me when you came to see me in hospital. I mean, it was you who came, wasn't it?"

"Yes, but I never said I was getting together with Simon. Where did you get that idea from?"

"The old guy in the bed next to me. When I came round, he told me that a pregnant woman had been to visit me and that he'd heard her say, and I quote, 'I'm going to say yes to Simon. It's what's best for the baby.' I assumed that meant you were getting back with him."

"I had no idea he was eavesdropping!"

"Yeah, Sam was a nosy old sod. He knew everybody's business on the ward." Dylan gave a small laugh, then turned serious again. "But what happened, then? What were you saying yes about?"

Libby paused, wondering how honest she should be with Dylan. Part of her wanted to tell him what had really happened: her moment of realization in the hospital that she was in love with him. But then she remembered his girlfriend.

"Simon asked me to move back in with him in Surrey, and

I very nearly said yes. But then I realized that I'd just be repeating the old pattern of making my life decisions based on what other people want me to do. Simon and my mum were so desperate for me to live with him again, and they'd almost convinced me that I couldn't do it on my own. But they're wrong. I can and I will."

"So where are you living now?"

"I've rented a tiny flat outside Guildford. My parents aren't far away, and they're helping me cover the rent until the baby's here and I can get a job again. They're being pretty good about it all, actually."

"And Simon?"

"He's involved. He's been coming to my appointments and stuff, and he's helping out with money too. Simon's going to be the child's father, but nothing more than that."

Dylan was watching her as she spoke, his dark eyes on her face. "So you're not with him, then?"

"Nope. I'm single and carefree, me. Out on the pull every night."

Dylan gave a soft laugh; then his shoulders fell. "Bloody hell, Libby. This whole time, I've thought you were in a relationship with him again."

"I'm so sorry. It never occurred to me that you'd think that."

"It's not *your* fault. I blame old Sam and his bat ears." He leaned back against the bench and exhaled.

"While we're talking about Sam . . ." Libby paused, chewing the inside of her lip. "When we were talking at the hospital, he told me that your girlfriend had been to visit you."

"My girlfriend?"

"Yes. And your dad told me about her too."

"Hang on a sec—you talked to my old man?" Dylan was

looking at her, his eyes narrowed. "He didn't come to the hospital, did he?"

"Not as far as I know. But that first day when you didn't turn up at Frank's, I went looking for you at your flat. And your father answered the door."

"Oh, Jesus," Dylan said, throwing back his head. "I had no idea."

"He told me that you'd run away with your girlfriend, and that was why you'd gone missing."

"What? That bloody man!"

Small red dots had appeared on Dylan's cheeks, and Libby was suddenly reminded of the first time she'd met him, when he'd shouted at her on the bus.

"He'll have done it on purpose," Dylan said. "He can't help himself; it's like he enjoys fucking up my life."

"Dylan." Libby reached out and rested her hand on top of his, and she heard him take a quick breath.

"Sorry," Dylan said, his voice dropping. "My dad has this ability to wind me up; he always has. What else did he say to you?"

"Not much, we didn't chat for long. But he did mention your mum."

Libby saw a flash in Dylan's eyes. "What did he say about her?"

"That she'd run away when you were little."

"He said that, did he?" Dylan gave a sharp laugh and shook his head. "She didn't run away; he drove her away. My father is a cruel bastard, and he made her life hell. In the end, she had to get out for her own safety. If she'd stayed, I don't think she'd still be alive today."

"Oh my god."

The rage had gone from Dylan's eyes, replaced by a weary sadness. "It wasn't just the violence, although there was plenty of that. He made her think that she was worthless, that she was a bad mother and wife. He ground her down so much that she started to think everything was her fault—every time he got drunk and hit her, she thought she deserved it."

"Your poor mum."

"It's a miracle she got out, really, and I'm grateful every day that she did."

"And you?"

Dylan let out a slow sigh. "She wanted to take me, but he said he'd kill her if she tried. And she was so scared of him, she believed him. I only found that out years later, though, when she got in touch again."

"How old were you when she left?"

Dylan blinked slowly. "Seven."

Above them, a solitary firework burst into the sky, its golden sparkles fizzing above their heads. Libby looked back at Dylan, but he was staring at his hands clasped in his lap.

"That's why I got so pissed off when Simon turned up at your birthday and tried to blame you for his shitty behavior," he said. "I know he's not the same as my old man. But that behavior when he tried to say that the breakup was your fault . . . It triggered something in me from all those years ago with my dad."

He stopped, and Libby wanted to reach across and put her arm round Dylan's shoulder. "You must be so angry at your dad."

"I was for a long time. I became a right tearaway, got expelled from two different schools. And then I fell in with the wrong crowd, got into drugs and all sorts of trouble. It was punk music that saved me. This might sound weird, but when I discovered it, what it stood for, I found somewhere healthy I could channel all that anger."

"But still, it's amazing that you're able to live with your dad now. I think if it were me, I'd never want to see him again."

"I didn't see him for a long time. But he got diagnosed with lung cancer last year; he's not a well man. And I know he's made a lot of mistakes in his life, but I can't abandon him now."

Libby watched Dylan as he spoke. She wasn't sure she'd ever met such a kindhearted, generous person, someone who was so willing to see the good in people.

"I think you're extraordinary, Dylan," she said, and she saw his cheeks color.

"I dunno about that. But we should really get you inside; you've started to shiver again."

"Okay. But before we go, can I check one thing?"

"Sure."

"Are you saying that your dad and Sam were both wrong about the girlfriend thing?"

"Of course they were wrong," Dylan said, sitting up straight. "The woman they were both referring to is Cass, an old mate of mine. She has a band, and she called me on that Monday to say her drummer had broken his arm and would I stand in for him? That's why I texted you to say I couldn't meet you that afternoon, because I was helping her out at a gig. And then I got beaten up when I was on my way home after the gig. Cass was there, so she saw it all, and she came to the hospital to visit me the next day."

Libby felt relief flood through her body so strongly that she was sure Dylan must be able to see it.

"Right" was all she managed to say.

"I would never have said those things I said at your birthday if I'd had a girlfriend, Libby. I'm not that sort of guy."

"I know. And I'm sorry for doubting you." Libby glanced down at her lap, feeling suddenly stupid. When she looked back up, Dylan was staring at her with a look that made her heart beat a little faster.

"What a mess this has been," he said in a voice so quiet it was almost a whisper.

"It would be funny if it weren't so tragic." For some reason, Libby found she couldn't take her eyes off his lips.

"I've missed you so much, Libby."

"Really?"

"I've wanted to call you every day and I nearly did a thousand times. But I knew what a difficult decision it must have been for you to go back to Simon, and I didn't want to make things any harder for you."

"And this whole time I've been convinced that the man I love had lied to me."

Libby realized what she'd said and flicked her eyes up to Dylan's, worried she'd see them fill with panic at the word "love." But instead, she saw his pupils dilate as they moved closer to hers. Libby's breath caught with anticipation, but then she pulled her head back.

"Dylan, I'm thirty-six weeks pregnant. Are you sure you—"

But she didn't get to finish her sentence, because suddenly Dylan's lips were on hers, his hands twisting into her hair as he pulled her toward him.

48

By the time they went back into the venue, the tables had been pulled aside and the dancing was well under way. Esme and Johnny were in the middle of the dance floor, surrounded by their friends and family. Frank was sitting in a chair to one side, talking to another of the older guests, and Libby and Dylan walked over to join him. He looked up as they approached, and Libby saw his face light up when he saw they were holding hands.

"Well, this is very good news indeed," he said.

Libby could feel her cheeks glowing with pleasure, and she was about to sit down next to Frank when Dylan suddenly leaped in the air.

"What's the matter?" she said.

"This song, it's 'White Wedding' by Billy Idol. Come on, let's dance."

"I'm not sure I'm really up for dancing in my state," Libby said.

"And I'm far too old," Frank said.

"Don't be soft. Come on, you two."

Dylan reached out a hand to pull Frank up, then led them

over to the dance floor. He spotted Esme and Johnny and po-goed across to them with such carefree abandon that several dancers had to move out of his way. Libby joined him, feeling self-conscious, but Dylan's enthusiasm was contagious, and before long she too was bouncing along to the music. Beside her, Frank was dancing with a young girl, spinning her round and round. Libby smiled, watching him, and then felt her hand being grabbed as Dylan spun her round and dipped her back, kissing her again, in front of everyone on the dance floor. Behind her, Libby could hear Esme cheering and whooping with delight.

They carried on dancing for several songs before Libby felt a twinge in her pelvis. She grimaced and Dylan was at her side in seconds.

"You okay?" he shouted above the music.

"I'm fine. I just need to sit down for a minute."

Dylan took her hand and steered her toward a table.

"There's really no need to fuss," she said as Frank came to join them. "You two carry on dancing."

"I'm done," Frank said, panting. "I can't remember the last time I had a good dance, but I'm exhausted."

"Shall we head off?" Dylan said. "We should probably be getting you back to Willow Court, Frank."

"Good point. I forget I'm under curfew now."

"What about you?" Dylan said to Libby. "Are you catching the train back to Surrey tonight?"

"Actually, I've booked a room in a hotel in Camden."

Libby looked at Dylan as she said this, and he smiled at her, a long, slow smile that made her chest tighten. For a moment neither of them spoke, their eyes locked.

"Well, in that case, I think we should all be getting out of here," Frank said, and when Libby turned to him, he winked at her.

They said their farewells to Esme and Johnny and then went to fetch their coats and Libby's bag.

"Shall I order us an Uber?" Libby said as they stepped outside. "That way we can drop Frank home on our way."

"Actually, would you mind if we caught the bus?" Frank said. "For old times' sake?"

"Of course."

They left the hotel and set off down the road, Libby in the middle. As they walked, she linked her arms with Frank's and Dylan's, and they strolled side by side in companionable silence, listening to the night sounds of the city.

"Are you feeling better now?" Dylan said as they reached the bus stop.

"Much better. I think I just overdid it a bit on the dance floor."

They waited five minutes before an 88 approached, half empty at this time of night. As the door opened, a familiar face was smiling out at them.

"Evening, Mr. Weiss."

"Patience, how lovely to see you again," Frank said, climbing on board.

"Have you been out partying?"

"We have indeed, a wedding. You remember Libby? And this is my friend Dylan."

"Of course I remember Libby. How's your search going? I spread the word round to all the drivers I know; everyone was talking about you."

"Ah, well, the search is over now," Frank said, and Patience's head snapped to look at him.

"Does that mean . . . ?"

"I found her, yes," Frank said. "I found my girl on the 88."

Patience let out a whoop, causing a dozing passenger in the front seat to jolt awake.

"I'm so happy for you, Mr. Weiss," she said. "And my parents will be too."

They moved toward some empty seats at the back of the lower deck. Libby and Dylan sat in one pair and Frank sat across the aisle from them.

"Wasn't that a wonderful evening?" he said as the bus set off.

"It was indeed." Dylan glanced at Libby as he said this.

"I'm sorry I'm such a party pooper," she said. "This little one has been pummeling the hell out of me this evening."

"You need to start taking it easy, Libby," Frank said.

"I will, I promise. There won't be any more dancing for me until the baby's here."

The bus pulled up at a stop, and an older woman in a woolen hat stepped on board, greeting Patience. Libby watched Frank instinctively scan her face, and then he turned back to her.

"I'm not sure I'll ever be able to stop checking. It's hard to break a habit of sixty years."

"Does it feel strange, finally knowing what happened to your woman?" Dylan said.

"A relief more than strange. I'm getting too old to be riding this bus every day anyway. Like Libby, I need to put my feet up more."

"Have you played bingo yet?" Dylan said.

"No, I have not, you cheeky bugger," Frank said, hitting his arm in mock outrage.

Dylan laughed, and Libby leaned back in her seat, enjoying the sound of the two of them chatting as the bus wound through Parliament Square. It felt wonderful to have Frank back in her life again. And Dylan . . . Libby thought of that smile earlier, the hotel bedroom waiting for the two of them, and felt a nervous flutter of excitement. It was followed by another sensation, a sharp stabbing in her lower stomach. She bent forward, inhaling.

"What's wrong?" Dylan said. "What happened?"

"I don't know. I think it might be Braxton-Hicks."

"What are they?" Frank said.

"Like practice contractions. I've had them before, so it's nothing alarming." But as she said it, Libby felt her pulse starting to race. She was pretty sure Braxton-Hicks didn't feel like this.

"Let's get you straight to the hotel," Frank said. "You probably just need some rest after a long day."

"Okay," Libby said.

She sat back and found Dylan's arm round her shoulders. She leaned into him, inhaling his wonderful, familiar smell. But as they approached the Cenotaph, she felt another pang and gasped.

"We should go to the hospital, get you checked out," Dylan said, reaching across Libby to ring the bell. "Let's get off at the next stop and jump in a taxi; it'll be quicker."

"But my notes and hospital bag are in Surrey. I don't have anything here."

"Don't worry about that," Frank said. "I'm sure you won't be needing all that tonight."

"I should never have come to the wedding," Libby said, shaking her head. "I should have listened to my mum; she told me it was too risky."

"Hey, calm down," Dylan said gently, and Libby felt his

hand squeeze her shoulder. "I'm sure this will be a false alarm, but let's get you checked out anyway."

Libby nodded, but as she did, she remembered Peggy's words. *When your time comes, you'll know it's for real.* When the bus approached the next stop, she stood up to get off, and as she did, she felt another sharp stab and let out a yelp.

"Is everything all right back there?" Patience called out.

"Yes, everything's fine," Frank called back. "It's just possible that Libby's in labor."

A murmur went along the bus.

"We'll get off at the next stop and get a taxi, nothing to be alarmed about," Frank said.

A woman who was sitting in the front row had stood up and was moving back toward them. "I'm a nurse. How many weeks are you?"

"Thirty-six," Libby said.

"And when did your contractions start?"

"I'm not sure. I've been uncomfortable on and off all evening, and then I had what felt like a contraction when I was dancing. Do you think it's Braxton-Hicks?"

"How often are they coming, darling?"

"I'm not sure. Every three minutes or so," Libby said, and as she spoke, she felt another wave of pain.

"Trafalgar Square," the electronic bus announcement said, but Libby could barely hear it over her own groan.

"That wasn't three minutes." The nurse was shaking her head.

"Do you want to get off here?" Patience called back.

"There's no time for a taxi; we need to get her straight to hospital," the nurse said. "These contractions are coming too close together."

"Oh, for Christ's sake!" a man sitting a few rows in front of them shouted. "Hurry up and get off; some of us want to get home."

The nurse turned and glared at him. "Sir, either we drive this young lady to the hospital now or she's going to give birth right here on this bus. It's your choice."

He started to grumble again, but Patience had stood up from her driver's seat and turned to face the passengers. "All right, everybody off here. This bus is on diversion!"

49

ibby felt another jolt of searing pain and clenched her fist to stop a scream coming out. Why was this so painful already? She'd watched enough episodes of *One Born Every Minute* to know it wasn't supposed to happen this quickly, especially the first time. This had to mean something was wrong.

The nurse, who'd introduced herself as Nikki, had moved to the other end of the bus and was having a muttered conversation on the phone. All the other passengers had been ushered off at Trafalgar Square, so the only people left were Dylan and Frank, the latter watching her now with a concerned expression on his face. When he saw Libby looking at him, he gave her a reassuring smile.

"No need to worry; everything is in hand," Frank said. "The 88 has never let me down before, and it won't today."

Libby glanced out of the window and saw they were crossing Shaftesbury Avenue. Why were they going so slowly? They needed to move faster.

"It's okay, breathe."

She heard Dylan's voice in her ear, calm and low. He had one arm behind her and was gently massaging her shoulder.

"This can't happen now, Dylan. It's too early."

"It's all right. Try and relax; we'll be at the hospital soon."

Another wave of pain came crashing over her, and Libby gripped tightly to something. When she looked down, she saw it was Dylan's hand, the skin white from where she was digging in so hard.

"I'm sorry," she said, releasing him, but he grabbed her hand back.

"Squeeze as hard as you like."

Libby looked round at him, tears stinging her eyes. "I'm scared, Dylan."

"You don't need to be. Everything's going to be fine."

"Will you stay with me when we get to the hospital? I don't want to be on my own."

Dylan lifted his spare hand and brushed a hair from her face. "I'm not going anywhere, Libby. You never have to be on your own."

"Right, I've called ahead to UCH and warned them to be ready for us," Nikki said, reappearing next to Libby. "Driver, how much longer do you reckon we'll be?"

"The traffic's quite clear, so hopefully ten minutes max," Patience said.

"As fast as you can, please," Nikki said. "Libby, how are you feeling? Any pressure to push yet?"

"Not yet, no."

"Great. Has anybody got water?"

"I've got a bottle up here," Patience said.

Libby saw the nurse move to the front of the bus. She returned carrying a two-liter bottle of water.

"And I've got this," Frank said, tugging off his suit jacket.

"What's going on?" Libby said, looking between them. "Oh my god, you think I'm going to have the baby on the bus!"

"Hey, calm down. It's okay," Dylan said, but Libby knew it was anything but okay. They were getting ready to deliver her baby and something was going to go wrong.

"No, I'm not doing it," she exclaimed, pushing Dylan's arm from around her and trying to pull herself up. "I'm not having my baby on the 88. I—"

But she didn't get any further as she felt another rip of heat through her torso. This time, with it, she felt a new sensation in her pelvis, as though she suddenly really needed the loo. She looked up at Nikki, who was watching her intently.

"You need to push, don't you?"

"I can't," Libby said, feeling the panic rising in her throat. "I can't."

"Yes, you can." Nikki leaned forward, bringing her face close to Libby's. "Listen to me. Women have been doing this for millions of years. We've given birth in fields and up mountains, in far harder conditions than this. So believe me, you can do this on a London bus."

"Damn, there's a holdup on Tottenham Court Road," Patience shouted. "I'm going to have to take us the long way round to avoid it."

"Whatever you have to do. Just get us there as quick as you can," Nikki said. She turned to Dylan. "Okay, Dad, I'm going to need you to support Libby so she can move into a more comfortable position."

Libby opened her mouth to say Dylan wasn't the father, but she could already feel him adjusting his position behind her.

"Libby, do you think you can take your underwear off?" Nikki said.

Libby looked at her in dismay. "Here? Really?"

"Well, it's a while since I did my training, but I seem to remember it's easier to do this without your knickers on," she said, smiling. "Your dress is long enough, so you'll still be modest."

Frank looked away and Libby wriggled out of her knickers. Thank god Dylan was behind her, so she couldn't see his face.

"Now, when your next contraction comes, if you feel the need to push, don't fight it," Nikki said. "And remember to breathe, okay?"

"Okay," Libby said.

"You can lean back on me. I've got you," Dylan said.

Libby leaned back, cautiously at first, but then she felt Dylan's body behind her, solid and safe, and she relaxed into him. He reached out his hand and she took it.

"You're doing amazingly, Libby," Frank said.

"We're going to be at the hospital in about four minutes," Patience said as they swerved round a corner at breakneck speed.

At that moment Libby felt another contraction hit her, harder than any so far. She closed her eyes and let out a long moan as she pushed down with all her might.

"That's good, well done," Nikki said, raising her voice to be heard. "Now stop and breathe."

Libby fell back on Dylan, panting.

"You've got this," he whispered into her ear, but she barely heard him for the sound of her heart hammering in her ears.

"I can see the hospital up ahead," Patience shouted a minute later as the bus made a sudden swerve to the right. "We're nearly there."

"There'll be a team waiting for us when we arrive," Nikki said.

Frank was leaning toward Libby, his eyes fixed on her face. "You can do this, Libby. I know you can."

Libby started to reply, then gasped as she felt another contraction rolling up. Out of the bus window, she could see a
flashing light and people in blue uniforms running toward the
bus, and then she threw her head back and let out a roar of
pain.

50

When Libby woke up, it took her a moment to work out where she was. Light was coming in through a thin curtain above her head, so it must be morning. It was quiet, unnaturally so, and when she looked to her right, she saw she was alone in the sparsely furnished room. Libby closed her eyes and leaned back into her pillow, listening to the distant sounds of traffic below.

There was a noise from outside the door, a clatter and the low sound of voices. Libby breathed deeply.

"*Shhh*, don't wake her up," said a voice coming into the room.

There was the sound of footsteps padding across the floor, and the edge of the bed creaked next to her. A second later, Libby felt something soft and warm against her skin.

"Mama!" came a high-pitched voice, and when Libby opened her eyes, a small, chubby face was pressed against her own.

"Frankie!" she said, wrapping her arms round her daughter and kissing her. "You woke me up!"

Frankie let out a gurgle of delight and squirmed out of Libby's arms, crawling across the bed away from her.

"Morning, beautiful." Dylan had climbed into the bed next to Libby and leaned over to kiss her. "Did you sleep all right?"

"Like a log, thanks." She lifted up her head and Dylan stretched his arm under it so that she was nestled against his chest. Frankie had settled between the two of them and was playing with her toy bunny.

"What time did she wake up?"

"Five," Dylan said, and Libby groaned.

"We need to get thicker curtains for her bedroom ASAP."

"That's top of my list of jobs, I promise."

They'd moved into their new flat yesterday. Before that, they'd been living in a studio flat near Euston Station, but now that Frankie had turned one they needed somewhere with a second bedroom. The flat wasn't much bigger than the studio, and the ceilings were so low that Dylan had to duck when he walked through the doors. But it had a small box room for Frankie, and with a lick of paint and some furniture, Libby was confident they could make it a proper home.

"Are you still seeing Frank this afternoon?" Dylan said, stroking her hair.

"Yes, today's the day for our bus outing."

After weeks of negotiations with the team at the care home, Libby had managed to convince them to let her take Frank out on the 88 this afternoon. She was planning to take him down into town to see the Christmas lights on Regent Street, and maybe stop for a coffee somewhere.

"Are you taking Frankie?" Dylan asked.

"It's probably easiest if I leave her with you. Last time I took her on the bus, she spent the whole time trying to crawl up and down the aisle."

"That sounds like my little girl on the 88." Dylan laughed.

Frankie had abandoned her bunny and wriggled back up the bed toward them. Dylan scooped her up and blew a raspberry on her cheek, making her explode with giggles.

"Shall we go to the park for a swing, little monkey?" he said.

"Ding!" Frankie said, bouncing up and down to imitate the swing, and Libby and Dylan both laughed.

"I think that's a yes," Libby said, kissing Dylan.

THEY spent the morning unpacking some of their belongings while Frankie crawled around their feet and tried to climb into all the boxes. The first thing they hung on the wall was a double picture frame that Dylan had given Libby for her thirty-first birthday. In the left-hand side was the sketch Libby had drawn of Dylan the first time they ever met on the 88, which it turned out he'd kept. In the right-hand side was the photo Libby had taken of Dylan that same day, the one that had caused him to shout at her. When Libby had opened the present, she'd suggested to Dylan that she could finally finish the drawing, but he'd refused, saying he wanted to keep it as it was, penis hair and all.

At lunchtime, Dylan made soup and the three of them ate it together at their small kitchen table.

"Do you really think we'll be able to fit everyone in on Christmas Day?" Libby said, looking round them at the tiny kitchen.

They'd invited Frank to join them for Christmas lunch, as well as Esme, Johnny, and Esme's mum, and then when Peggy had mentioned she was going to be on her own for Christmas, Libby had invited her too. It had felt like a good idea at the time, their first chance to entertain friends in their new home, but now Libby realized it was going to be extremely cramped.

At least Simon had turned down their invitation, so that was one less person. He and his new girlfriend were spending the day together, and then he'd see Frankie on Boxing Day, when they went to celebrate at Libby's parents' house. Rebecca and her family would be there too. Frankie adored her cousins, Hector and Emily, and Libby and Rebecca had settled into a cautiously friendly relationship, forged through sleep-deprived coffees and late-night text chats during breastfeeding.

"Christmas lunch will be fine; we'll just have to all get cozy," Dylan said as Frankie enthusiastically dunked a piece of bread into her bowl, splashing soup everywhere. "Do you think you'll be able to finish the presents in time?"

"I hope so."

Libby had spent the past few weeks doing sketches of Frankie, which she was planning on framing and giving to everyone for Christmas. She felt a bit self-conscious about doing it, but after her first term at art school, her drawing had already come on in leaps and bounds. She was especially proud of the sketch she'd done for Frank. It was taken from a photo Dylan had snapped of Frank and Frankie together, back in the summer. Frank was holding Frankie on his lap, and the two of them were looking at each other, grinning. It was one of Libby's favorite photos of her daughter, and she knew that Frank would love it too.

"Right, I'd better get going," Libby said once they'd cleared up.

She put on her winter coat and twisted her hair up inside a thick bobble hat. Then she kissed her partner and daughter good-bye and stepped out into the cold December wind.

51

Libby spotted him through the front window as the bus pulled up at the stop. Frank was sitting in his usual seat on the top deck, and she boarded the bus and bounded up the stairs. A volunteer from Willow Court was sitting across the aisle from him, and Libby nodded hello to her as she slid into the seat next to Frank.

"Hello, Frank."

She saw his shoulders jerk at the sound of his name and he turned to her in surprise. Then she saw his dark brown eyes twinkle. "Hello! I like your bobble hat."

"Thanks very much. How are you?"

"Good, good. Isn't it a beautiful day? Perfect weather for a bus ride."

"Isn't it? I wanted to see the Christmas lights, if you fancy that?"

"I've always loved the lights. I used to take Clara every year when she was small."

The bus turned into Royal College Street and made its way down toward Camden Town. A group of carol singers huddled outside Sainsbury's, wearing Santa hats and serenading shoppers with "Good King Wenceslas." Frank nodded along to the tune as the bus drove past.

"Dylan sends his love," Libby said, watching to see his reaction.

"That's nice."

"He starts on his Access to Nursing course in January. It turns out, helping to deliver a baby on a bus has got him over his blood phobia! Don't tell him, but I've bought him a stethoscope for Christmas."

Frank smiled at this, so Libby continued, encouraged.

"He's at home with Frankie today. She's trying to walk already. Can you believe it?"

"They grow up in the flash of an eye," Frank said. "How old is she?"

"Thirteen months now. It was her birthday last month. Do you remember? We brought you some of her chocolate cake."

"I bake an excellent chocolate cake; it's my mother's recipe. I baked one last week, actually."

"Oh, wonderful. Have you been doing the baking class at Willow Court?"

"Willow Court? What's that?"

"It's where you live now, the care home."

"I don't think so. I live on Makepeace Avenue."

"You moved last year, remember? You have that nice room with the view of the garden."

Frank turned to look at Libby, frowning. "I'm sorry, but have we met before?"

Libby's heart sank. For a while there, she'd really thought he remembered. "Yes, we have. I'm Libby."

"Libby . . ." She could see him trying to place the name.

"Are you one of Clara's school friends? I'm sorry; you girls all look the same to me."

"No, we met on this bus." Libby watched Frank's face to see if there was any flicker of recognition, but he was looking at her with his brow furrowed. "I drew you, Frank."

"Are you an artist? I knew an artist once, years ago. We met on the bus too."

"Your girl on the 88."

"Yes, did you meet her as well?"

It had been months since Frank had mentioned the girl on the bus; Libby had assumed she'd been lost in the fog of dementia, along with so much else.

"What do you remember about her, Frank?"

"Oh, she was very beautiful. She had bright red hair, the most extraordinary I've ever seen. I have to admit, I rather fell for her. And then I lost her telephone number."

"I'm sorry to hear that."

"She changed my life, that girl, and I never got to say thank you. I often wonder what happened to her."

"I'm sure she lived a happy life. Perhaps she became an art teacher and grew old with her best friend."

"Perhaps." Frank was staring out of the front window again, and Libby could sense that he was slipping away.

"We're looking forward to having you at our new place for Christmas." Libby hoped that talking about the present might ground Frank, but he didn't react. "Dylan's cooking turkey and Peggy's bringing a trifle. It's going to be quite a party."

Frank was sitting motionless now, his eyes staring blankly forward. Libby sank back in the seat, trying not to feel too disappointed. She'd hoped that being back on the 88 might help anchor him a little, but it didn't seem to make any difference.

Although at least they'd had some conversation today; there were times recently when she'd visited Willow Court and he hadn't even registered her presence.

As the bus made its way down the side of the park, Libby pulled her sketchbook out of her bag and found a clean page. They'd been working on shading this term, and she tried to put her new skills into practice as she drew Frank now. She wished he could see how much she'd improved since her first drawing on the bus last year.

Libby was so absorbed in her work that they reached Regent Street before she knew it. Christmas lights had been suspended between the tall Georgian buildings, huge angels whose lights twinkled like stars over the shoppers' heads. The bus pulled up at a stop and more people boarded, lugging heavy bags of shopping. It was getting warmer now, the windows steaming up as passengers filled the top deck. Libby was beginning to regret wearing her thick hat, and she pulled it off, shaking out her long hair. She stuffed the hat in her bag and then turned to check on Frank.

He was staring openmouthed at her.

"Frank, are you okay?"

He looked at her for a moment longer, speechless; then his face broke into a smile. "Oh my goodness, it's you."

"Yes, I'm Li—"

Libby stopped as it dawned on her what was going on.

"I knew I'd recognize you again," Frank said. "Your hair is exactly as I remember it. And you're still at art school, I see." He indicated the sketchbook on her lap.

"Yes, I am."

"That's marvelous! People said I was mad to keep looking for you, but I never gave up. I knew we'd find each other one day."

Libby didn't say anything, just took in the joy on his face, this flash of the old Frank she so desperately missed.

"Where are you going now?" he said.

"Oh, nowhere in particular."

"Well, in that case, I don't suppose you'd like to accompany me to the National Gallery, would you? I believe I owe you a visit." He laughed then, and Libby laughed too.

"I'd love that."

"Wonderful." Frank reached out and took her hand, squeezing it. "It's so good to see you again."

Libby looked down at Frank's trembling hand, the skin a mosaic of wrinkles. She squeezed his fingers back. "It's good to see you again too."

Acknowledgments

Writing a first book is a lonely endeavor. You sit on your own in front of a computer, typing up words that you never know if another soul is ever going to read. I therefore found writing my second book a much more collaborative process, and I'm extremely grateful to all the lovely, talented, and enthusiastic book people around the world who have helped bring *The Lost Ticket* to life.

I have to start by thanking my agent, Hayley Steed, who has been there every step of the way, since I first sent her an e-mail saying, "What about a book set on a London bus?" Her expertise, passion, and endless reassurances have been invaluable as I've navigated the debut-author experience, and I feel incredibly lucky to have her on my side. Thank you to the amazing team at Madeleine Milburn Literary Agency, who work so hard for all their authors. Special thanks to Elinor Davies, Liane-Louise Smith, Georgina Simmonds, Valentina Paulmichl, Giles Milburn, Emma Dawson, and Hannah Ladds.

Thank you to everyone at Bonnier Books for using so much creativity and flair in bringing this story to UK readers. To my editor Sarah Bauer, who not only is talented, smart, and kind but also finds the word "flaps" as funny as I do. To Jenna Petts, my brilliant UK publicist—there's no one I'd rather run around London pretending to be a fairy with. To Vicky Joss, marketing manager and creative genius. And also my heartfelt thanks to Katie Meegan, Lucy Tirahan, Alex May, Eloise Angeline, Laura Makela, Alex Schmidt, and the whole sales team. Finally, my eternal love and gratitude to Jenny Richards and Anna Morrison for the gorgeous cover.

In America, my hugest thanks to everyone at Berkley for their phenomenal support of my books. To Kerry Donovan, who is not only a superb editor but also one of the calmest people I've ever worked with—thank you for making this whole process so smooth and enjoyable. To Bridget O'Toole and Elisha Katz from the lovely and endlessly hardworking marketing team, and to my publicist Tara O'Connor, who has blown me away with her work to promote my book—I will never forget that e-mail about *Good Morning America*! Thanks as well to Mary Baker, Christine Legon, and Dan Walsh. And once again, I am in absolute awe of Anthony Ramondo's cover design and Sanny Chiu's beautiful artwork.

I am extremely lucky to have not one but two fantastic writing groups who supported me while I worked on this book. In the UK, love and thanks to my friends from the Faber Academy class of 2018. Four years later, we still meet regularly, and they are the first to read my work and give feedback on it. Particular thanks to Lissa Price, Hannah Tovey, and Laura Price, who were my beta readers and gave me invaluable notes.

I'm also indebted to the Berkletes, a group of my fellow Berkley authors, who have provided me with endless encouragement, advice, and laughs over the past year and a half. I honestly don't think I would have survived the debut-author experience without you all. Special thanks to Lesser Chris Evans, the knot that ties us all together.

I'm very grateful to Jacqui Cannon from the Lewy Body Society for talking to me about Lewy body dementia, and to Chris Maddocks, whom I heard speak so eloquently about living with dementia. I'd also like to thank Loan Tray and Jane O'Connell for their advice and feedback on writing the character Esme.

On a personal note, thank you to Jenny, without whose child-care help I'd never be able to write a word. Thank you to my wonderful parents and brother for always being my biggest supporters and most enthusiastic readers. To Olive and Sid for being the funniest and most welcome distractions from my writing, and for loudly telling strangers in bookshops that they should buy my book. I love you both to the moon and back. And to Andy, for being my companion and best friend on this crazy, exciting, surprising journey. There's no one I'd rather ride the 88 bus with.

Finally, I would like to save the biggest thank-you for all the booksellers, librarians, book reviewers, bookstagrammers, and bloggers who have championed my work, and for every single reader who has picked up one of my books. Writing stories had always been my dream, and it's thanks to all of you that it continues to come true.